JIM BÆN PRESENTS:

PHILIP JOŚE FARMER

Includes Two Bonus Stories:

THEY TWINKLED LIKE JEWELS
and
RASTIGNAC THE DEVIL

TOR

A TOM DOHERTY ASSOCIATES BOOK
Distributed by Pinnacle Books, New York

THE LONG WARPATH

A few miles outside of the city, Joel Vahn-dert challenged Benoni Rider.

The tension between them had been high enough before they left Fiiniks with the mule-train to the Iron Mountains. But it had been confined to not-so-good-natured kidding; practical jokes which could have crippled or killed, and boasts about which one would marry Debra Awvrez.

The older men on the expedition had inter-vened more than once to prevent blows. They did not want to lose one of the warriors-to-be. Too many had died last year from snakebite, valley fever, and raids by the Navahos.

When the train got to the Iron Mountains, the leaders had seen that the two eighteen-year-olds were kept apart as often as possible. This was not difficult to do, for every man had to work hard all day long. By evening, all were too tired to do much besides slump around the fires, talk a while, then go to sleep. And Chief Wako had assigned Benoni and Joel to different work parties.

So, the two did not see much of each other. They were too busy with the digging of the ore, the melting, refining, tempering, and hammering of the metal into weapons and tools. Under expert guidance, they learned how to make swords, daggers, spearheads, arrowheads, iron stirrups and bits, hammers, nails, and plowblades. The months passed while they sweated under the hot Eyzonuh sun. Three months they struggled with the pick and shovel, the furnace, the flame and forge, the hammer and anvil. And when Chief Wako thought that the two youths still kept too much energy after the day's labor, he assigned one of them to night guard.

But the end of summer neared. All the weapons and tools that could be carried by the mules were fashioned. The mules were loaded with the steel handicrafts, the smoked meat the hunters had killed and prepared, and water from the springs. Then, the train began its slow and dangerous trip over the mountains, through the desert, and eventually to Fiiniks in the Valley of the Sun. So far, they had been lucky, for no wild Keluhfinyanz or Indians had attacked them and they made the journey back to the city without losing one man.

On the way back, there was not enough work to keep Benoni and Joel apart. Chief Wako watched them, and he or one of the sub-chiefs interfered when one of the gamecocks pushed the other too far.

A few miles from Fiiniks, nevertheless, Joel Vahndert began telling all within hearing of his loud voice what he and Debra would do on their wedding night. The men walking beside him did not like this. You did not talk of such things. At least, not about your wife and the other free women in the valley. Perhaps, if no preachers were around, you might talk about your exploits with the Navaho slave girls. But never about the Fiiniks women.

Joel knew this, and he must have hungered deeply for a fight with Benoni to have risked the disapproval and perhaps punishment of the older men. He disregarded their glares and tight-lipped frowns and continued talking in ever greater detail. He could see the flush spreading over Benoni's skin, the flush replaced by paleness in a few minutes.

Joel did not seem to care. He walked beside the mule that was his care in a long-legged stride. He was a big man, six feet four, with heavy bones and muscles to go with the bones. His long, thick black hair was bound in a red band around his forehead. His face was broad; his nose, long and slightly aquiline; his lips, thin; his chin, thick and seemingly hard as the end of a warclub. There was not a youth his own age in the valley he had not wrestled and thrown, not a man for twenty miles around Kemlbek Mountain who could throw a javelin as far as he. He made a splendid figure in his red cotton shirt gathered around the waist with a belt of turquoise beads and his puma-skin shorts and leggings.

Benoni Rider was a different sort, impressive in his own frame of reference but puny compared to Joel. He was about six feet tall, had broad shoulders, a tapering waist (Joel was thick there) and long legs. His waist-long yellow hair was held by a black band around his head; his blue eyes were now narrow; the nostrils of his straight nose were flaring; his normally full mouth was clamped to a thin line. He was strong, and he knew it. But he was not the bear that Joel was. Rather, he was a mountain lion, a slim but swift creature, or a deer. He could run faster than any one born in the shadow of Kemlbek. But here, obvious to all, was a situation which did not demand running. Not if he wanted to be worthy of taking the First Warpath.

Benoni listened to Joel for several minutes, meanwhile looking around to see if the older ones would speak to Joel. When it became apparent that he was expected to be the one to take action, Benoni did not hesitate. The only thing that had kept him silent so far was the realization that Joel Vahndert was baiting him. And he had not wanted to give him the satisfaction of knowing that he had the power to infuriate him. Also, he had hoped that one of the sub-chiefs would rebuke Joel and so humiliate him.

But the sub-chiefs were at the head of the train conferring with Wako about the order of dress as they marched into the nearing city of Fiiniks. No help from them.

Now, Benoni walked up to Joel. Joel stopped talking and faced Benoni, knowing from the fury on Benoni's face that he would be challenged.

"What's the matter, jack rabbit?" he said. "You look pale. Been out in the sun too long? Maybe you should lie down in the shade of a sawaro until you recover. We men will go on ahead of you and tell the slaves to bring out a stretcher to fetch you. I'll tell Debra that . . ."

Benoni did not follow protocol. Instead of

slapping Joel in the face and then formally challenging him, he kicked Joel. He kicked him where it hurts a man most, with feet that had never known shoe or moccasin, with soles the skin of which was half an inch thick and hard as rock.

The big man screamed, clutched himself, and fell to the ground. There, he writhed and rolled and yelled with agony.

Wako, though distant, heard the screams, and he came running. Joel was still making noise when he arrived, but Wako shouted at him to keep quiet, to bear himself like a warrior—which he would be some day if he lived that long.

One of the men explained what had happened. Wako said, "Serves the filthy young fool right."

But he swung towards Benoni, and he said harshly, "Why did you strike him without warning? Or without first making sure that one of us was a formal witness to the challenge?"

"When a man talks like he does about a woman, he should have his filthy mouth shut as a slave's is shut," said Benoni. "Besides, why should I give him the advantage of a formal challenge? He's much bigger and stronger than I am; I'm not too proud to admit it. Why should I give him an advantage? I fight to win, and letting him get a chance to get a bear hug on me isn't the way to win."

Wako laughed and said, "I wouldn't have permitted you two to kill each other if you had challenged him. What's the matter with you young fools? Don't you know that in less

than a week you'll be going on the First Warpath? And that you'll get all the killing you
want? Maybe more than you want."

Joel, still holding himself and bent over,
struggled to his knees. Glaring at Benoni, he
said, "You fight like a dirty Navaho! Wait
until I recover, you . . . !"

"Both of you will wait," said Wako sternly.
"There will be no serious fighting among the
unblooded until you return from the uplands.
And, by then, you'll have more than your belly
full. Now, listen to me. I told you what you
can't do. If either of you disobey, you'll stand
before the Council of Kemlbek. And that may
mean that you'll have to wait a year before
you're allowed to go on the warpath. Do you
want to do that?"

Both young men were silent. They wished
this punishment no more than any one of their
age would have. To continue to be treated like
boys while their friends became men!

"It's settled then," said Wako. "You two
shake hands and swear you won't tangle again
until after you're set on the trail. Otherwise . . ."

Joel Vahndert, who had now risen to his
feet, half-turned away as if he had no
intentions of shaking hands with Benoni,
ever. Benoni watched him, his hands on his
hips.

Wako said, loudly, "You had that coming,
Vahndert! And you, Rider, wipe that smile off
your little boy's face! Now, shake! Or I'll see
that you have some trouble getting initiated
this year!"

Vahndert turned back, held his hand out,

and said, "I'll shake if Rider is man enough."

"I'm man enough to do anything you do," said Benoni. His hand disappeared in Joel's, and Joel squeezed down with all his strength.

Benoni's arm muscles became rigid, but he did not wince nor try to withdraw.

"All right, don't try to make the other holler uncle," said Wako. "And get back to your mules. We'll be in Fiiniks by noon if we push hard."

The train started again. Benoni was still too angry to feel the joy of homecoming. He looked to the south across the rocky plain and saw a reflection of his own smoldering fury in the sky. Thin black clouds of smoke rising from a volcano ten miles away. Last year, when he had left his native city for the mountains, that volcano had just been forming. Now, it was high enough for him to see that the lava and cinders had built a cone at least two hundred feet high. The earth-demons had been busy while he was gone.

His anger faded away, replaced not by the pleasure of returning to his family, but by fear for them. He could remember, when he was a very little boy, hearing his father tell a friend that the first of the volcanoes had broken the crust of the earth only two years before Benoni was born. That fury had been forty miles to the west; its birth had accomplished an earthquake that shook down the walls and houses of Finniks and killed many. Now, there were ten volcanoes in the Valley of the Sun. Sometimes, when the winds were right, smoke from all ten lay over the valley and made the sun a ghost.

Benoni looked to the east where the strange form of Kemlbek Mountain lay. From this distance, the mountain did appear as a sleeping beast with a high-humped back, a very long neck, and a long-snouted head. The preachers said it got its name from the keml. Benoni had never seen a keml; neither had the preachers. But there was a beast called the keml (spelled camel in the archaic writing of the ancients) which was mentioned in the Found Books. Benoni wondered if it were as large as the mountain named for it. If so, he was glad it was as dead as the leviathan and the unicorn also mentioned in the Found Books.

At midday, the adobe walls of the city which ringed the foot of Kemlbek appeared. An hour later, the men of the train saw the crowd waiting outside the Gate of the Fiiniks (a huge bird that had lived long long ago but which would some day rise from its ashes and come whirling over the desert bearing Jehovah on its back).

Benoni, after being formally dismissed by Wako, went home with his father and step-mother, his two younger brothers, his two married sisters, their husbands and his little nephews and nieces. Everybody was talking at once. Benoni could only partly answer the many questions hurled at him. He was in a glow of happiness. Even though he could not help thinking of Debra Awvrez and was impatient to get to her, to be loved so by his people made him love them very much. And, in the eyes of the younger members, he was a hero because he had been so far away and had brought back the much-needed tools and weapons.

After they had walked about a half mile down the broad street, they came to his father's home. This was a two-story adobe house painted white. It had a tower at each corner and an embrasured roof from which the Fiinishans could shoot at any invaders. A ten-foot adobe wall around it gave them privacy; also, if attackers ever entered the city, a place from which to fight until they were forced to retreat to the house.

Here the dogs, big wolflike beasts, bounded out barking, and leaped upon Benoni. The household cats, aloof, clad in stripes and dignity, sat on the walls and watched the proceedings. Later, when there were not so many people and so much commotion, Benoni's favorites would come down and rub against his leg and purr to be picked up.

Benoni had to eat a big supper, or at least to sit down at a loaded table of fruhholiiz, toriya, refried beans, beef, and Mek beer. He talked too much to get a chance to eat, but he was not hungry. He trembled at the thought of seeing Debra that night, and he wondered also how he could get away decently from the family.

After supper, he put on his church clothes and went with the family to church. There they stayed for an hour while the preacher gave innumerable prayers of thanks for the safe return of the men and boys who had gone to the Iron Mountains. Benoni tried to keep his mind on what the preacher said, but he could not resist the temptation to look around. She was not there. Or, if she were, he could not see her.

He went back to his house. His father and brothers-in-law asked him many questions, and he answered as best he could with his mind on Debra. Finally, as he was beginning to despair of finding a polite way of leaving the house, his stepmother came to his rescue.

"You men will have to excuse Benoni," she said, laughing so they would not be angry at her. "I'm sure he's dying to visit the Awvrez. And they will think he's very impolite not to drop by there for at least a few minutes."

Benoni looked at this woman with gratitude. She had taken his mother's place only six years ago, and he loved her as much as he had his own mother.

His father appeared disappointed, and he opened his mouth to protest. But Benoni's mother said, "I don't interfere much, Hozey, you know that. I do know that Benoni has been itching to leave for hours now. Have you forgotten how you were when you were eighteen?"

Benoni's father grinned. He slapped his son on the shoulder and said, "Get going you young stallion! But don't stay out too late. Remember! Your initiation might start at any time! And there are things you must do before then."

Benoni's mother looked sad, then, and Benoni felt a pang. He had seen her weep two years ago after Benoni's older brother had left for the First Warpath—and his last.

Benoni excused himself, kissed his mother, and went outside to the stable. There he put a gold-chased Med leather saddle on Red Hawk, a fine roan stallion. He led the horse to the front gate, shouted to his nephews to open the gate and mounted.

He was no more astride than he heard the bellow of an Announcer.

"Wait a minute, Benoni Rider! I have a message for you from the council of Kemlbek!"

Benoni reined in Red Hawk, impatient as himself to get going. And he said, "Announcer Chonz! What message? I hope it's not bad!"

"Good or bad, it's well to mind it," said Chonz. "I just gave the same message to Joel Vahndert, and he did not think much of it. But he swore on The Lost Books and The Found that he would obey."

"Oh?" said Benoni. "Well?"

"The chiefs have heard of the quarrel between you and Joel Vahndert and what happened afterwards. They have met and decided that you two would undoubtedly meet at Debra Awvrez' house. And there you might spill each other's blood. So to make sure that you save your blood for the Navahos —may God smite them blind—the Council forbids you two to see the girl until you return with a scalp at your belt. Then, being men, and responsible for your actions, you may do what you wish. But, until then . . . have you heard?"

Sullenly, Benoni nodded and said, "I have."

Chonz urged his horse through the gate until he was beside the youth. He held out a book bound in Mek leather. "Place your right hand upon it and swear upon it that you will obey the Council."

Benoni hesitated a moment. The full moon, which had just come over the faraway Supstishn (Superstition) Mountains, showed him gritting his teeth.

"Come on, son," said Chonz. "I ain't got all night. Besides, you know the Council won't do anything but what's good for you."

"Can't I even see her once before I go?" said Benoni.

"Not unless you go to her house," said Chonz. "Her father is making her stay at home. Old man Awvrez is mad. He says you and Joel have shamed her by bandying her name in a public place. If it wasn't so close to initiation, he'd horsewhip both of you."

"That is a lie!" cried Benoni. "Why, I never once mentioned her name! It was Joel Vahndert! It's not fair!"

Sullenly, Benoni placed his hand on the book. He said, "I swear by The Found—and The Lost—Testaments to obey the will of the Council as charged in this matter."

"That's a good boy," said Chonz. "Good luck to you on your first warpath. God be with you."

"With you," said Benoni. He watched the tall lean Announcer ride away, then he rode Red Hawk back to the stable. After unsaddling the horse, he did not return to the house. He wanted his fury to die out first. Instead, it became stronger, fed by images of Debra and Joel. After elaborating various forms of exotic punishment for Vahndert, if Vahndert ever got into his power, he felt somewhat better. Then, he went back into the house and explained what had happened. To his relief, he was not kidded. His father and brothers-in-law did speculate on the chance of bad blood between the Riders and Vahnderts, and they talked with gory detail of some honor-battles that had taken place between Fiiniks frats in the remote and recent past.

Until now, the elders of both families had been on good terms. They went to the same church. They lived not more than five blocks apart. The heads of both often had amicable and mutually profitable business.

"If Peter Vahndert belonged to our frat," said Mr. Rider, "we could submit the dispute to the Inner Lodge. But the Vahnderts don't, so that way is out. However, nothing will happen to cause us to draw our swords until after the boys come back. Then, God alone knows. That Joel is a loudmouth; he's been nothing but a trouble maker since he was a child. Give the child of Seytuh his due, though, he throws a mighty javelin."

The men began to heap abuse on Joel. Benoni did not join them. It would not have been correct for him to do so when others present were. Besides, he did not want to think of the lout. He wanted to think about Debra. After a decent interval, he excused himself and went upstairs to his room. Here, he soaked some clothes in water and hung them over the window in the hope the breeze would be cool enough for him to sleep. After an hour or more of tossing and turning and futile efforts to get Debra out of his mind, he fell asleep.

Benoni dreamed that he had been captured by the Navahos. They were about to pour a

great kettle of scalding hot water over him
before inflicting more localized injuries. To
give him an idea of what the entire kettle
would be like, they were letting a few drops of
the skin-burning water drip on him. By doing
this, they also hoped to unnerve him and
make him beg for mercy.

He swore to himself that he would act like a
man, a true Fiinishan, and would make them
admire him. After it was over, the Navahos
would send a message to Fiiniks that the
white youth, Benoni Rider, had died bravely,
and they would compose a song in his honor.
Debra would hear of this. She would weep,
but she would also be proud of him. And she
would scorn Joel Vahndert when he came
courting. She would call her father and
brothers. They would drive him from the
house with whips and dogs.

Benoni woke to see his stepmother's profile
against the moonlit square of the gauze-hung
windows. She was sitting on his bed and was
bent over him; her tears were dripping on his
chest.

"What's the matter?" he said.

"Nothing, really," she said, sitting up and
sniffling. "I came in to sit by you, to look at
you a while. I wanted to see you once again."

"You'll see me in the morning," Benoni
said. He was embarrassed, yet touched. He
knew she still grieved for his dead brother
and that she was worrying about him.

"Yes, I know," she said, "but I couldn't
sleep. It's so hot, and I . . ."

"A mother's tears cool the hot blood of the
young warrior on his first warpath," said

Benoni. "A smiling mother is worth a dozen knives."

"Don't quote me proverbs," she said.

She rose and looked down at him. "It's because I love you," she said. "I know I shouldn't be crying over you; you'll feel bad because I do. But I couldn't help myself. I just had to see you once more, before . . ."

"You talk as if you'll never see me again," he said. "Think of death, and you're a ghost."

"There you go with your old proverbs," she said. "Oh, I'm sure I'll see you again. It's just that you've been gone so long, hardly come home. And in no time at all, you'll . . . never mind. I'm doing what I promised not to do. I'll go now."

She stooped over and kissed him lightly on the lips, then straightened up.

"I'll stay home tomorrow and talk to you," he said.

"Thank you, son," she said. "I know how much you want to go into the marketplace and tell your friends about the Iron Mountains. And you *will* go tomorrow, act as if tomorrow is any other day. Besides, I'll have too much work to do to talk. Thanks very much, anyway, son. I appreciate your offer and what it means."

"Goodnight, mother," he said. Her voice had trembled so much that he was afraid she was going to cry again.

She left the room. Afterwards, he had trouble getting back to sleep. It seemed to him that, when he did succeed, he had just fallen out of wakefulness only to be dragged back into it.

This time, the moonlight showed four shadowy figures of men around his bed. They wore carved masks of wood with long curving beaks of ravens and black feathers standing out from three sides. Though the faces behind the birdmasks were hidden, he knew they were his father, two brothers-in-law, and his mother's brother.

"Get up, son of the raven," said his father's muffled voice. "It is time for you to try your wings."

Benoni's heart beat fast, and his stomach felt as if a dozen bowstrings were vibrating inside it. The time for his initiation had come sooner than he had expected. He had expected he would be given a week to rest from the long trip back from the Iron Mountains. But, he remembered, it was supposed to come unexpectedly, like a lion out of the night.

He rose from bed. His father secured a blindfold around his head. Somebody wrapped a cloth around his waist to cover his nakedness. Then he was taken by the hand and led out of the room into the hall. He heard a woman's soft weeping and knew that his mother was crying behind the closed door of her bedroom. Of course, she would not have been allowed to see the men in their masks nor him blindfolded. Nor would she have been warned that tonight was his time. Somehow, she had expected this. Women were supposed to be able to sense such things.

Benoni was led down the steps and out into the open air. Here he was placed on a horse and then the horse began to canter. Another horseman—he supposed—had his horse's reins and was pulling him along.

He gripped the horn of the saddle and felt very helpless riding in such a manner. What if his horse stumbled and fell and he, Benoni, were hurled off the saddle? Well, what of it? He could do nothing to prevent it.

Nevertheless, he felt uneasy. When, after perhaps half an hour's ride, they stopped and told him to dismount, he felt better. Then he was helped into a wagon and placed on a bench which ran the length of the wagon. On both sides, naked shoulders and arms and hips pressed against his. These, he presumed, belonged to other initiates.

The wagon started with a jerk and began rolling and bumping and lurching over a rough road. Having been warned to be silent, he did not speak to his companions. The ride lasted for perhaps an hour. Then, the driver shouted, "Whoa!" and the wagon stopped. There was silence for about five minutes. Just as he was wondering if it was part of the ceremony to sit on the hard wooden bench all night, a man barked a command.

"Come on out! And keep silent!"

Benoni was helped off the wagon and guided to a spot where he was told to stand still.

A drum began beating a monotonous four-beat; this continued for about ten minutes.

Suddenly, a horn blew, and Benoni started. He hoped that no one had noticed his nervous reaction.

A hand ripped off the cloth around his waist; he opened his mouth to protest against being naked, then shut it. He did not know for sure, of course, but he had heard that when the unblooded were let loose in the desert, they wore nothing.

His blindfold was untied and removed, and he blinked in the full moonlight. Then, since he had not been forbidden to do so, he looked around. He was standing in the middle of a line of naked youths, twelve in all. In front of him were many adult men, their bodies clothed in furs and feathers, their faces hidden by the animal masks of the various frats. One of them was going down the line, giving each youth a drink of water from a gourd. When the gourd was handed to Benoni, he drank deeply. Unless he was mistaken, this would be the last water he would taste for a long time.

The ceremony that followed was short and simple; so much so that Benoni could not help feeling disappointed. He had not known what to expect, but he had thought that there would be much beating of drums, long speeches exhorting them to go into the Navaho country, take as many scalps as possible, and return to their honor and that of Fiiniks. He had also expected that their heads would be shaved, leaving only a roach of hair and that their bodies would be daubed with warpaint. Or even that there would be a bloodletting ceremony during which his blood would be mixed with that of the adults of his frat.

Chief Wako, in a few words, dissolved those preconceptions.

"You boys will go as you are, naked as when you came into this world. You will go East or North or South until you come to enemy territory. There you will take at least one man's scalp. How you get food, water, shelter, and weapons is your problem. After you return—if you return—you will be initiated as men into the frat. Until then, you are only fledglings.

"If this seems hard to you, to let you loose with bare hands and feet, remember that this custom was established many many years ago. The first warpath weeds out the unfit. We want no weaklings, cowards, or stupid ones to breed their kind among us.

"Later, in the fall, the eighteen-year-old women will go through a similar test in the desert, the main difference between their tests and yours being that they do not have to go into enemy land.

"Now, when the drum begins beating, your elders in the clan will drive you into the desert with whips. You will run a mile, will be dispersed in all directions so you will not band together. Not that we can forbid you to band together afterwards, for you may do anything outside the area of Fiiniks. Even kill one another, if you wish."

Benoni heard a youth near him snort and mutter, "Good!" and he did not need to look to know that Joel Vahndert had spoken.

He did not have time to think about the implications of the remark, for Chief Wako raised his hand, held it a moment, then lowered it.

The drums broke out into a frenzy. The men in the masks, whooping and screaming, raced behind the youths. Then, whips cracked, and Benoni leaped into the air at the burn of a whiplash on his buttocks. He began running, and he felt no more cuts, for there was not a man in Fiiniks who could run as fast. But, behind him, the whips cracked and the yelling continued, and he ran for at least a mile until his pursuers had dropped far behind. Then he continued dog-trotting for several more miles, heading northeastward.

Benoni planned to trot for about five more miles, then hunt a while for a kangaroo rat or a jackrabbit to furnish him with blood and meat. Afterwards, he would find a place to sleep during the day. Travel by night was the only sane way. The sun would burn up the water in his naked body and make him more easily seen by any Navahos who might be in the area. Besides, hunting was better in the night when most of the beasts were out.

He paused on top of a high hillock of malapi to get his bearings, and then he heard, or thought he heard, somebody in the rocks below. At once he slipped behind a huge black malapi boulder and gripped a stone as a weapon. The man, or whoever it was, seemed to be in a hurry, which puzzled Benoni. He did not think it likely that a Navaho would be this close to Fiiniks, though it was possible. And if the follower were a Navaho, he would not be making this much noise. Chances were that it was one of the initiates. Either one who had happened to be taking the same path as himself, or one who was purposefully tracking him.

Joel Vahndert?

If it were Joel, he would not be one bit better armed than himself. It would be better to face him now, get it over with, rather than wait until he had fallen asleep and Joel could take him by surprise.

Benoni crouched behind the boulder. And he, whose ears could detect the lizard running over the sand and whose nose could smell a rabbit a quarter mile away upwind, knew at once that this was a sweating man. There was tobacco in the odor, which relieved him. It could not be Joel; youths were not allowed to smoke until they took their first scalp.

However, if this were the case, then the man could be a Navaho. And he might be careless because he thought that he, Benoni, was much further ahead.

The man came by the boulder, Benoni leaped around it, ready to catch him in the side of the head with a thrown stone.

He stopped, restrained his arm, and said, "Father!"

Hozey Rider jumped away, whirled, his long knife in hand. Then he relaxed, put the knife back in its sheath, and smiled.

"Good work, son!" he said, "I knew you must be some place close. I'm glad I didn't catch you unawares. I'd have felt very bad about your chances among the Navahos."

"You made a lot of noise," said Benoni.

"I had to catch you," said Hozey.

"Why?"

Benoni looked at the knife and wondered, for a second, if his father planned to give him the blade so he would have a better chance. He dismissed the thought as dishonorable.

"What I'm doing isn't according to ritual," said his father. "And it's actually a last-

minute thought on the part of the chiefs. I'll
be brief, because it's not good to hold a young
unblood back from the warpath.

"You know, son, that your older brother
went out with a scouting party about two
years ago, and we never heard of him again.
Possibly, he may be dead. Then, again, he
might just not have come back from wherever
he went to. You see, the mission he went on
was secret, because we didn't want to stir up
our own folk. Or let word to the Navahos what
we might be doing in the future."

"I never did know what the party Rafe went
out on was looking for," said Benoni.

"It was looking for a good place for us to
move to," said his father. "A place where
there is no valley fever, no earthquakes, no
volcanoes, and plenty of water, grass, and
trees."

"You . . . mean out of the valley?"

Hozey Rider nodded, and he said, "You
must not tell anybody. The Council sent the
scouting party out two years ago but told nobody why they went. We thought that there
might be emotional upsets. After all, Fiiniks is
our home. We have lived within the shadow of
the sacred Kemlbek Mountain for hundreds
of years. Some people might not want to
leave, even if Fiiniks was knocked flat by a
quake twenty years ago and ten volcanoes not
over thirty miles away formed in the last
twenty years. They might make a lot of
trouble. But we decided that it would be for
the good of the people if we did find another
home. For one thing, besides the fever, which
has been getting worse since I was a child,

and the threat of quakes and of volcanoes, there is another thing. That is, that this valley can only feed so many people because there is only so much water available. Despite our heavy mortality, the population has been expanding. Food is getting increasingly scarce. Oh, you haven't suffered, because you're the son of a rich farmer and slaveholder. But there are plenty of poor people who go to bed hungry every night. And if they keep getting hungrier and more numerous, well . . . I saw the Great Slave Revolt of thirty years ago."

"But those were slaves, father!"

Hozey Rider smiled twistedly and he said, "That's what you've been told, son. That lie has been spread about so successfully that even those who know better believe it now. But the truth is that the lower classes tried to storm the granaries. And only after much blood-shed on both sides was the revolt settled. The granaries were opened, the courts and laws were reformed somewhat, and the lower classes were given more privileges."

"Lower classes?" said Benoni.

"You don't like to hear that word? Well, it's part of our way of life to deny that there are such things as classes. But any man who wants to blink two or three times can clear the mist away from his eyes. Would you think about marrying the daughter of a cotton-chopper? No, you wouldn't. And there are other things. Some people don't like the idea of slaves."

"Any slave who serves fifteen years gets his freedom and becomes a citizen," said Benoni.

"That's very fair. The Navahos never give their slaves freedom."

"And so the ex-slave joins the ranks of the poor, is not fed, and loses all his security. No. Anyway, I didn't puff and pant after you just to discuss our social system.

"Shortly before you and the others were initiated, we Councilmen talked about asking some of you to extend your first warpath."

"Extend?"

"Yes. Remember, this is not an order. It's a suggestion. But we would like some of you young bucks, after you've taken a scalp or two, not to return at once. Put off your moment of glory. Instead, go east. Look for a place where there is water, perhaps the Great River so many talk about but have never seen.

"Then, when you report, we can start thinking about moving our people, starting anew there."

"Everybody?"

"Everybody!"

"But father, if I do this, I may not get back for a long, long time. And . . . and . . . well, what about Debra Awvrez?"

His father smiled and said, "You think Joel Vahndert may have married her by the time you get back? Well, what about it? She isn't the only good looking girl in the valley."

Benoni gasped in astonishment. He said, "Weren't you ever in love?"

"Six or seven times," said Hozey Rider. "And I loved both my wives. But if I hadn't married them, I would have met some other women and married them and loved them just as much. You think I'm cynical, son. But that's only because you're so young. Anyway, if you have your fiery young man's heart set on this particular blonde, think of the honor that will be yours if you discover a new country. How can a Navaho scalp compare with this? She will be yours for the asking; any girl in the valley would be yours."

"But Joel may have returned and have her! You forget that!"

"If Joel's father can catch his son, and he shouldn't have any trouble following the tracks of that lumbering bear, he will tell him the same thing I'm telling you. If I know Joel, the idea of so much glory will be irresistable. He'll go on to the East, too."

"Perhaps. Why didn't the Council think of this before?"

"Then we wouldn't have to be tracking you down? As I said, it was decided suddenly. It *was* ridiculous doing it so impulsively and so late. But a suddenly made-up mind moves quickly, and Wako told us to track our sons down if we could and ask them."

Benoni envisioned the older ones frantically chasing down the young men to give them a last-minute message. He did not know whether to feel sick or to laugh. All the dignity and importance of the ceremony was gone; he doubted the wisdom of the Council, which he had looked up to all his life. His father, as if he had read his thoughts, said, "Yes, I know. It's ridiculous. but when you take your place on the Council, son, you will find yourself doing just such stupid and hasty things."

"I don't know about this exploration trip,

father," he said. "I'll have to think about it
later. Now, I'm going to be too busy keeping
alive."

Suddenly, tears appeared in his father's
eyes; the moonlight glinted off them. And his
father put his arm around him and said, "God
go with you, son. And bring you back home as
soon as possible."

Benoni was embarrassed. It was bad
enough for his mother to weep. She could be
excused because she was a woman. But his
father . . .

Nevertheless, after gently saying good-bye
to his father and watching him disappear into
the boulder strewn hills, Benoni felt better.
He had not known that his father cared so
much for him. Men took so many pains to
conceal emotions, to deny they even had any.
Besides, no one had seen them, it was not as if
his father had broken down in public.

Benoni headed toward the northeast,
keeping the towering bulk of the Superstitions, twenty miles away, to his right. His
goal was the beginning of the Pechi Trail, the
path of the uplands and Navaho country. To
get there, he had two choices. Take the easy
but much longer road which curved southeast
and then back north just at the foot of the
Superstitions. Or cut straight across the
country or rock strewn, wash-gashed, hilly
country. The easier path meant that he would
have to pass by farms and the fortress-town of
Meysuh. Even though his going would be at
night, he would be in danger of being shot by
his own countrymen or having dogs set upon
him. The naked youth on his first warpath

was taboo. A man's hand was lifted only to strike a blow at him, to send him more swiftly on his way. There had been cases where boys had taken the easier road, were detected, and killed or crippled. Nobody felt sorry. A youth who was captured was obviously unfit to be a warrior of Fiiniks.

Benoni cut across the desert. He climbed the steep walls of several cut washes. One of which, so said legend, was an irrigation canal dug centuries before white men had ever come to this land. Hohokam, the ancient Indians were called. Their descendants were the Papago and Pima, long since absorbed into the white majority in the Valley of the Sun.

He skirted several small mountains where he could, climbed where he could not go around. Near dawn, he had covered about ten miles.

Then, thirsty and hungry, he thought of hunting. First, he needed a knife. That meant finding a piece of chert or some satisfactory substitute. He would be lucky if he found even chert. There was no better grade of flint in this area. And, after an hour of straining his eyes in the moonlight and picking up many rocks and rejecting them, he found a chert. This, he chipped away at, though he hated to make any noise. And he fashioned a crude cutting tool, one that would be refined when he had more time.

After choosing two small stones for throwing, he looked for jackrabbits, cottontails, kangaroo rats, pocket mice, or anything else that he might see before it saw him.

After an hour of slow and silent search, he came across a pack of kangaroo rats. These long-legged, strong-tailed little creatures were playing in the moonlight in a coliseum formed by a ring of malapi boulders. They bounded high into the air, chased each other, rolled and tumbled in the dirt that was the floor of the coliseum. Benoni waited until one was chased close to the boulder behind which he crouched.

Then, his left hand fired the stone at the unsuspecting creature.

Sixteen years of practice propelled the missile. It struck the rat on the side and bowled it over. Benoni shifted the rock in his right hand to his left and threw it. The rat rolled over a few turns from the second blow and kicked out its little life.

Suddenly, the coliseum was empty of all but the victim.

Benoni ran up to it, picked it up, and cut its throat with the chert he had sharpened an hour ago. He held the beast upside down, allowed its blood to drain into his throat. Some ran over his lips and down his chin and dripped onto his chest, but he was too hungry to pay any attention. Later, he would scour himself with sand.

When he finished drinking all the rodent had to offer, he skinned it. His rough tool of chert made the skinning a tough job, but he was not concerned with damage to the skin for he had no use for it. Then, he cut off the long heavily muscled legs, cut out the heart and kidneys and liver. And he chewed up the warm tough meat. This he did with some distaste; he did not like raw meat of any kind. But a man had to eat, and he had been doing just this for some years in preparation for this day and more to come. To light a fire was to invite a Navaho knife at his throat, or an arrow in his back; too high a price to pay for cooked meat.

Gingerly, Benoni cut open a barrel cactus, not without being stuck several times with the long spines, though he was careful. He gouged out several pieces of the pulp and sucked on them. It was not like drinking from a cup of water or a spring. In fact, the pulp held no more moisture than a piece of raw potato. But it was moisture, though in limited quantities and somewhat bitter.

Afterwards, he dug out a foxhole under a palo verde tree near the banks of a wash. Curling up in the hole, he composed himself for sleep. Sleep came swiftly.

But as swiftly, dawn with its whiteness and heat awakened him. Thirsty again, he crawled out of the hole, cut some more strips of barrel cactus. These he took back to the hole. Some he buried deep to use later during the day; the others, he sucked. He covered himself with sand to cut down on the moisture loss and went back to sleep. Several times during the day, he awoke and dug up the cactus pulp. Still, the water he got from the pieces was far from enough to replace that drawn from his body by the dry and burning air.

Fortunately, a sidewinder wiggled its crazy path near to his hole. All Benoni had to do was to reach out, seize the rattler by the tail, and crack it like a whip. Back broken, the sidewinder managed only to writhe as it tried, vainly, to sink its fangs into him. Benoni hacked its head off, then drank the blood and ate some of its back-meat. The rest he buried beneath the sand, for he did not want to attract any buzzards or hawks. Their circling might also bring some curious Navahos.

No birds came. But the ants did. For an hour, he scooped them up and crunched them between his teeth or swallowed them whole. Finally, they quit coming, and he settled back to sleep.

Dusk came. Benoni, itching all over from insect bites, crawled out of the hole. He took a sand bath, cut some more cactus pieces, and set off toward the northeast. The moon, diminished to a sliver, rose over the Superstition. It was huge and bloody. As it went higher in the cloudless sky, it became smaller and silvery. Benoni had the light he needed. He found a nest on a branch of cat's-claw tree; two wrens slept in it. A leap upwards, ignoring the thorns sticking into his hand, and clutching the branch with one hand, he swooped downward upon the nest with the other hand. His hand closed upon the birds, squeezed them, cut off their sudden cries and their lives. Their blood went to quench his thirst; their meat stilled the rumblings of his stomach. He spat out the feathers and pin-feathers that had escaped his hasty plucking, and went on.

The rest of the night, Benoni walked swiftly toward his goal. Toward dawn, he found a dying palo verde and spent some time tearing a branch loose. When he had cut and twisted it off, he sliced off the bumps along its length and sharpened one end.

He had no trouble finding jackrabbit holes. Down the entrance of over twenty holes, he thrust the sharp end of the stick. Finally, the jabbing stick caught in the body of an animal. Quickly, he twirled the stick; it caught the loose fur of the rabbit and wound tightly around the stick. Benoni pulled the kicking animal out of the burrow and hit it in back of the head with the edge of his palm. He cut its throat and drank its blood. He took more time skinning the creature this time. After he had cut the animal up, he buried part of it deep in the sand and ate the rest.

He spent several days near the spot where he had caught the jackrabbit. With the animal's own fat and with his urine he tanned the fur, though it was stiffer than he liked, he was able to make a sun-hat for himself. He also caught two other rabbits with the same technique of the pointed stick, a trick known by the Navaho name of *haathdiz*. He made himself a loincloth and a belt, found another piece of chert. This he intended to use to make a spearpoint, but he fractured the chert with a blow that was not quite at the right angle.

At night he moved on. He ate chuckwalla and gecko lizards, pocket mice, ants, an armadillo, a diamond-back rattlesnake, and a ring-tail cat. Once he caught a desert turtle and drank water from the two little sacs it carried under its shell.

He went up the hills, began climbing up slowly, going up a tall hill or small mountain, then going down again before tackling the next. But he was at a higher level than the Valley even when he was going down, and on the evening of the fifth day he rose from his sleep to see his last sawaro. The fifty-foot cactus stood on the side of a hill and was outlined blackly against the setting sun.

Straight it stood, a pillar with one outstretched arm and one dropping downward. It looked like a man bidding him farewell.

Impulsively, Benoni waved good-bye at it. He could not help thinking that, perhaps, this might be good-bye forever, that he would never again see these stately and sometimes weird plants that grew only in the Valley of the Sun.

Then he continued climbing, came to the ancient trail leading around the sides of the mountains, and decided to follow it for a while. Certainly the chances of Navahos waiting here during the night time seemed remote. Even if they were, they would have a hard time seeing him. He was, he boasted to himself, a ghost. He drifted along in the darkness like a coyote, a lion. Besides, he had heard that the Navaho always stayed close to their camping site at night, that they feared demons and evil gods. On the other hand, his father had told him that was nonsense. The Navahos feared the dark no more than the Fiinishans. Proof was that they had often attacked outlying farms and lone travelers at night.

All that night, Benoni followed the trail. Now and then, he came to a broken piece of strange rocklike stuff, rotten, crumbling at the touch. This, he supposed, was the stuff the old ones had paved the Pechi Trail with. His father and others had described it and said what they thought it was. Of course, Benoni told himself, their saying so did not necessarily make it so. Whatever the truth, the trail was not a wide road now as it was supposed to have been. It was narrow, sometimes so narrow that he had to stand with his back against the cliff and edge along facing outwards. Other places, it was broad, though even here boulders had fallen down from above to the road, partially blocking it. The spring torrents had cut washes and grooves into it.

When dawn threatened, Benoni left the road, climbed up a steep cliff to the top, and found a place he could dig into under the shade of an ironwood. Here, he slept uneasily all day. In the dusk, after careful reconnoitering, he descended to the trail. He wondered if he was doing the right thing. Perhaps, he would be much safer if he ignored the easier path and cut across the mountains and valleys between them. His progress would be slower. But he would not meet any of the *Dine*, not likely.

He met no-one, heard nothing except the screek of a night-hawk, the scream of a bobcat, the whoopbark of a coyote. Several times he came across the big tracks of lions, but he did not worry overmuch about these. From childhood, he had seen hundreds of lion tracks in washes and other places and had yet to see a live lion.

At dawn, he came to the top of a big hill. And he saw, far below and away, the glitter of blue water.

This, he knew, must be the lake that lay a few miles outside of the really dangerous territory. Here, it was said, the old ones had once built a dam, oh, so big that Benoni's head swam trying to imagine it from the descriptions. Once, this lake had been much larger than the one he now saw. Here the ancient whites sported, swam (something he could not do), sailed (something he had to strain his imagination to picture), and enjoyed all the benefits of a ruling and powerful race. Now, Navahos, or the threat of them, made the place deadly.

Yet, Benoni was determined to sneak down at night, to take a bath, and wash off the grime and stink of the desert, to drink cool water to the fill. And here he would find and fill a calabash with water to carry along. He was sick of blood and cactus pulp moisture; his throat was dry and aching.

Shortly after dusk, Benoni Rider was on the shore of the lake. He did not rush in, though every cell of his body craved water. He felt an unexpected sensation, one he had never imagined because of lack of experience. Fear of water.

This hollow between the mountains was deep, and he could not swim. If he went in very far, he might step off a ledge and sink into the black depths. The thought sent him into a near panic.

For a long time, he crouched by the shore and watched the lake lap at the rocks on the edge. Then, calling himself a coward, unfit to be a man, he walked into the water. Slowly, he slid his foot ahead and tested the pebbly bottom to make sure there was not a break in its continuity. When he was knee deep, he decided he had gone far enough. Now, forgetting his terror, and sighing with ecstasy, he sat down. He scrubbed himself with his hands and with sand he brought up from the bottom. He made sure that the dirt and sweat was gone from his body and from the hair on top of his head. Afterwards, reluctantly, he left. His calabash filled with water and hanging from a strip of rabbithide around his waist, he followed the trail. An hour before dawn, he caught a gecko lizard and ate it raw, crunching the delicate bones between his teeth.

He was looking for a place far enough off the path to be safe for sleep when he heard a horse snort.

He hit the ground, lay still a moment, then snaked into the scanty vegetation. Since the snort had come from above, and since he had heard no other noise, he was fairly confident he had not been seen. However, he was slow and cautious in getting to the little mesa above the path. He went around the side, first cutting down a wash, then starting to climb up. The slope on this side was even steeper than the side along the trail, so he knew that the horse and rider must have come up a much gentler climb on the side opposite the one he was ascending.

After crawling up between two large rocks on the edge of the mesa, he peered through them. He saw more than he had expected.

Four horses and a pack-mule, all hobbled and grazing on the sparse grass. Under the green branches of a palo verde tree were four sleeping men. Navahos. No. Three Navahos. One was lighter in color and was naked. Big.

The white man turned over, and Benoni saw that he was Joel Vahndert.

Joel's hands were tied behind him; his ankles were roped together.

There was a fourth Navaho, a squat man who sat on a rock about forty yards from the others. His back was to Benoni, and he was obviously supposed to be watching the trail from his position. Why he had not seen Benoni, Benoni did not know. Perhaps the Navaho had fallen asleep for the few minutes Benoni needed to escape detection. Whatever the reason for his lapse, it was going to be fatal if Benoni had anything to do with it.

Benoni put the chert knife in his teeth, picked out two stones, placed one in each palm, and began crawling toward the sentinel. The Navaho never looked his way until Benoni was within twenty feet. Then, the Indian stood up and stretched. Benoni leaped to his feet and threw the first stone. It caught the Navaho in the back of the head with a loud crack.

The Indian pitched forward and fell down on the face of the slope with a clatter of loosened rocks. Benoni whirled towards the others, expecting them to be awakened. But they did not stir, and the horses and mule only continued to eat.

For a minute, Benoni hesitated between two choices of action. Take the scalp of the man he had just killed and return with honor to Fiiniks. Or cut Vahndert loose and, with him, attack the other Navahos.

The first choice was the easier. To cut and run would not be to lower himself in the eyes of his people—even if they found out. Joel Vahndert was his enemy. Joel wanted to marry Debra Awvrez, and he had proved himself an inept warrior by being captured. If Benoni cut Joel's throat before he left, he would be within his rights. Anything an un-blood did on his warpath was permissible, anything at all. He had no one to account to but himself.

That was the trouble. Discretion and logic told Benoni that the best thing he could do for his own interests was to scalp the Navaho and take to the hills. There, the Navahos could not easily track him.

But Benoni could not see himself doing this. He could not leave a fellow Fiinishan to be tortured to death. Besides, the more scalps he brought back home, the more honor to himself. And when the story of Joel's rescue was told, Joel would be in disgrace.

Weighing of the factors took only a few seconds. He was scarcely aware of them as fully expressed and considered thoughts. They came up from the unconscious like flashes, the barely visible peaks of thrusts from the deep below. He picked up the knife fallen from the Navaho's hand—it was about nine inches long and of good and sharp steel—and walked towards Joel. He did not run because he did not want to startle the beasts.

By the time Benoni had reached Joel, Joel's eyes were opened. He was pale, his mouth hung open as if he did not believe what he was seeing. Benoni did not bother to make a sign cautioning him to keep silence. Joel would not be stupid enough to make a noise. If he were, he deserved to die.

The keen edge severed the ropes around Joel's hands, which were tied behind him. Joel began flexing his fingers, his face twisted as the returning circulation drove agony through his veins. Two slashes, and the ropes around the big youth's ankles were cut.

Benoni asked him, very softly, if he could go into action.

"I can't do anything for a minute," said Joel. "I don't think I can walk."

He rose and took a step like a man with frozen legs. "Wait just sixty seconds, then . . ."

But there was a cry from behind them, and a Navaho bounded to his feet. He was the one closest to the two, well within good knife range. The rising sun flashed on his blade as he threw it.

Benoni reacted automatically; his own knife flew.

Suddenly, the hilt of the knife struck out from the pit of the Navaho's stomach. The stricken man fell backwards, his hands around the hilt. At the same time, Benoni felt a blow in his side, and he staggered back from the force. Though he felt no pain, only a numbness, he knew he was wounded. Looking downward, he saw the Indian's knife sticking out from between his right ribs. It was not in more than an inch, but blood was welling out from around the steel.

The other two Navahos, yelling, had also gained their feet by now. One picked up a short spear from the ground. The other grabbed up a bow with one hand and an arrow with the other. Benoni, screaming, picked up a rock and rushed at the bowman. The Indian fitted the notch to the bow and raised the bow and arrow as a single piece, pulling back as he did so. Benoni threw his rock; it flew straight and smashed into the man's throat. But not before he loosed the arrow.

Benoni felt another blow, this time in the chest just below the shoulderbone. He fell backwards upon the ground, then sat up. The Indian must not have had a chance to draw the arrow back to the head, for the arrow had not gone in deeper than the head. Nevertheless, Benoni was out of the fight.

The only Navaho standing raised his spear as if to throw. Then, changing his mind, he lowered it, gripped it with both hands, and charged Joel.

Joel looked desperately around for a weapon. None was within reach, none except the arrow and the knife sticking from Benoni's flesh. And it was one of them that Joel took, tearing the knife from between Benoni's ribs. Benoni cried out, but it was done so swiftly he could not resist. If he had had time to think, he would have told Joel to do it. Otherwise, both would be dead.

Joel stooped, picked up a rock, and ran at the Navaho. A few feet from him, he threw the rock. The Navaho ducked; the rock shot past

his head. Joel shifted the knife to his right
hand, and his left hand shot out. The Navaho
came up out of his dodging maneuver a little
off balance. Joel caught the spear shaft with
his hand but not without closing it around the
head first and cutting his hand. He jerked
backwards. The Navaho, clinging to his spear,
was pulled headlong. Joel pulled the spear
towards him as he fell, twisted, and the spear
drove between his arm and body. His right
hand came up with the knife. The blade drove
into the Indian's belly. The Indian screamed
and fell beside Joel. Joel pulled the knife out
and plunged it into the Navaho's throat.

Then, there was silence. Even the horses,
which had been screaming, were quiet.
Benoni looked down at the ravaged place on
his side from which the knife had been so
savagely jerked. The blood was flowing fast
now, and the pain was beginning to come.
Also, he was starting to feel the arrowhead in
his shoulder.

There was nothing to do but try to work the
arrow loose, even if it meant more loss of
blood. He batted the flies away from the two
wounds and closed his left hand around the
shaft and began to move it slowly.

Joel, breathing hard, came up to him, and
he said, "You'll never be able to do that by
yourself."

He pulled the arrow loose with one easy
motion. Benoni clenched his teeth to keep
from screaming, and he felt faint. For a
moment, the world swam, then it came back
into focus. He saw Joel standing over him
holding the bloody knife and arrow and

smiling. Smiling.

"Looks as if you won't make it, friend," said Joel. "Too bad, too."

"I'll make it all right," said Benoni. "I'll live to take those scalps back to Fiiniks."

"I don't see how you can say that," said Joel. "Since I'm taking those scalps."

"You!" said Benoni. "You only killed one man. The rest are mine."

Still smiling, Joel said, "Now, how are you going to scalp a man when you haven't even the strength to walk? And'll be dead in an hour or so? No, it'd be pure waste to leave all that fine black hair here to rot."

"Maybe you should take my scalp, too," said Benoni. He fought to keep his consciousness.

"I would if it wasn't yellow," said Joel. "Of course, I could tell them back home that it was taken off a blond Navaho. They say there are some. But I think they might find that hard to swallow. Besides, it wouldn't be right, would it?"

Laughing, he turned and walked away and began the business of cutting and peeling back the dead men's scalps. When he had four hanging from a belt he'd taken off a Navaho, he put on one of the men's loincloths. He selected a horse, the best bow and arrows, a spear, and the best knife. He unhobbled the other animals, too, saying, "Couldn't leave them there to die of starvation or be caught by the lions."

Benoni watched him make preparations to move on. One thing he was determined not to do was to beg for help. It was obvious that

Vahndert meant to give him none. Even if
Vahndert would, he was not going to get
Benoni Rider to plead. Benoni would rather
die. Probably would die, too.

After putting the choicest food in the saddle
bags of his horse, Joel returned to Benoni.
"By rights, I should put a spear through you,"
he said. "You're no damn good, and you might
possibly live. Though I doubt it. However, I'm
a very forgiving person, I'll let you make it on
your own."

He paused, then said, teeth bared in hatred,
"Not before I pay you back for what you did
on the way home from the Iron Mountains."

He drew his foot back and kicked Benoni
between the legs. Benoni felt agony, then he
fainted.

When he came to, he found himself sitting
up on his knees, bent over, and clutching at
the source of pain. Blood was running down
his side from the two wounds, and the flies
were swarming on that side of his body,
forming an almost solid mat of blackness and
buzzing. Benoni scraped them away, then
began crawling towards a pile of goods beside
a Navaho. Painfully, he made the short
distance, though he had to stop four times to
fight off unconsciousness. Once at the pile, he
chose two ceramic water bottles. These were
not filled; the water that Joel had poured from
them was fast drying on the rocks. However,
Joel had not bothered the food. Benoni chose
strips of dried meat, mesquite beans, and
some hard dry bread. Then, he put on one of
the dead men's pants. They were tight, but
they covered him.

He wrapped several bandannas around the wounds in a very clumsy but effective job to stanch the blood. Armed with a knife, a bow, and a quiver of arrows, and carrying a sack of food, he managed to mount a horse. He almost fell off from weakness and dizziness, but he held on. And he urged the horse down the slope and across a wash and back onto the trail. Then he rode back to the lake, where he dismounted and filled the water bottles.

After these preparations, he had only one thing to do. That was to find a cave in the mountains where it was cool, where he could command a view of the trail below, where he could recover from his wounds. He hated to loose the horse, for he could use it when he felt well enough to go back on the warpath. But if another band of Navahos found a hobbled horse, they would search the territory and might unearth him. He could not take a chance.

He took the saddle and reins off and gave the beast its freedom. Then, slowly, panting, full of pain, he climbed the mountain. And, within three hours, he had found one of the caves that pockmarked the face of the mountain. He crawled into its entrance over a pile of dried choya branches left there by rats, ignoring the pain of many little barbed needles. At the rear of the cave, he collapsed. He did not come out of his sleep until early next morning.

He drank some water and ate some smoked meat and the sweet beans. He waited for a fever to come, knowing that if he became infected from the wounds, he would probably die. But the fever did not come.

And, on the evening of the third day, he left the cave. He was very weak and stiff from the wounds and thirsty because he had drunk all the water on the second day. Painfully, he made his way down the mountains. At its foot, he drank water and refilled the bottles. Then, he began walking toward the northeast. A week later, he was able to run and to work the arm in which the arrow had sunk. He killed game with his arrows, and he built a small fire in the most secluded spots and cooked his meat.

Always, he looked for Joel Vahndert. If he had found the youth sleeping, he would have cut his throat on the spot. But he did not find him.

One night, he almost stumbled into a Navaho sentinel. This man was placed on a cliff high above the trail. After studying him, Benoni decided that this was the first in a chain of sentinels placed near the town that guarded the end of the trail. There was a big lake beyond it, the beginning of a series of lakes which ended in the body of water beside which Benoni had been wounded. Benoni worked his way over the mountains. At the end of the second night, he saw the lake and the stockaded village beside it. To the east were the beginnings of pine forests. He knew that north and east were many small Navaho settlements. About a hundred years ago the Navahos had come into this area, killed or driven off the Apaches then living there.

Benoni stood on top of the cone-shaped peak in the shadow of a jumper for a long

time. What to do? Skulk around the town, kill
a man, then leave for Fiiniks with a scalp at
his belt? Or go east for a long distance, maybe
to the edge of the earth, searching for a well-
watered earthquake-free country to which the
Fiinishans might migrate?

Finally, he decided that it was too soon to
make up his mind. He would go much further
east, however. He did not think it would be
good to try to take a scalp here. Doubtless,
Vahndert and some of the other youths had
already been here. They would have stirred
up the Navahos, put them on their guard. It
would be better to go through here at night
and strike at some of the towns or farms
where the inhabitants were not so cautious.

That night, he left the mountain and struck
across the forests. He traveled for two weeks,
hunting on the way. He passed many Navaho
farms with their rock hogans and straight or
circular rows of maize, beans, pumpkins,
squash, and muskmelons and little herds of
sheep, goats, and a few cattle. Several times,
he had a chance to take the scalp of some
farmer working in the field, but he refrained.
Two more weeks passed, and always he
traveled into the rising sun. Now that he had
many trees and bushes to hide him, he walked
by day.

Then, one morning, a lone Navaho youth
riding a horse came close to his sleeping
place. The horse was a fine roan stallion; the
saddle was chased with silver. The youth was
singing a song about the maiden whose hand
he meant to ask for.

Benoni admired the song and the fine voice

of the youth. But he admired the saddle and
the horse even more. He shot an arrow
through the youth, cutting off his song in the
middle of a word. He took the scalp and the
horse and set off towards the east. Knowing
that he would be tracked, he pushed the horse
for several days. He went up as many streams
as he could find and many times took the
horse carefully across rocky places. Never
did he see any pursuers, but he did not
breathe easily until he had come to the edge of
the forest.

On the edge of the Navaho country, where
the desert began again, at the time of the sun's
setting, Benoni heard something. What it was
he did not know. Only a murmur from
upward that told him of something
dangerous. He tied his horse to a branch of a
tree beside a wash and worked his way on his
belly northwards.

After fifteen minutes of cautious progress,
he came to the top of a low ridge. He looked
through the sparse grass and down into a
little amphitheater. In its center sat Joel
Vahndert, Joel Vahndert cooking a rabbit
over a tiny fire. His horse was a few feet from
him and was feeding upon the tough brown
grass.

Benoni's heart had been beating fast before.
Now, it thudded under his breastbone,
hammered. But he moved slowly in order not
to make any noise, the ridge concealing him,
and his hands were steady as he fitted an
arrow to the string of his bow.

He planned to stand up, call to Joel, and
thus give him a fighting chance. No one—not

even himself, the only surviving witness (he hoped)—could accuse him of cowardice. Of magnanimity, yes, for he did not have to warn the treacherous Joel. No, not magnanimity, for he wanted Joel to know that he, Benoni, had lived and now was taking vengeance.

But he did not rise at once, for he was savoring the look that would appear on Joel's face when he saw him. Luckily for him, he crouched those few seconds. Just as he started to rise, to spring upon the top of the ridge, he froze.

A whoop from half a dozen throats rose from the opposing rim of the amphitheater. And, over the rim, six Navahos rode.

Joel dropped the meat into the fire, jumped up, caught his horse by the saddle just as it began to run away, and hoisted himself upon its back in one flowing motion. Fortunately for him, the horse was headed at right angles from the Navahos, and it passed four scrubby pines. The arrows of the attackers struck the branches or were deflected, and they lost some time by having to round the trees. By then, Joel was gone, though whether he could keep ahead of them was another matter. Huge, Joel burdened any horse he rode, and his animal was no larger than those that ran after him.

Benoni, unable to restrain himself, shot at the last Navaho in the line of pursuers. His arrow entered beside the youth's lower spinal column, and the youth fell backwards off his horse. The others did not see him tumble, for their eyes were on the quarry.

Benoni ran out, scalped the corpse, and ran

back to his horse. Then, instead of riding away from the party, he decided to follow them. A foolhardy move, but if the Navahos lost Joel, he intended to find Joel for himself. And, perhaps, he could pick off another of the enemy. He liked the idea of hunting them while they chased Joel.

When day came, he was deep in the desert, and he saw no signs of the hunting party or of Joel. The night had been moonless, and the ground was rocky.

Nevertheless, Benoni pushed eastwards, imaging that Joel would have fled in that direction and hoping that he would again run across him. He believed in events happening in three's; he was sure he would meet Joel again. Next time, he would not delay.

The desert was somewhat different than the one he had known, but not too different. He rode the horse until it became apparent that there would be no water for it. Then, reluctantly, he killed it. After smoking as much of its meat as he could carry, he set out on foot. And here he had the same problems facing him as in the Fiinishan desert. These he solved in the same way, living off the plants and animals. A man who had not been born and bred there would have died in two days. But Benoni, alone and on foot, made fifteen miles a day. And, though he did not grow fat, he maintained his weight and his health, grew hard as the shell of a desert tortoise.

Now, he cut towards the northeast at night and slept during the heat of the day. The flat-land behind him, he began going around mountains where he could, over them where he could not. Generally, he followed an ancient trail. Doubtless, it had been one of the stone roads of the old ones. When he came to a place where dirt and sand was piled up in many hummocks for miles, he knew he was in the ruins of a city of the old ones. He did not sleep in the ruins but walked all night. He was very nervous, for he had heard that the ghosts of the old ones and earth demons flitted through the spaces between the hummocks. And, sometimes, they possessed the person unlucky enough to fall asleep.

He wondered if the stories were true about the old ones. Had they once been so numerous they filled this land, drank water piped in from the sea (which he had never seen), flown through the air in magical wagons, lived to be two hundred years old, talked to each other at great distances through magical devices? Was the story true that the old ones had fallen out among themselves and devastated each other with weapons so terrible it made his flesh crawl to hear of them? Or was the other story, that the demons of the earth had destroyed civilization, true?

The preachers said that almost all the knowledge of the old ones had been lost, that their books, even, were destroyed. Some parts of ancient scriptures, telling of the creation of the world, of Adam and Eve, of the wanderings of the lost Hebrews across the desert (this one?) and of Our Savior had been found. But these were incomplete, parts of them were lost. And it had taken half a century for the preachers in Fiiniks to decipher the spelling of the old ones. And even now they were very uncertain of the meanings of many words. In fact, disputes over the interpretations had led to a religious war about ten years before Benoni was born. The losers had fled westward through the desert. Their goal was the great ocean said to exist beyond the mountains.

Benoni could not read the Found Testaments; he had been lucky to be born in the ruling classes and given enough schooling to read the writing of Fiiniks, which differed from that of the old ones. The preachers said the writing of the old ones, though having an alphabet similar to the demotic, had different values in many cases. To master the old ones' writings, a man had to spend almost all his time in the attempt. It was not worthwhile unless a man wanted to be a preacher. Benoni envied the power the preachers had, but he intended to become a big man in Fiiniks through other means.

Next dusk, Benoni walked onwards. A week later, he was almost surprised by a band of horsemen. They came around the corner of a mountain, and Benoni was almost caught in the open. He heard them about thirty seconds before they came into view, enough time to hide above the trail behind a boulder.

The riders were all men and dressed strangely. They wore clothes tied around the head that fell halfway down their back, and their bodies were covered in loose robes of many colors. Their standard-bearer carried a white flag on which was a golden hive and large golden bees swarming from the hive. By this, Benoni guessed that the men were a war

party from Deseret. He had heard about
Deseret from Navahos he had talked to in the
market-place during the December-January
trade-truce. They said that the white men of
Deseret had once been a small community on
the Great Salt Lake, that they had a strange
religion something like that of the Fiinishans.
That during the past hundred years they had
increased in numbers, were pressing upon the
Navahos, and had conquered much territory
to the east.

Benoni watched them go by regretfully. To
take the scalp of a Deseret man would bring
him much honor at home.

He went on, and two days later passed near
the remains of a village of Indians. The
Indians were dead, probably victims of the
Deseret war party that had passed him. Every
corpse had been stripped of its scalp. Benoni
felt contempt for the Deseret men. It was all
right to kill enemy women and children, for
that meant the women would bear no more
males, the male children would not grow up
to kill you, and the female children would not
grow up to bear males. But there was nothing
about the deed to warrant honor. You left
those scalps untouched.

Four weeks later, after going over a great
mountain range, Benoni left the desert. It was
almost like stepping from one room to
another. On one side, sand and rocks and
cacti. On the other, grass and trees.

He was in a country of great plains cut
occasionally by creeks and, now and then, a
small river. There were many trees along the
waterways; not so many on the plains. Yet

even here there were enough to make him
think this land rich in wood. Here began the
great herds of antelopes, deer, wild horses,
longhorned cattle, and huge pigs. Here also
were flocks of birds in such number they
darkened the sky as they flew overhead. Here,
naturally, were the packs of wild dogs, big
wolfish creatures, and, not so naturally, here
were lions. Benoni was surprised to find
them, for he had always thought of the lion as
a mountain beast. But these lions were not the
slim animals he had seen. These were great
cats weighing at least four hundred pounds,
thick-limbed, and seven to eight feet from tip
of nose to tip of tail. Aside from their size and
more massive legs, they looked just like the
cats at home, and he wondered if they were
not descended from them. On the plains, they
had changed into creatures large enough to
stalk and kill the dangerous longhorns.

He gave them a wide berth. At night, though
he did not like to attract human eyes, he built
a ring of fire to keep the lions away.

However, it was the wild dogs who almost
got him. One dawn they came sweeping
silently over the horizon just as he was arising
from sleep. He ran like a deer, and managed
to get up a tree which was fortunately nearby.
He stayed there for a day and night while the
dogs howled and leaped vainly. In the
morning, the dogs left. He came down.

The following evening, Benoni built a bed in
the branches of a tree. And, before going to
sleep, he considered what he was doing.
Almost without thinking about it, he had
pushed so far east that he might well be past

the point of returning. Not that there was anything to keep him from going back. It was just that the lure of the distant grassy horizons was getting stronger with every mile. He had planned to stop short many scores of miles back and make a decision whether he should look for a new country or take his scalps back to Fiiniks. Day had succeeded day, and he had put off the final decision. Now, he wondered if the Great River he had heard his father and the preachers talk of was only a short distance away. No-one, as far as he knew, had ever come this far from the Valley of the Sun. This adventure alone would be enough to make him the talk of Fiiniks. He would be able to tell tales about it the rest of his life. And, perhaps, his children—and Debra's—could some day travel the same path and even go on to the Great River.

Debra! Was she now pledged to marry Joel Vahndert because Benoni had not come back and she thought him dead?

He fell asleep wondering. In the morning, when he came down from the tree, he decided to put the choice of his path in the hands of Jehovah God. After washing himself thoroughly in a nearby creek, he got down on his knees and prayed. Then, he stood up, took his knife out of its scabbard, and flipped it high into the air. He stepped back and watched it turn over and over, flashing in the morning sun. If it came down point first to stick in the ground, he would continue east. If the butt of the knife struck first, he would turn back towards Fiiniks.

The knife whirled. And its butt hit the grass, and it bounced up to fall on its side.

Benoni put the knife back in its scabbard. Aloud, he said, "You have shown me what I should do, Jehovah! And I hope I am not doing wrong by changing my mind. But I intend to go straight ahead. I should not have asked You, because I knew in my heart secretly what I wanted to do."

Uneasy because he had ignored the omen, he walked on. For several days, he expected something terrible to happen: an attack by one of the huge lions, a bite from a rattlesnake, an arrow from behind a bush. But nothing out of the way occurred. After a week, he lost the uneasiness.

During the next two months, he had many adventures. But he always escaped from death or injury. Many times he had to hide to evade human beings. Usually, these were Indians. Four times, however, the danger was white men. A pack of wild dogs chased him, and again he barely made it to a tree. Once, a lion walked out of the dense vegetation surrounding a waterhole, and Benoni prepared to fight to the death: his death, he supposed. But the lion merely belched and stood his ground, and Benoni walked on.

A few days later, Benoni was peering from behind a bush at the strangest habitation he had ever seen. It was huge, perhaps four-hundred feet long and forty-feet high, wide in the middle and tapering to a point at one end. The other end was covered with the dirt of a hill. Its curving sides rose from the ground in a manner suggesting that only the upper half could be seen and that another half was buried under the ground. It shone in the morning sun, reflecting like Navaho silver. It had no doors or windows that he could see, and he circled the entire structure to get a good look. If it had an entrance, he decided, it must be behind the high log walls and gate of a stockade butting against the curving sides of the south side. Another log stockade mounted the central portion of the top of the structure; this, obviously, had been built as a look-out.

He dared not come any closer, for people were coming out of the open log gates. Some of them were tall husky men armed with bows and arrows, spears, and short, broad bladed iron swords.

The inhabitants looked like Navahos except that their noses were flatter, almost bridge-less, and they had folds of skin over the inner corners of the eyes. These folds gave them a slant-eyed look. Moreover, when several got close enough for him to hear, they spoke a harsh sing song tongue no more like Navaho than Navaho was like Mek or Ingklich.

Benoni knew that the buried metal cone must contain many people. The narrow log enclosure by its side would not hold them if they stood on each other's heads. Soon, the men, women, and children moved out to work the fall crops and became so numerous that he had to leave the vicinity.

He went eastward but not without puzzling for a long time over the weird metal building and its weird inhabitants.

Two months later, he had put the plains

behind him and was deep into a heavily
forested land of rolling hills with many water-
filled washes and rivers that was noisy and
bright with birds he had never seen before. He
passed the ruins of a farmhouse that had only
recently been burned, for the ashes were
warm. The corpse of a man, two women, and
three children lay outside the ruins. Benoni
knew that he was in a country of different
customs, for every body lacked its head.

An hour later, he picked up again the tracks
of horses which had led away from the bodies
but which he had lost. He told himself that he
should go at right angles to the war party. But
he was too curious; he could not resist following.

Just before dusk, Benoni saw the light of a
fire ahead. He worked his way through the
tall grass and brush very slowly. By nightfall,
he was behind a tree only twenty yards away
from the war party. He gasped, and he began
shaking. Never before had he seen men with
such black skins, such thick lips, such kinky
hair. It was not just that he had not
thought of such men. As a child he had heard,
and believed, tales of black giants who dwelt
far to the east near the Great River. These ate
flesh, would eat him if he did not behave as a
good child should.

These men were tall but not the twelve-foot
giants his mother had told him about. They
did look ferocious, however. They wore red
and white warpaint and headdresses of long
white feathers. They also wore human hands
strung on a necklace. One man had a pole
mounted with a human skull, and some of the

bags on the ground looked just the right size to carry heads.

Benoni watched them for a long time. He crawled closer, unable to resist his curiosity about their speech. This sounded like his, yet not like it. Sometimes, he thought he could identify a word, but he could never be sure. They were laughing and drinking from quart jugs, which he supposed they had taken from the farmhouse. They did not seem to worry at all about pursuit.

The September moon rose, and the black men kept laughing and joking until the jugs were empty. They threw these into the weeds and lay down to sleep. One youth was appointed guard; he stationed himself with spear and short sword a few yards outside the range of the fire, which had died down.

Benoni waited for an hour, then he made his way towards the sentinel. Easily, he crept up behind the nodding youth and chopped against the side of his neck with the edge of his palm. He caught the youth as he fell and eased him to the ground. Then, using the fellow's shorts, he gagged him. Using his belt, he tied his hands behind him. A few minutes later, he silently saddled two horses. After he had hoisted the youth belly-down onto one of the animals, he cut the hobbles around the other. Two whinnied and shied away, and he froze, waiting for the sleeping blacks to awake. They slept the sleep of the half drunk.

When he was mounted, he shouted, screamed, and rode among the other horses to spook them. Then, he urged his animal out into the forest while he held the reins of the horse on which the unconscious youth sagged.

He rode as swiftly as he dared in the night while behind him shouts arose. After an hour, he settled for a canter; another hour, for a walk. Morning saw them far away from the scene of the thievery.

By then, the black youth was awake. Benoni took him off his horse, hobbled the animal, and removed the gag from his captive. It took some time to convince the youth that Benoni did not intend to kill him. After he had calmed down through signs, Benoni started the task of learning the stranger's language. He interrupted the lessons twice to feed the youth. After eating, the youth seemed to be less reticent.

Benoni speeded up his learning when he found that part of the strangeness of the youth's speech came from a vowel shift. Also, that Zhem's tongue had unvoiced all word-final voiced phonemes. Where Benoni said *dog*, Zhem said *dahk*. For *stown* (stone), Zhem said *stahn*, and for *leyt* (late), *liyt* (as in seat). *Kaw* (cow) he pronounced *ku*. Thin, in Benoni's tongue, was *tin*. There were other differences. Some words were unknown to Benoni; he could not find any in his vocabulary to match Zhem's.

The following morning, Benoni tied Zhem's hands in front of him and allowed him to take the reins of his horse. He warned Zhem that if he tried to escape, he would be shot. They rode slowly, while Benoni practiced talking to the black youth. That night, he told Zhem why he had kidnapped him instead of killing him.

"I need someone who can tell me about this country," he said, "And especially about the Great River."

"The Great River?" said Zhem. "You mean the Mzibi? Or, as the Kaywo say, the Siy?"

"I don't know what it's called. But it's supposed to be the biggest in the world. Some say it circles the edge of the world. That if you go to its other side, you fall off."

Zhem laughed and then said, "*Ee de bikmo ribe iy de weh.* It's the biggest river in the world, yes. But there's land on the other side. Tell me, white man. If I answer your questions, what you going to do with me?"

"I'll let you go. Without a horse, of course. I don't want you tracking me down and killing me."

"You're not going to take my head home to show your folks, your woman?"

Benoni smiled and said, "No. I had thought of taking your scalp. It'd bring me much honor in Fiiniks because they've never seen one like that. But you're not a Navaho; I've no reason to kill you. Maybe you'll give me a reason."

Zhem frowned and looked sad. "No," he said, "if I did bring your head back with me, it wouldn't do any good. I'm in disgrace because you captured me. No Mngumwa can never go home again if he is cowardly enough to be taken prisoner. When Mngumwa goes into battle, he either dies or wins the victory."

"You mean your people won't take you back? Why? It wasn't your fault!"

Zhem shook his head and said, hollowly. "It

makes no difference. If I tried to rejoin our war party or go home, I'd be stoned to death. They wouldn't even dishonor their steel with my blood."

"Perhaps you'd be better off dead," said Benoni. "A man with no home is no man. And then your scalp . . . it's so woolley."

"I don't want to die!" said Zhem. "Not as a captive, anyway with my hands tied. It'd be different in battle. And I feel sad because I'll never make love to my wife again. But I want to live."

"You might be a help to me," said Benoni. "I don't know the land. But why should I trust you?"

"You shouldn't," said Zhem. "I wouldn't trust you either. But if we became blood-brothers . . ."

Benoni asked what blood-brothers meant, and Zhem explained. Benoni considered. He looked steadily at Zhem for a long time. Zhem fidgeted, frowned, smiled. Finally, Benoni said, "Very well. I don't like the idea that I have to fight for you no matter what you do. I don't know you. Maybe you'll do things I won't feel like defending you for . . ."

"You'll be my older blood-brother," said Zhem. "I will obey you in all things, unless you do something dishonorable."

"O.K." said Benoni. And he put out his arm for Zhem to cut and to apply his own wound to it . . . so their blood was red. He had thought it would be black; indeed, this thought had held him back from accepting Zhem's offer. He had not liked the idea that he might become half-black.

But, now that he thought about it, Navahos were very dark, sometimes, and their blood was as red as his.

Zhem chanted some words so fast that Benoni could only understand several. Then, they applied clay to the cuts. And Benoni untied Zhem's bonds. Until they were made blood-brothers, he had not trusted Zhem. He had watched him while he cut his, Benoni's, arm for fear the youth would try to stab him. A hint of a wrong move would have sent Benoni's knife plunging into the black skin. Zhem must have known this, for he had moved very slowly.

They mounted and rode on. Zhem explained that they were two days' horse-travel from the Msibi. This country belonged to the Ekunsah, a white nation. To the northeast lay the great nation of Kaywo. Its capital city, Kaywo, was at the meeting place of the Msibi and Jo rivers. Or, as they were called in the Kaywo tongue, *Siy* and *Hayo*. The Kaywo were a mighty nation, they had huge houses and temples, roads of smooth stone, and a great navy and army. They had just won a ten-year war with Senglwi; they had slaughtered the citizens of that city. And now they were turning their attention to the great city of Skego. Skego, once a small town on the shores of the Miys Sea, had become big, too, and was extending its empire southwards, towards Kaywo.

"I would like to see this great city," said Benoni, wondering if it were half as large as Fiiniks. "Can we go there without their killing us on sight or enslaving us?"

"I've been thinking that we could go there and enlist in the Foreign Legion," said Zhem. "If we fight for Kaywo, we get much booty. Women, too. If a man serves five years in the Legion, he is made a citizen of Kaywo. That would be worth fighting for. A man would have a home again."

"I would not mind going there if we would be allowed to leave again," said Benoni. "But, I must get back to my home sometime."

"You could always desert," said Zhem. "But you will not be allowed to enter the country as a free man unless you join the Foreign Legion."

Two days later, they reined their horses back upon the top of a high hill. Below was the Msibi, or Siy, the Great River. Benoni stared at it for a long time. He had never seen so much water before. It must be at least two miles, maybe more, wide. He shivered. It was like a giant snake, a snake of water. And that much water had to be dangerous.

"It's worth walking across half the world to see this," said Benoni. "Debra will never believe it when I tell her of it."

"*De po e de wote*," said Zhem. "The Father of the Waters. Do you want to ride toward Kaywo, elder brother?"

"Kaywo it is," said Benoni. "I can't wait."

They rode northwards along the shore of the great river. After half a day, they came to a rough dirt road and followed it. They went around a small stockaded village. Zhem said they could skirt a certain number. However, according to what he understood, the villages and farms became very numerous. They would encounter an army fort. Then, what happened would be in the hands of The Great Black God.

Benoni was a little jolted to hear this. He had always thought of Jehovah as being white. But, now he thought about it he had never seen Jehovah. Nor did he know anyone who had seen Him. So, how did he know what He looked like?

Benoni and Zhem had crossed the Kaywo border at a point above the frontier forts. According to Zhem, there were forts along every major road in the empire. It was inevitable that soldiers would find them. So, it would be best to present themselves at the first fort they came to. After a half day's riding, they found their chance. They came to a little valley the entrance of which was walled with boulders cemented to a height of twenty feet. Two guards challenged their right to go through the big iron gateway. Zhem, speaking Kaywo hesitantly, asked to see the officer of the guard. Two other soldiers were called. These conducted the strangers through the gateway. Outside a large stone building, Benoni and Zhem dismounted. They were led into the building, through several rooms, and finally faced the commandant of the fort.

The captain was a big dark man with a snub nose, thick lips, and curly hair that hung down the back of his neck. He wore a shiny silver-embossed steel helmet topped by a scarlet roach of dyed horsehair, a cuirass molded to fit his torso, a green kilt, and yellow leggings. He asked them what they wanted. Benoni could understand a word here and there, but the main sense was lost to him. Zhem translated for him.

Zhem replied that he was from the kingdom of Mngumwa. His blood-brother came from a place nobody had ever heard of. It was called Fiiniks, and it lay in the middle of a burning desert a thousand miles or more to the south-west.

The captain, Viyya, looked at Benoni with interest. He rose from his desk and walked staring around Benoni. Then he laughed and said something to Zhem.

"He says he's never seen anybody with skin like iron on the soles of his feet," said Zhem. "He says your name should not be Rider, for he sees no callouses on your buttocks. It should be Ironfoot."

"So you two want to join the Foreign Legion and fight for the glory of Kaywo and the Pwez Lezpet?" he said. "What crimes have you committed that you had to flee your native countries?"

Zhem told him the story of his capture by Benoni, though he neglected to mention that his war party had murdered a farmer and his family. He explained also the reasons for Benoni's presence here.

"A strange tale," said the captain. "A suspicious tale. If it were not for his ironshod feet, I might doubt it. However, we'll see. You two will be conducted to the capital where the Usspika might be interested in your story. He had ordered that anybody from the unknown lands be taken to him. I do not know why, nor am I supposed to know."

He then gave orders for the two to surrender their arms. Tomorrow, they would start their journey, under escort, to the capital. There, they could begin their training as rookies in the Foreign Legion. If they could qualify as worthy fighting men, they would be sworn. If they did not, they would be sold as slaves. If they misbehaved, their heads might be cut off and placed on poles.

Benoni did not understand the full meaning of the last remark. Next day, after he was put into a cage on a wagon, and the wagon drove along the smooth highway with its great slabs of stone, he understood. On both sides of the road, spaced every twenty feet, were ten-foot high wooden poles. A human head, in varying stages of rottenness, or a skull, topped every pole. Ravens flew around them or sat on the pates and picked off shreds of flesh. Along every one of the hundred miles to the capital, the skulls grinned and the heads stared emptily. Most of the heads were those of black men.

"The Fifth Army brought back thousands of captives when it defeated the invading barbarians of Juju," said one of the prisoners sitting beside Benoni. "Many were sold, but over half were beheaded. We couldn't afford to have so many savages working for us. If they revolted, they might cause us much trouble. We remember the slave revolt of six years ago."

The prisoner added, proudly, "Kaywo is mighty indeed, wild-men. While the First, Second and Fourth Armies stormed Senglwi, the Fifth defeated the Juju in the south. And

the Third hunted down and destroyed the
Hayo River pirates."

Fascinated and awed, Benoni watched the
display of the might of Kaywo for a long
while. Then, as the wagon rolled on, he began
to notice the countryscape. The farms were becoming more numerous and closer together.
The structure of the farmhouses and the
barns remained fundamentally the same: very
steep double roofs, no windows on the first
story, narrow windows on the second story, a
three or four-story narrow round stone tower,
built for lookout purposes, near to every
house. And, in every front yard, a twenty-foot
high wooden totem pole on which were carved
animal and human faces. Every pole was
topped by the double-headed wolf, the patron
beast of Kaywo.

He began to see more villages. These were
always surrounded by high stone or wooden
walls with many watchtowers. Every now and
then he saw a small fort of stone on top of a
hill; these, he was to find out, belonged to the
kefl'wiy, the aristocrats. The kefl'wiy and
their families and soldiers and their families
lived in these.

The road followed the contour of the Great
River, called *Siy* by the Kaywo. There were
hundreds of boats, some military, most
commercial, on the *Siy*. A few were sailing
craft, but the majority were propelled by oars
pulled by men.

Benoni talked, as well as he could, to the
other occupants of the wagon. These were
criminals going to the courts of the capital,
where they would either be sentenced to serve

in the galleys or mines or would be placed in a special work-battalion in the army.

By the time they reached the capital city, Benoni could speak Kaywo with fifty per cent efficiency, as long as the conversation stayed on a simple level.

On the evening of the fourth day, the wagon rolled through the famous Gate of Lions. Benoni stared at the towering limestone block statues of bearded lions guarding the gates, which were a hundred feet high.

"*Dhu wya*," he said to the man who sat next to him. "*Those lions*. Are they just figures of imagination? Or do lions with beards really exist?"

"*Zhe*," said the man. "*Yes*. I have seen them. They are like the lions of the great plains to the west except that they are smaller and have short dark-red beards, both male and female. There are some in the woods to the north, between Kaywo and Skego. But there are many in the forests of the east."

Benoni continued to look wide-eyed at the broad streets, the buildings reaching as high as six stories, the crowds he had never seen in such numbers even during the Truce Market in Fiiniks.

The wagon went down the two-hundred yard wide Avenue of Victory and entered the Circle of the Wolf. This lay in the heart of the city; in the middle of the Circle was a thirty-foot high pedestal topped by four granite statues. These represented the legendary founders of Kaywo: the giant man Rafa and his mate, the double-headed timber wolf Biycha, and their twin sons, Kay and Wo.

According to the Kaywo religion, the she-wolf
had given birth to a two-headed infant. After
Kaywo had reached manhood, he fought the
arch-enemy of mankind, Lu, the giant
cannibal from the Northern Seas. Lu had split
Kaywo with his sword and left him for dead.
But their mother Biycha, had restored them
to life. Now two individuals, they fought Lu
again and killed him and buried him on the
very spot where the statue was. Then they
built the city of Kaywo, prophesying before
they died that Kaywo, though small then,
would some day grow big enough to rule the
world.

Around the Circle of the Wolf were the *Pwez
Paleh* (the President's Palace), the Temple of
the First (a colossal flat-topped pyramid), and
many governmental buildings. A mile past the
Circle, the wagon stopped at the entrance to
the Kaywo Legions. Here, Benoni and Zhem
were taken into a barracks. They were put in
the care of a tough sergeant charged with
shaping the "wild-men" into disciplined
soldiers.

Benoni had expected to be called before the
usspika (the Speaker of the House of *Kefl'wiy*)
at once. But weeks went past, and he was busy
from sunrise to sunset with drill, arms
instruction, indoctrination, parade, weapons-
cleaning and sharpening. There was, however,
no kitchen duty. Slaves performed that
menial task.

The days were getting shorter, and the
nights were colder. Benoni asked Zhem about
the winters. He knew what intense cold and
high snows meant. As part of the toughening

every Fiiniks youth went through, he had
spent several winters in the mountains to the
far northwest of Fiiniks. But he had not liked
it, and the prospect of being sent off to
garrison duty in some remote snowbound
forest made him wonder if he should not
desert now. How could he serve Fiiniks by
doing such duty?

Zhem replied that, when he was a very little
boy, he had been told by his grandfather that
winter had once been very cold and snowy.
But they had been getting warmer for a long
time now. If the increasingly temperate
weather kept on getting more temperate, a
man would not be able to tell when summer
left off and winter began.

Oh, Benoni would see some snow, and he
would freeze his buttocks off at night on
maneuvers. But it was not too bad.

A few weeks after this conversation, the
recruits were given a weekend pass. Before
they were released from the walls
surrounding the Legion Grounds, their
sergeant, Giyfa, told them exactly what they
could and could not do. Specific about their
limitations, Giyfa was even more detailed
about what would happen to them if they
strayed outside the proper area and behavior
of a rookie wild-man on leave. Punishment,
varying according to the degree of offense,
ranged from a light flogging of ten strokes of
the lash to beheading. However, it was better
to lose one's head than be roasted slowly over
a fire. And so on.

Giyfa advised that, if they had to find a
release for their cooped-up spirits, they

should not stray outside the Funah section of the riverfront. This area, inhabited mainly by the very poor, sailors, resident foreign merchants, traders, and ex-slaves, was more tolerant of wild-men's actions. Moreover, a crime committed there was not as grave as one elsewhere. Provided, of course, that no Kaywo citizen of reasonable wealth or standing was offended or injured.

"You think Giyfa meant all that?" said Benoni to Zhem as they left the barracks.

"I hope we never find out," replied Zhem. "You know what a mean man he is with a whip. He could take every inch of your skin off with ten strokes."

Benoni looked at the pay in hand. Twenty new hexagonal steel coins. Stamped on one side with the eagle profile of the late Pwez of Kaywo and on the other with the two-headed wolf and the rayed eye of Kaywo's god, the First. "We can't do much with this," Benoni said.

"When we run out, we can always take some from a drunk," said Zhem. "Catch him in some dark alley."

Benoni said, "Be thieves?"

"You don't mind robbing an enemy, do you?"

"But we are guests," said Benoni. "In a way, that is. You don't rob your hosts."

"We are prisoners," replied Zhem. "It's true we're willing prisoners; how else could we visit Kaywo? If we had told the border guards we just wanted to see Kaywo, we would have been arrested. No, we may be serving this country, but this country is the enemy of my people and yours. Don't you ever forget it. When Kaywo has conquered Skego, Kaywo will look to the south for new conquests. And when the south is laid low, Kaywo will conquer your desert country, if she thinks it worthwhile."

"What you say is undoubtedly true. But as long as I take Kaywo's pay, I serve her," said Benoni. "And that means that I will not be a thief."

Zhem shrugged and said, "You have some peculiar ideas, Ironfoot. But you are my elder blood-brother. And if you say that we do not rob, then we do not rob. But that means we do not have much fun."

"What is your idea of fun?"

"The beer of my people is good," said Zhem. "But I understand that the beer of Kaywo is even better. and they have something called *vey*, made from grapes, that is sweet and makes your head spin. And they also have, so I've heard a much stronger drink called *vhiyshiy*. Half a bottle of that, and a man thinks he is a god."

"I have never tasted any of those," said Benoni. "We do have a drink called *kiyluh*. The Mek call it *takil*. And we have another, *puk*. But these are drunk only during religious ceremonies and then only by men. I am forbidden to touch any such stuff until I have returned to Fiiniks with a scalp at my belt."

"You said something about beer once."

"We get that from the Mek during Truce Market," said Benoni. "But I have noticed that men who drink beer get short-winded and fat-bellied. That isn't for me."

Zhem threw his hands up in the air and rolled his eyes.

"*Gehsuk*! Then there is nothing left for you but women! Not that that is bad, but you don't have enough money to buy more than one woman for one hour—if that!"

Benoni turned red, and he said, "When I was confirmed, I swore an oath of chastity to Jehovah. I would not think of betraying my god."

Zhem goggled at Benoni as if he were a monster. "But, but, your god is a long distance off!"

"He can see everything," replied Benoni. "And even if he could not, I have given my oath."

Zhem burst into loud laughter and slapped his thigh again and again. After he had controlled himself, he said, "You mean every youth in your country remains a virgin until he takes a wife? Every one?"

"There are some who break their oath with a slave-girl," said Benoni, thinking of some stories he had heard about Joel and others. "But if they're caught, they're whipped. And they must take wives from among the freed slaves, for honorable fathers would never allow their daughters to marry such men. And . . ."

"Tell me no more, blood-brother," said Zhem. "You frighten me. Your people must be inhuman! To ask hot-blooded youths to deny their natures!"

"It is what our god asked of us," said Benoni stiffly.

"Your souls must be as hard as the soles of your feet," said Zhem, and he laughed again. "Well, never mind, let's go to the Funah. But you must not ask me to obey the strange laws of your strange god. Or," he said anxiously, "would I dishonor my blood-brother by following the ways of *my* people?"

"When you mingled your blood with mine, you swore only to fight for me, as I swore to fight for you," said Benoni. "You may do what you wish. After all, I wouldn't ask you not to eat a certain food because I am forbidden to."

They were silent for a while after, too intent on watching the buildings and the people in the streets. By noon, they had walked to the Funah district. Here they found the variety of dress and speech even more exotic than in the citizen's section of town. Within the space of a block, they heard three languages, not a word of which they recognized; saw men wearing high-piled turbans, masks over the eyes, and long beards; saw others wearing helmets with bull horns and clothed in skins; saw women with rings in their noses, and one man whose face was covered with blue, green, and red tattoos.

"Kaywo sits at the meeting of two great rivers," said Zhem. "The Father of the Waters, which runs from the north to the south and cuts the world in half. And the Hayo, which runs from the east to the west and cuts the world in half until it joins the Msibi. Far to the east are two great nations: the Iykwa and the Jinya. These are too far away for the Kaywo to make war against. That is, as of now they are. But they use the

Hayo to send their trade goods to this nation.
And even the Skego, who are at war with
Kaywo, use the L'wan River and the Msibi to
trade with Kaywo. The Skego dominate the
Miys Sea, and the other Northern Seas are
ruled by the Skanava."

Zhem pointed at a tall, broad-shouldered
man with a long red beard and a bullhorn-
helmet.

"A Skanava. They say his people came over
the great river far to the east about two
hundred years ago and over-ran the Kanuk in
the North. They speak a tongue such as you
never heard before. Some say the river they
crossed is even wider than the Msibi, but that
I do not believe. Everyone knows that the
Msibi is the Father of the Waters and that all
other rivers are his little children."

Near the riverfront, the two saw a building
with a sign hanging over the door. On the
board was a crudely painted image of a
creature half-cock and half-bull.

"Any time you see that *kabuh*," said Zhem,
"you know you're standing in front of a
tavern. Let's go."

Benoni, feeling very self-conscious, and also
somewhat guilty, followed Zhem into the
tavern. He went down a flight of six steps and
found himself in a low-beamed room about
fifty by seventy feet wide. Coming in from the
bright sunlight, he could not, at first, see very
well. The room had only two small windows,
and, though several lamps burned on a table
in the middle of the room, the light was over-
come by the thick clouds of tobacco smoke.
Benoni sniffed these and the strong odor of

beer and liquor, and he said, "This place stinks."

"Smells good to me," said Zhem. He went to the bar and placed one of his coins on the counter and bought five cigars. Then, he spent another coin to buy a stone mug filled with dark beer.

Benoni turned down the cigar offered by Zhem. Zhem shrugged and lifted the heavy mug and drank. And drank. His Adam's apple rose and fell, rose and fell. Not until the huge mug was half emptied did he lower it to the bar. And he belched loudly.

"At that rate, you'll spend all your money before the sun quarters the west," said Benoni.

"Can't be helped. I built a giant thirst while we were in the barracks. Let's sit down. Get waited on by one of these pretty girls."

Benoni did not think the girls were so pretty. They were too old, there could not have been one under twenty-six, and their big flabby breasts and bulging stomachs told of too many tipped mugs. He felt a pang, then, thinking of the beautiful face, clear eyes, and trim figure of Debra Awvrez.

Zhem, who must have seen Benoni's grimace, said, "Drink some of this. They'll all start looking like queens, then."

Benoni shook his head and wondered if he would have to sit here all day and possibly half the night. He would have no fun doing this. He wanted to get outside, where he could breathe and walk around, see the wonders of this metropolis. Also, find out the weak spots in its defenses, just in case the Eyzonuh ever did storm Kaywo. It was a fantastic idea, he had to admit, but he had seen so many strange things since leaving Fiiniks.

At least, he could eat. He called over a waitress and tried to give her an order. But she asked him if he wanted to go upstairs before ordering anything, and he suddenly was unable to remember the words for the dish he had intended to order.

Zhem, seeing Benoni's red face, laughed and then told the woman they would like to eat.

Benoni felt like walking out. Not only because he was digusted but also because he felt that Zhem was laughing at him and that, perhaps, Zhem doubted his manhood. But he stayed. If he deserted Zhem, he might be thought a coward.

Within a few minutes, the waitress placed before him a wooden bowl containing steak, fried potatoes, and a salad of lettuce, tomatoes, and onions. Benoni's mouth watered, and he began to cut the thick meat. But he never got the tender juicy piece into his mouth. As he raised it on the end of a two-pronged fork, he heard a voice behind him. A loud voice, speaking Kaywo with a barbarous accent.

"Joel!" said Benoni, and he dropped the fork into the bowl.

He rose from the stool, turned, and saw Joel standing at the foot of the steps. Joel was blinking, his eyes unaccustomed as yet to the twilight. He wore the bobcat skin vest and the helmet fashioned to look like a bobcat's head, so that Benoni knew that Joel was a sworn-in

soldier of the wild-man Feykhunt (Five
Hundred). His scabbard was empty, for
nobody was allowed to carry weapons inside
the city walls unless he was a soldier on duty
or a member of the *kefl'wiy*. His companions,
four wild-men, stood by him, also blinking.

Benoni, growling, unable to articulate,
charged Joel. Out of the twilight and the
tobacco smoke, he charged, and he caught
Joel around the throat with his two hands,
and Joel fell backwards against the stone
steps.

Joel's face, red above the two hands
choking him, twisted, and he gasped out one
word, "Benoni!"

He could not have been more surprised if he
had seen Jehovah appear.

Benoni lunged forward and rammed the
back of Joel's head against the edge of a step,
lifted Joel, and smashed his head down again.

Then, Joel's face swam before him, and
Benoni felt himself slumping down by the
side of his enemy. He looked up and saw one
of Joel's companions standing over him, a
stone mug in his hand. Confused through he
was, Benoni knew that the man had struck
him on top of the head with the mug. He felt
wetness on his head and crawling down his
face, but he did not know if it was blood from
a cut or beer from the mug. It did not matter;
he was too stunned to defend himself. He was
done for; the man raised the heavy stone again
to crush his skull.

But the man stiffened, and the mug fell
from his hand. Two mugs struck the floor, one
of them aimed expertly by Zhem at the back of

the man's neck. The man pitched forward,
falling on Joel and knocking him backward
again. Benoni, beginning to recover his
senses, rolled to one side, away from the
steps, and closed his hand around the leg of a
stool.

At the same moment, Zhem flew into the
other three companions. He kicked one
between the legs, caught another under the
chin with an elbow, and grabbed the third by
the wrist. Turning, he brought the unlucky
fellow over his back and sent him upside
down through the air. But a stranger,
probably not caring what the quarrel was
about or who won, but wanting to get into a
brawl, hit Zhem on the jaw with his fist just as
Zhem straightened up. Zhem staggered
backwards, and the stranger followed,
throwing two more punches, one of which
went wild.

Before Zhem could reply, a second stranger
locked his arm around the neck of the first
and began pummeling his face with his left
fist.

That was enough. In a few seconds, every
male in the place was fighting.

Benoni got to his feet just as Joel charged
him. He brought the stool down on Joel's
back. But Joel had caught Benoni in the
stomach with his shoulder, lifted him up in
the air, and carried him backwards until he
rammed him into the wall.

The breath went out of Benoni; he felt as if
his entrails had been squeezed out of his
mouth.

Then, he was falling, for Joel had not only

smashed Benoni into the wall but had dealt
his own head a hard blow against it.

Joel got up first, and his huge frame loomed
over Benoni. He drew his sandalled foot back
to kick Benoni in the ribs, and then he fell
heavily. Zhem, coming up from behind, had
kicked Joel hard in the ankle.

Zhem kicked Joel in the ribs and knocked
him down again. A figure soared out of the
smoke and carried Zhem face-forward to the
floor. Benoni struggled to his feet, picked up
another stool, and brought it down on the
man on top of Zhem. The man quit trying to
bend Zhem's neck backward until it would
break, and he crumpled.

Benoni whirled to face Joel, saw Joel had
removed his belt and was holding it by one
end and preparing to use it like a whip. The
buckle on the other end, probably sharpened
for just such an occasion as this, would slash
like a knife if it caught Benoni.

Benoni loosened the strap around his chin,
took his steel helmet in hand. As he saw Joel
flick the buckle-end of the belt back before
lashing it out at him, he hurled the helmet at
Joel's face. The helmet struck Joel a glancing
blow on top of his head, for Joel had ducked.
Benoni was on him, inside the reach of the
belt, before Joel could recover. He struck at
the face, felt his fist hit the big jaw, and then
was enfolded inside Joel's arms. His arms
were pinned to his sides in the bear hug.

"I'll break your back, you sidewinder!" said
Joel. "How the hell did you ever get *here*?"

"I'd find you in hell!" said Benoni.

"So now what're you going to do with me?"

And Joel began squeezing.

There was nothing Benoni could do except try to bring his knee up, and Joel was too good an infighter to allow that. Benoni did begin to hammer the top of his head against Joel's chin, but he was so close to knocking himself out that he quit. Then he began tearing at Joel's neck with his teeth, and he ripped the skin and tasted the blood on his mouth. But the breath was being forced from him, and his ribs felt as if they would collapse. His senses dimmed. If he did not do something at once, he would die in Joel's arms. And those arms were the last he wanted to die in.

Then, the arms fell away from him, and Joel was backing up to the wall, a swordpoint against his belly driving him.

Benoni turned and saw that the tavern was filled with armed soldiers. These wore stuffed hawks on top of their helmets. The civilian police.

Benoni was herded with the other brawlers outside the tavern and allowed to collapse against the wall while the police waited for the wagon that would bear the culprits to prison. By the time the wagon arrived, he was feeling well enough to stand and ask Zhem if he were all right. Zhem's woolly scalp was bloody, but he laughed and said that this fight was better than the tankards of beer and a woman.

Benoni got into the big cage on top of the wagon and sat down. Joel was the last to climb aboard. He made a lunge for Benoni as soon as the cage door was shut. Benoni leaned back, kicked out with his feet, and his steelhard soles caught Joel's jaw and drove him backward. Joel fell heavily to the floor and lay there, unconscious and breathing hard. He did not come back to consciousness until shortly before the wagon halted in front of the prison-tower. He glared at Benoni but did not offer to attack again.

One by one, the prisoners were taken out of the wagon, shackled by the wrists to each other, and led into an office. There they were identified, searched for weapons, relieved of their money, and led off to individual cells.

"Good thing we're military," whispered Zhem to Benoni just before they went behind the bars. "If we were civilians, we'd all be put into a den. And a man's lucky if he comes out of one of those alive. The professional criminals beat you up, maybe kill you, just because they don't like non-professionals. They gang up on you or wait until you fall asleep."

Benoni was hungry, but he almost failed to eat when he saw the bowl of mush that was to be both his supper and breakfast. There was a blue mold over it, and he suspected there might be worms within. He ate anyway, knowing that he needed something to give him strength for whatever tomorrow might bring.

At dawn, he was awakened by a club scraped against the bars of his cell. He had time to eat the little left over from supper then was taken with the rest (six who had not fled out the back way of the tavern) before the judge.

The judge was a big white-haired man with

a face like a lion's. He wore a scarlet robe and
a green three-cornered hat, and he held in one
hand a baton topped by two wolves' heads. He
sat behind a big desk on top of a platform; two
spearmen stood at attention beside the desk.

None of the prisoners were allowed to plead
guilty or innocent. A policeman read out the
charges; the judge asked the captain of the
squad that had made the arrests to identify
the guilty.

"According to the laws of Kaywo, you
soldiers are under my jurisdiction if you
commit crimes while off duty," the judge
said. "There is no doubt you are guilty of
drunken and disorderly conduct and of
damaging the property of a private citizen.
Now if you cannot pay for the damages, which
amount to six hundred *owf*, and the fines,
which amount to six hundred *owf*, twelve
hundred *owf* in all, then you will suffer the
full penalty of the law.

"The full penalty is a flogging of thirty
lashes, and losing your status of free men.
You will be sold as slaves to pay for damages.
And for every *owf* that is lacking from the
sale, each of you will spend one year as a
slave. Of course, after the flogging, you must
be turned over to the military to be officially
discharged and suffer any punishments they
have for you before being sold as slaves."

The six looked at each other helplessly.
Their money had been taken before they were
led to the cells. The amount had been written
down, and the sergeant-of-the-day had told
them they would get it back—minus the
amount needed to house and feed them—after

they were released.

Benoni started to open his mouth to protest that his money had not been returned, but he closed it when Zhem rammed his elbow into his side. Benoni, startled, looked at Zhem. Zhem put his finger to his lips and shook his head to indicate silence.

"Captain," said the judge, "are these men penniless?"

"There isn't a coin among the six," said the captain.

"So? Then I find you guilty as charged."

And the judge banged the end of his baton on his desk.

Benoni, furious at the injustice but knowing that Zhem must have his reasons for warning him, ground his teeth together. He marched behind the others out of the courtroom and back to his cell. On the way, he whispered to Zhem, "What about the money they took from us?"

"Wouldn't have been enough, anyway. And the captain would have denied taking any from us. He'll split it with his men, maybe with the judge, though I doubt that. The judge is *kefl'wiy*, and they think it a dishonor to steal. But he's just as guilty as the police; he supports the system. I was trying to tell you not to open your mouth, because the captain would have knocked your teeth down your throat for contempt of court. And the judge would have doubled the lash-strokes. You aren't allowed to speak unless requested to do so."

"When will we be lashed?" said Benoni.

"If we weren't military, we'd be getting it

now," replied Zhem. "But the civilians, no
matter how high and mighty the judge talked,
can't do a thing to us until our case has been
reviewed by our officers. We may get off with
a few lashes, or we might end up on the block.
Depends on how badly they need soldiers. I'd
say that, with the Skego war getting hotter
every day, we're needed."

Benoni had time to think about the Skego
war, for he spent the next two days in the cell.
He knew that, though the two nations had
never officially declared war, fighting on a
small scale took place every day in the forests
to the north. Skego feared Kaywo now that
Kaywo had devastated Senglwi. Skego
wanted to fight before Kaywo recovered from
her losses in the taking of that city. Trade between the two was being carried out as before
the Senglwi war. That is, it was on the Siy and
L'wan rivers. But the overland caravans no
longer conducted business; too many from
both cities had been robbed and the
merchants and beasts of burden abducted. No
official complaints were made; both sides
seemed to accept the explanation that wild
men or bandits were responsible. But each
knew what the other was doing.

Perhaps, because Kaywo needed every
sword she could get, Kaywo would give the
six a suspended sentence. Or a few lashes.

Benoni nourished that hope, but it died the
dawn of the third day when he was marched
out with the rest into the open courtyard and
saw the lashman waiting for him.

"We've had it," said Zhem. "See that
officer?"

He pointed at a captain of a Feykhunt sitting on his mount near the whipping post. "He's here to see that we get just what the civilian court ordered and no more. Then off we go to the barracks to get it from the military."

Benoni watched while the first of the six was stripped of his bobcat skin shirt and shackled to the post. He winced with each crack of the whip and wished that he had been first. Then, he would have been so concerned with his own pain that he would not have to suffer while the others were being lashed.

Two others followed. One of them, a burly yellow-haired Skanava, walked away from the post; the others had to be dragged away by their heels. Benoni, as next in line, waited.

But the officer on horseback spoke, and the three; Joel, Zhem, and Benoni, were marched out of the courtyard and into a cage on a wagon.

"What happened?" said Benoni softly to Zhem.

Zhem shrugged and muttered, "Don't know. Maybe something good. Maybe something worse than the lash."

Benoni had expected to be taken to the barracks. but the wagon stopped before the Pwez Palace, and the three were ordered to get out of the cage. The captain dismounted, and, as two guards with short spears kept the prisoners in order, he led them into a side door of the great building. Here, they waited a while in an office. Benoni still did not know what to expect. The captain merely announced that he had brought the three wild-men as ordered. After a half an hour, an officer, splendidly uniformed, appeared and relieved the captain of his charge. The shackles were taken off the three. Two palace guards replaced the Feykhunt, and the officer led the three through many rooms and up two flights of steps. He paused before a door, outside of which stood four fully armed soldiers, and announced that he had brought the prisoners. One of the soldiers went inside the door and reappeared a few minutes later.

"You wild-men behave," he said. "The Usspika and the Pwez herself are going to speak to you. Don't forget to bow as soon as they notice you. And don't speak unless it's clear that one of them expects you to do so. Too bad we didn't have time to wash the prison dirt and stink from you before bringing you in, but we didn't. No help for it. Now, follow me, and try not to disgrace yourselves."

Benoni did not feel awed or ashamed; he was burning from the injustice of the judge. Moreover, though impressed by Kaywo's superiority over Fiiniks in population, area of sovereignty, and military might, he still felt that one man from anywhere in the Eyzonuh desert was equal to three men elsewhere. Besides, what kind of people could these be that allowed a woman to rule over them? They might be great warriors, but they must have an effeminate streak in them.

He was led into a room which was twice as big as any room in Fiiniks, twice as large as the council-cave hollowed out of rock in Kemlbek Mountain. There were only four persons in the huge chamber besides the officer and the three wildmen. Two were spearmen who stood at attention, each at the end of a desk curved like a quarter-moon. The desk was made of some dark, red close-grained polished wood Benoni did not recognize. Two people sat behind it. On a chair set at floor level was a small white-haired and very wrinkled old man with a face like a fox's.

On another chair, raised by a platform several inches above the other chair, sat a woman. A young woman. Very beautiful. Dark-skinned, dark-haired, and blue-eyed.

The officer leading the three halted six paces before the desk and saluted by bringing a clenched fist to his chest.

"Captain Liy, Pwez! Reporting with three wild-men as ordered!"

"You may go, captain," said the Usspika in a voice surprisingly deep for the thin neck and narrow chest.

The captain saluted again and spun smartly and marched out. Benoni wondered why the old man and the young woman would allow themselves the danger of being closeted with three wild-men and only two soldiers. It was true that the soldiers were heavily armed and the three wild-men were weaponless. But the three, if they wanted to sacrifice one of their number, could get to the Pwez.

Benoni looked around him and saw that, high up along the walls, were many narrow openings. He did not doubt that behind each one stood an archer with arrow fitted to the string.

He transferred his inspection back to the Pwez, Lezpet. Now, there was a woman! Beautiful, regal. She showed in every motion, in every aspect of her bearing, that she came from a long line of men and women accustomed to wealth, power, and schooling in how to conduct one's self. She wore her long hair piled in a Psyche knot and bound with a silver band. A golden chain set with diamonds hung around her long slim neck; her curving body was tightly clothed from the neck down in some light blue and shiny cloth. The chair she leaned against was covered with jaguar fur. Benoni, seeing this, knew that Kaywo's trade extended far to the south or else some wandering merchant had brought the specimen to Kaywo. From conversations he had had with his barrack's mates, he knew that the jaguar was not native to this area.

Lezpet, unsmiling, returned his frank stare steadily.

The Usspika, Jiwi Mohso, took some papers from the top of his desk. He glanced through them and said, "I have been aware for some time that you three were in Kaywo. I had intended to bring you in to get some information. But to be frank, I had forgotten you. Until these papers, asking me to authorize your punishment, came to my attention yesterday."

The old man leaned back, looked long and hard at them, and then said, "We are interested in your story because it may have some bearing on the welfare of Kaywo. If that is true, we may want to place you under an obligation. A strange—to you—obligation."

There was a silence, for all three wild-men remembered the captain's warning not to say anything unless definitely requested to do so.

The Pwez smiled slightly, lifted her hand, and pointed a finger at Joel Vahndert.

"You," she said in a husky voice, "the largest. You speak first. Tell your story. But don't be longwinded. Where do you come from? Why did you come here? What are your people like? What kind of land were you born in? What do you plan to do in the future?"

Joel, speaking Kaywo fluently but with a wretched accent, told his story. He told of being born at the foot of Kemlbek Mountain in the midst of the Eyzonuh desert, of growing to young manhood with the sawaro, the jack-rabbit, the coyote, the rattler, the sharp rocks, and burning sun molding him and his playmates. He told of raids made on outlying farms of Fiiniks by the Mek from the south and the Navaho from the north and of the raids his elders made against the Mek and the Navaho. He told of the earthquakes, the lava bursting loose from the bowels of the earth through the throats of volcanoes long thought dead and of the birth of volcanoes from flat plains. He told of the custom of sending each Fiiniks youth out to prove his manhood by bringing back a scalp.

And he told of finding Benoni captured by a group of Navahos, of killing the Navahos, freeing Benoni. Only to have Benoni treacherously stab him and leave him for dead.

Benoni's eyes grew round, and his face flamed.

"That is a lie!" he roared. "He is telling just the opposite of what happened! It was I was freed him, and it was he who left me to die, and . . ."

"Silence!" the Usspika shouted. "Were you not warned to speak only when spoken to!"

"But he lies!" shouted Benoni. "Why do you think I tracked him so far? Why do you think he fled so far? This is the first time any Eyzonuh have ever gone so far on the warpath!"

"One more word, and I will have you cut down!" said the Usspika. "One more word!"

Benoni strangled on the hot words that tried to escape, but he knew death when he saw it. The old man was ready to raise his arm, to signal to the archers behind the windows high up on the walls.

"That is much better," said the Usspika. "I can see you need more discipline. However, we do not expect as much from a non-citizen as we do from those born of Kaywo. You are forgiven, provided you do not repeat the offense."

The Usspika told Joel to continue his story from the point at which it had been interrupted. Joel told of having waylain some Navahos, taking their scalps, and continuing eastwards. Apparently, he had had the same misgivings as Benoni. Though he went to the edge of the desert east of the Navaho land, he was not sure that he would continue. Then, he said, he had decided that he wanted to see the world and, at the same time, do a great service for his people.

So, he had crossed the great desert, and the

great plains. Finally, after many adventures, he had come to Kaywo. On the border, he had fallen in with several merchants. He discovered that he could not enter Kaywo unless he was a merchant with documentary proof of his origin and trade or else would join the Foreign Legion. So, he had become a mercenary. On a weekend pass, he had entered the tavern and been attacked without warning by the man who had tried to kill him.

There was silence for a moment after the story. The Pwez and the Usspika stared at Benoni so long and so hard that he wondered if he were already judged.

Finally, Jiwi Mohso, the Usspika, said "What have you to say for yourself, Rider?" He pronounced Rider as Wadah.

Benoni said, "My countryman's story is true . . . up to a point. But it was I who freed him from the Navaho war party, and it was he who left me to die. I did not die, as you can see, but regained my strength and went on into Navaho country. Not so much to get a Navaho scalp as to get his. And . . ."

"Tell me, Fiiniks boy," said the Pwez, Lezpet. "Is it not true what Vahndert said? That a youth on the warpath may do whatever he wishes, even to killing another Fiiniks youth? That he will not be held responsible? That, if he had slain you or you him, it would not be murder but lawful?"

"That is true, Excellency," said Benoni. "And we have been enemies for a long time. But I could not stand by and see a Fiiniks killed by a Navaho. I saved him, yet he repaid me by leaving me to die. I could not forgive that. That was not the deed of a warrior; that was the deed of a mad coyote."

"And so you crossed the desert and the plains to kill him?" said the Pwez. "Barefoot and alone. Your hate must have been great. Was it not so?"

"It was so. But I had also been asked to find the Great River. I do not think I would have come looking for it if I had not wanted so much to kill Joel Vahndert. On the other hand, if I had not thought of the need of our people to find a new land, and, I must admit, the glory that would come to me if I did find the Great River, I would not have tried to track down the treacherous coyote."

Lezpet laughed, and she said, "You are, at least, frank. Well, we do not have all day. We have many other affairs of business to conduct, running the greatest nation in the world is not easy. You have found the Great River. Now, what will you do? When you go back to the Eyzonuh desert—if you go back—you cannot tell your people to leave the Valley of the Sun and come here can you? Your people are not strong enough nor foolish enough to try to dispossess us? They would be swept away as a strong wind sweeps away the chaff of the harvest."

"No, your Excellency," said Benoni. "I could not tell them to come here. But the Great River is a long one, and Kaywo rules only a very small part of it. We could go to the south and settle there. Or we could go to the north."

The woman smiled, and she said, "You could not settle to the north, for the Skego control a good part of that. And the savage tribes of the Wiyzana, and the Mngumwa, and many others live along the Siy south of our borders."

"We would take it away from them," said Benoni.

"Perhaps. But the day would come when you would have to face the might of the armies of Kaywo. When we have settled with Skego, we shall turn southward. Not soon, but not too much in the future, either. And what then?"

"Though I have been confined," said Benoni, "I have kept my ears open. And I know that Kaywo took Senglwi at great cost and that she conquered the Juju only after losing half the Fifth Army. And that she now faces a much more formidable foe than Senglwi. Skego with her Skanava allies. Who knows if Kaywo will even exist in the near future?"

Lezpet sucked in her breath, and her skin turned pale. The old man, however, smiled.

"You are a brave man, Fiiniks. Or a stupid man. Or both. Or else intelligent enough to know the truth and speak it, trusting to the greatness of the Pwez not to be offended.

"Yes, what you say is true. Kaywo can use help at this time. Not that we would be defeated if we did not get help, for the First has blessed us and promised us that we will rule the world. But we are practical, and we will use all the help we can get. After all, the First may have sent you here to us. That is why we called you wild-men in. To find out if you can be of any use to us. And, of course, if we can be of use to you."

There was silence again. Benoni, Zhem, and
Joel did not speak, for neither of the Kaywo
had given permission. But Benoni burned
with impatience and curiosity. What could
they want from the likes of him?

"If the Eyzonuh left the desert and came
here," said the Usspika, "how many fighting
men would they bring?"

"Eyzonuh?" said Benoni. "The entire
confederation? I would say about eight
thousand from Fiiniks, three thousand from
Meysuh, half a hundred from Flegstef. But I
do not know if the entire confederation plans
to leave Eyzonuh. Or that they would come
here."

"I think we could induce them," said the
Usspika. "I will be brief. If the Eyzonuh leave
their desert, and come here, man, woman,
child, horse, dog, and whatever possessions
they can carry, and they swear loyalty to us,
we will give them land. Land of their own to
hold forever. They may have their own rulers,
their own laws."

"May I speak?" said Benoni.

The Pwez nodded, and Benoni said, "Where
would we live—if we accepted your offer?"

"In a land free of earthquakes and
volcanoes. Far from the dry dust and burning
sun. In a land by a broad river, a land with
rich black earth, not the sand and rock you
know so well. A land cool and shady with
many trees, alive with deer, pig, turkey.

"To the north of Kaywo?" said Benoni.
"Along the L'wan River? Between you and the
menace of Skego?"

The Usspika smiled again, and he said, "You are not unintelligent, wild-man. Yes, in the L'wan forest. Between us and Skego. You would constitute a march, a borderguard. In return for this rich and lovely land, you would repel any who might wish to march upon Kaywo. Not alone, for the might of Kaywo would be at your side."

"May I speak?" said Zhem.

The Pwez nodded again, and Zhem said, "What have I to do with these two of the desert? Why am I here?"

"If you can talk your tribe into leaving Mngumwa and living on the southern limits of our border, as the Eyzonuh would on our north, you could help us against the Juju. It is true that we decimated the army they sent against us. But we know that the Juju are many and that they have formed an alliance with the white nation to their north, the Jinya. It's not much of an alliance; the two may be fighting each other before they ever reach us. They are planning to send several armies against us, even if we live a thousand miles from them. We suspect the Skego are behind this, that the Skego have falsely warned the two that we plan to march on them as soon as we conquer Skego.

"They are wrong, of course. It will be some years before we will be in a position to make war against them."

Benoni could not help thinking that Jinya and the Juju were just being foresighted in waging war now against the Kaywo, in trying to crush them before they became too strong and while they were fighting for their survival against Skego. But he said nothing.

"If you think that there is a chance your people will accept our generous offer, we will send you with our ambassadors to your countries, you will speak on our behalf. You will tell them of the might of Kaywo, of how we shattered the Juju savages and the civilized Senglwi. You will tell them that they have much to gain and little to lose."

Except our lives, thought Benoni.

"Before you go," continued the Usspika, "you must spend some time learning our language better. Not too much time, for we do not have much. But enough so that you can speak of us to your people with authority. And our ambassadors must begin learning your language. They will continue the lessons while riding towards your lands.

"Now, what do you say?"

"I say yes!" said Joel loudly. "I am sure that my people will accept your offer!"

There was nothing after that for Benoni to say but that he, too, thought the offer might be acceptable to his people. In any event, nothing could be lost by making the offer.

He did not say he really thought that, even though the Kaywo might be sincere, they might also be presenting a very dangerous temptation to the Eyzonuh.

"Good!" said Mohso. "Now, Zhem Smed, what do you think?"

"I think that my people would consider the idea. But that I cannot take it to them."

The Usspika's white eyebrows rose, and the Pwez's dark eyebrows bent in a frown.

"Why not?" she said sharply.

"I allowed myself to be taken prisoner," said Zhem. "I am in eternal disgrace. I would be slain on sight if I set foot inside the borders of my tribe's territory."

"Even if you were accompanied by many of our soldiers?"

"Even then."

"We will make you a citizen of Kaywo," said Usspika. "Surely, your people would not dare slay one of us."

"Perhaps," replied Zhem. "But you would have to explain very carefully just what my being a citizen meant before they saw me."

"We will do that. Although, it is not as necessary in your case that we have you as a guide because we would not have much difficulty in locating your people. But these two," he added, indicating Joel and Benoni, "come from a land so far away we have never heard of it. We need them to show us the way and also to act as intermediaries."

"May I speak?" said Benoni. Seeing the Pwez nod, he said, "On our way to Fiiniks, I would like to investigate a very strange thing I saw on the great plains. That is a great house, or fort, or some kind of building, made of a silvery seamless metal. It is shaped like a needle, and it is inhabited by a strange people. It . . ."

"The Hairy Men from the Stars!"

It was the Usspika who gasped out those words and who rose and clutched the edge of the table with his gnarled hands.

"The ship of the Hairy Men from the Stars!"

"Wha . . . what?" said Benoni.

The Usspika sat down again, and, after

ceasing to breathe so hard, regained some of
his composure and said, "You do not know
what I am talking about?"

"No," said Benoni.

The old man looked thoughtful but did not
offer to explain. The Pwez, whose face had lit
up at Benoni's description of the metal
building but who had maintained more self-
control, said, "We will discuss that later. Not
that we are not interested but that we must
take one thing at a time.

"Now, my honored uncle may have given
you the impression that both of you Fiiniks
would be sent as bearers of our offer. But he
did not mean to give that impression, I am
sure."

Benoni saw the Usspika's eyes flick in her
direction, and he was sure that the old man
had meant to give that impression. But the
Pwez did not want them to think this nor to
know that she was over-ruling her uncle. That
the Usspika did not object showed Benoni
that she was the ruler, although a woman and
young. It also showed him that she probably
depended upon his wisdom and counsel and
did not wish to offend him by blatantly acting
in an autocratic manner. Nevertheless, when
she made a decision, she would follow it
through.

"One of you is lying," she said. "One of you
is vicious, untrustworthy. We would not want
to send such a man to act for us, for we could
only expect him to betray us the first chance
he got to better himself by so doing. Therefore, we must determine who is telling the
truth and who is lying. The liar will be killed,

for he has dared to lie to the Pwez, which is the same thing as lying to the people of Kaywo and the god of Kaywo."

She paused, and Benoni felt the sudden sweat trickling from under his armpits and down his ribs. He had seen enough of the customs of this nation to know that even proving one's innocence might be very painful. Besides, how could either he or Joel prove or disprove anything? There were no witnesses to Joel's treachery.

The Usspika spoke. "If my beloved niece and revered superior will hear an old man, in private, she may learn within a short time how to determine which is guilty. And it will not be necessary to go through a long and perhaps fruitless attempt to wrest the truth from these two. They both look tough and as hard as the skin on the soles of their feet. They might die, and we would be left without a guide. Even if one survived, he might so hate us, because of the ordeal, that we could never trust him. No, if I may be forgiven for interceding, I can clear this up within a short time."

"Since I was a little girl, I have listened to my uncle," said Lezpet. "I am not offended."

She spoke to the three standing before her. "You may go to apartments that have been prepared for you, for we expected that you would accept."

We would be fools if we had not, thought Benoni. Probably dead fools.

"You will be taken care of there. I imagine," she said, smiling briefly, "that you are hungry after your prison fare. Tomorrow, we begin an intensive training. Within two weeks you should know enough to speak for us. That is," she added, "two of you will be our guests. One of you will not be concerned with our affairs. Or, indeed, your own."

Benoni began to sweat even more. He knew that she, like most of her people, was cruel. Far better to have gotten the suspense over with inside a few minutes, as the Usspika had said it could be, than be tortured with uncertainty all night. And she could speak so calmly of the possibility of taking his life. He could not imagine Debra, soft and oh, so kind Debra, speaking in such a manner.

A few minutes later, Benoni and Zhem were inside the suite of rooms that would be—for one of them, at least—permanent quarters for the next two weeks. Joel was taken to another suite, the one next door to theirs. Apparently, the Pwez or whoever had ordered their domiciling had decided that the wisest thing to do would be to keep them separated. Otherwise, one might be dead before night fell or dawn broke.

Benoni and Zhem were not alone for some time. Two slave girls washed their hands and faces for them, as was required by Kaywo religious custom, before they sat down at the table. Then, two other girls served them their meals. And Zhem, famished from little and bad food during his stay in prison, ate as if he would never eat again. He also drank heavily of the wine offered him, so that it was not long after eating before he went to sleep sitting up in a chair and talking to Benoni.

Benoni did not eat nearly as much as his

companion, for he had been taught from childhood that it was an offense against himself and his God to stuff his belly. A man could not be quick and also be fat. Moreover, food had never been overplentiful in the Valley of the Sun; necessity had made a virtue of moderation. He wandered about the suite, inspecting each room and the furnishings. These consisted of three large chambers: the anteroom and two bedrooms. The stone walls were concealed by scarlet and gold draperies, the floors were covered with thick rugs into which were woven scenes from Kaywo's early history, and the furniture was of a dark brown dense-grained wood that must have been imported from some land to the south.

The most interesting item, to Benoni, were the windows. These were tall and narrow, just wide enough for a man to slip through sidewise, if they had not had two iron rods barring his passage.

Benoni finished his inspection just before the slaves returned with a portable wooden bath tub and many buckets of water. Much to Benoni's relief, the slaves were not girls, but men. He did not like the idea of being bathed by men but it was better than being scrubbed by women. Later, he found that some of the *kefl'wiy* males were bathed by women but that this was a new custom, not widely spread. In the palace, which was governed by the rigid morality of the old-style aristocrats, such a thing would not have been permitted.

Zhem was awakened and bathed; Benoni took his bath and the clean clothes given him. His long hair, which fell to his shoulders, was

oiled and combed. Then, their new tutors
arrived, men to teach them more of the
Kaywo language, of the origin and rise of the
nation, the religion, and the destiny of Kaywo,
which was to be glorious.

An hour before supper, their teachers left.
The two, wanting exercise, asked the guards
before their door if they could go down into
the courtyard. They took them to the ground
floor and into the huge inner court of the
palace. Here, the two practiced with dull-
edged swords and shields until they could
hardly lift their arms. Then, they tried
wrestling, two falls out of three. Benoni won
two but lost the third. Panting, sweating, but
feeling fine, they returned to their rooms,
bathed again, and ate. Zhem duplicated the
feat of eating and drinking himself to sleep;
this time, Benoni took his hand and led him,
stumbling, to his bed. Zhem sank into it and
was snoring before Benoni went to his own
room.

Benoni took a book left by a tutor and sat
down under the oil lamp to read a history. Or
try, for the Kaywo alphabet differed somewhat from the Fiiniks, and the vocabulary
used by the author was based on the literary
dialect, the form of Kaywo that had ceased to
be spoken a hundred years before except in
the *Uss a Spika* (House of Speakers) and
during public religious ceremonies.

After struggling for an hour, he realized he
would be able to read only with the help of an
educated Kaywo. So, rising, he ate an apple
from a large bowl of fruit on the table. Then
he went to bed. But he could not sleep. He was

too worried about what might happen to the Eyzonuh if they did accept the Kaywo offer to become a borderguard people, a march.

First, there was the migration of a whole nation across the cruel desert and the broad prairies. It was one thing for a lone man or a small war party to traverse those dangers; they could move swiftly without attracting much notice. But a whole nation with small children and women, their dogs and cats, their cattle, sheep, and chickens, their wagons, bedding, clothing, and everything they needed for the exodus!

For one thing, they would have to move very slowly, no faster than the slowest wagon could go. Then, they would have to fight their way out of the Valley of the Sun, for he was sure that the Navaho would know of this great move and would summon all their strength to attack. Having battled against the Navaho, the crossing of the desert between the Eyzonuh mountains and the great plains would be next. They would need much water to bring them across. And they would be harried by Navahos. Possibly, by raiders from the land of Deseret to the north. Then, having reached the plains they knew not what other dangers they faced. He did not think the lions and the wild dogs were much to dread; the presence of so many people would make them scurry, though it was likely they would try to stalk anybody who left the main body. But there were many nomadic tribes on the plains; he had seen enough of them to be sure of that. And the news of this great mass moving eastward would reach the ears of the savages living along the line of travel.

But, if the Eyzonuh did survive all the
dangers, what then? Would they not be in
even more peril than in their earthquake-and-
volcano-ridden land? Was not the chance very
strong that they would be crushed in the war
between the Skego and Kaywo? Exterminated
or worse, taken as slaves? Oh, the Eyzonuh
could fight, they would make their
conquerors pay bitterly. But he had to be a
realist. If the Skego land was as thickly
populated as the Kaywo, and if, moreover,
they had a horde of Skanava allies to draw
upon, the Skego could overwhelm the
Eyzonuh by numbers.

The Kaywo must know this, must be
expecting this. They were willing to sacrifice
the Eyzonuh, hoping that the desert people
would check the men from the Northern Seas
long enough for Kaywo to rebuild her
strength, that the Eyzonuh would inflict such
losses that Skego would be weakened.

But, suppose, that the Kaywo supported the
Eyzonuh so that Skego was repelled?
Suppose, that Kaywo even won the war? Then
what?

If peace came, if the Eyzonuh settled down
on the rich black soil along the L'wan River, if
they built villages, grew crops, multiplied,
became rich in food and in trade goods? To
the south of them, and close, would be their
mighty patron, Kaywo. The borders of
Kaywo, with its swiftly growing population,
would move northwards, touch upon the
Eyzonuh march. And she, with her superior
civilization and numbers, would insidiously

influence the Eyzonuh. Kaywo customs and language would be admired and adopted. The religion would attract the young Eyzonuh. Within a generation or two, Eyzonuh would be, in everything except name, Kaywo. And the next step would be to offer the Eyzonuh citizenship in Kaywo.

Or, as was unlikely, if the Eyzonuh were stiff-necked and resisted all these influences, retained stubbornly their own customs and culture, then what? Once the danger from Skego was past, the gratitude of the Kaywo would last no longer than spring snow under the noon sun. It would be easy to pick a quarrel and to march upon the Eyzonuh, crush them, enslave them to add to the wealth of Kaywo. And to send their own citizens to live in the L'wan.

Benoni tossed and turned in bed a long while before he finally fell asleep. His last thoughts were that he would advise his people against accepting the offer. Migrate, yes, but not to L'wan. They could go elsewhere; the world was a large place and had many fine lands. Of course, their rejection of Kaywo would anger Kaywo, and they would be classed as enemies. But Kaywo might not survive the Skego war. And, if they did, they would be too busy licking their wounds for a long time to turn their attention to the Eyzonuh. Especially, if they did not even know where Eyzonuh were.

He fell into a sleep that was not so deep that he did not dream of Debra Awvrez. But Debra's face melted, became Lezpet.

"Let us . . ." she said, and she never

finished. He was awakened by shouts and the
clang of steel upon steel.

Benoni rolled out of the great bed and ran
from the bedroom and to the door of the anteroom. He pulled on the upright hook
furnished to swing the door inwards and
found that the door would not move.
Evidently, the bar on the outside had been
shot into the socket in the wall to lock the
door.

He put his ear against the thick wood to
hear the commotion in the corridor, could
make out voices but could distinguish only a
few words here and there. The ring of sword
against sword was still making a din; twice, it
was punctuated by shrieks.

Behind him, Zhem said, "Wha . . . what's
going on?"

Benoni turned to see him standing close to
him, his face thick with sleep and his eyes
bloodshot.

"I don't know," he said. "But such a battle
inside the walls of the palace could mean only
one thing. Treason. An attempt to assassinate
the Pwez. Or, maybe, Skego agents managed
to force their way in and are trying to kill
her."

Zhem spread out his hands before Benoni.
"We are unarmed, and the windows are
barred. What can we do?"

"I'm not sure we should do anything even if
we could," said Benoni. "Yet, we've accepted
the hospitality of the Pwez, we are under her
roof, eating her food."

"Have you forgotten that she may have you
killed in the morning?" asked Zhem. "You are

her prisoner, not her guest."

Benoni said, "If this is an assassination attempt, if Skego is behind it, the Skego would not want either of us to live. They would not care for us to take the offer of the Pwez to our people. So, they would probably kill us."

"Besides, if we fight for the Pwez, we show we are to be trusted."

"You can't expect gratitude or trust from her," said Zhem.

"I'll do what I can to earn it," said Benoni. "If I am rewarded with the beheader's blade, I will still be in the right."

"Right does a dead man no good," said Zhem. "You are a stiff-necked man, Benoni; you were born in a strange and hard place of strange and hard people."

"Do what you want to," said Benoni. "I am getting out of here and into the fight."

He walked to the end of the hall between the two bedrooms, pulled the heavy drapes to one side, and looked out the window at its end. The two bars across it were each twice as thick as his thumb, and the end of each was buried deep in the shafts in the massive stone blocks that formed the window.

"What could you do if you were able to remove the bars?" said Zhem, who had followed him silently and closely as a shadow.

Benoni stuck his face against the bars and looked to either side as far as he could. The night-sky was cloudless, and the half-moon was high. He saw that the wing of the palace in which they were joined another wing to his left at less than a forty-five degree angle.

Looking straight across, he could see torches
and lamps illuminating many of the narrow
tall windows. Beneath the windows ran a
narrow ledge almost the length of the wing.
But it stopped about ten feet before the
windows closest to the juncture of the two
wings.

"Maybe you weren't checking your location
from the moment you entered the palace," he
said. "But I did. And I am sure that the Pwez's
chambers are at the corners, behind those
windows. And, while I can't see them, I am
sure that a ledge runs below our windows,
just as it does beneath those directly across
from us."

Below him rose the ring of swords against
swords and shields and the shouts of fighting
men and the screams of the wounded and the
transfixed.

"So?" said Zhem.

"So, will you help me remove these bars?"

Without a word, Zhem grasped one of the
bars in the middle. Benoni gripped the same
bar, and they braced their feet against the
edge of the window and bent their backs.
Slowly, slowly, the bar began to bend.

"We are stronger than I thought," said
Zhem, panting. "Stronger than Kaywo steel."

"Save your breath," said Benoni, and he
pulled until his muscles ached and his back
seemed ready to break. Four times, he and
Zhem had to quit and lean against the wall
until they regained their strength and breath.
But, each time that they went back, the bar
was curved more like an archer's bow. And,
just as they thought they would have to quit

for a fifth time, the two ends of the bar
slipped from the stone sockets, and they fell
upon their backs on the carpeted floor.

Benoni did not rest but climbed into the
window and tried to squeeze his body
between the stone and the remaining bar. "No
use," he said, groaning. "We have to take the
other one out."

"I do not think I have enough strength left
to get off my back," said Zhem. But he rose
and gripped the bar and bent his back again.

This time, they had to take six rests. Finally
the bar, screeching as the ends slid over the
lips of the shaft, shot out, and they fell again
on the rug.

Benoni wanted to rest, but he could not. He
leaned out the window and saw that his guess
was right. Three feet below the window ran a
ledge of stone two inches wide.

"Not much, but it will do," he said.

"What will do?" said Zhem from the floor.

"I don't know about you, but I am going to
help the Pwez," said Benoni. "It's only logical
that, if what we hear is an assassination
attempt, the assassins are trying to get to the
Pwez's rooms. She may be dead by now; I may
be too late. I must try. I can't get through the
door; we could never batter it down. And if we
did get into the hall, we might be cut down.
But if we went through the Pwez's
window . . ."

Zhem gasped, and he leaped to his feet.

"Are you crazy? How could we do that?"

Benoni, noting Zhem's use of the plural,
smiled slightly.

"I don't know that we can, but we can try.

Now, let's see if we can walk like a cat. And
then fly like a bird."

"You go first, blood-brother. Not that I am
afraid, it's just that I would not know what to
do."

Benoni went through the opening in the
wall sideways, putting out one foot and
feeling for the ledge with it. Touching the cold
stone, he eased his weight down on one leg,
and, grasping the edge of the stone with his
fingertips, brought his other leg down.
Flattening himself against the outer wall, the
left side of his face pressed against the wall
and both arms out and his fingertips against
the stone, he began to go crabwise along the
ledge. It was slow work but not cold. Despite
the winter chilliness of the night, he was
sweating. Only his toes and the balls of his
feet were on the ledge. The rest of his feet
projected over the air. It was a five-story fall
to the limestone-block surface below.

Zhem, also on the ledge, was muttering
strange names to himself, doubtless calling
on his gods or the various names of his god or
else chanting some formula to invoke divine
protection.

It seemed to take a long time before he felt
the ledge end. But he knew that it could not
have taken over five minutes. He had not
dared to stop, even though now he wondered
if he had not been a fool to take such a chance.
Some of his hot impulsiveness had cooled;
what had looked easy, if daring, now looked
suicidal.

Perhaps, if Zhem had not been along, he
might have turned back. But he could never

do that when another man was watching. Especially, his blood-brother.

At the end of the ledge, he had to turn around so that his back would be against the wall and his heels would be the only part of his feet to have support. It was not something to do quickly, for the chance of losing his balance was too strong. He saw that he had rushed into this, that he should have taken more time to plan better. If he had, he would have left the window facing outwards and inched his way with his back against the wall. Thus, though he would have been staring outwards and downwards, he would have been set for the next big step in his plan.

He must turn around now.

Cursing himself for a fool, he began the slow task. He stood on the toes of his right foot while he lifted the left foot. Slowly, grinding his body into the wall to forestall loss of balance, he brought his left leg behind him and then around. When he felt the ledge under the foot, he lowered it until it was firmly resting against the right side of his right foot. Then, he began the slow and agonizing turning. There was no way to get away from it; he had to twist so that the bulk of his body would be supported by nothing but air and he would lose most of his contact with the wall.

He twisted. As he did so, he saw that Zhem was not waiting but was going through the same maneuver.

Zhem grinned, and he said, "If we fall, I hope we fall on one of those *beystuh* below. Won't be a totally wasted death, then."

Benoni did not reply but continued turning. When he had reached the point where his left foot could be turned, where the toes could turn over the task of support to the heel, he advanced his right foot at a parallel angle to the wall. Then, his right arm high up, its palm flat against the stone, he pivoted on the ball of his left foot.

And he turned his right foot, twisted his body, and both heels were on the ledge and his back was against the stone.

He looked to his right, at Zhem.

"You're all right. Fine."

"What do we do now?" said Zhem.

Benoni looked across the gap at the face of the wing opposite theirs. He could see directly into a window. It lay at the end of a hall, much wider than the one in his quarters and much longer. It led into a brightly lighted room. Three or four women were standing at the extreme wall by a huge door. All carried a sword or spear.

Lezpet appeared from the right side, and she was holding a rapier in one hand and had a small round shield strapped to her left arm. She wore a helmet and a cuirass.

"They haven't got in yet," he said to Zhem. "Maybe they won't ever. From the way the women are acting, I'd say somebody is hammering at their door now."

"How're we going to get across?" said Zhem. "And, if we do, how're we going to remove the bars?"

"One thing at a time," replied Benoni.

With his eye, he measured the distance from his ledge to the window opposite. Close to seven feet. Easily within his power if he were standing flatfooted on the ground and just jumping to clear a mark. But here, five stories up, with only stone to shove against and the bars in the window to grab and no second jump if he slipped or missed . . .

He rose on his toes, his heels against the stone and higher than his toes, bent his legs, and shoved against the stone. Outwards he shot, his eyes fixed on the iron bars, his hands held straight out in front of him. His right hand closed on a bar. His left hand missed. His body slammed into the wall, knocking the breath from him.

Frantically, he clawed with his left hand, scraping the stone. Then, it closed around the same bar he clutched in his right hand, and he was hanging outside the window.

His arms were rigidly extended before him and were pulled down by the weight of his body. The bars, set deep within the window, were just far enough away so that the edge of the window cut into his body under the armpits. An inch or two deeper, and he would not have been able to seize the bars. Now he hung with no support for his feet.

He made no effort for a minute, did nothing but recover his breath and his strength. Then, flexing his arms, he pulled himself up over the edge of the window with sheer strength. After he was inside, he released the bar and began to shake.

But he had no time for the luxury of after effects. He could hear the deep thumps of something hard and heavy being rammed against the door to the Pwez's chambers. The door held, but every time the ram, or whatever it was, slammed into the wood, the wood bent inwards. A few more such blows, and the great bar holding it in place would be burst asunder along with the door.

"Jump, Zhem," said Benoni. I'll hang onto the bar with one hand and snare you with the other."

Zhem's teeth gleamed in the moonlight as he smiled with bravado, or fright, or because he thought he ought to do so. And he braced himself against the ledge and the wall and leaped.

Zhem's hands would have missed the bar; he was not quite as long-armed as Benoni.

But Benoni's free hand caught Zhem's left arm, and he pulled him forward and up over the ledge of the window. Pulled him with so much force that Zhem's hands socked into the bar, and he scraped the skin off his face and chest.

Benoni hoisted him upwards, and Zhem was standing with Benoni inside the cave formed by the window. Fortunately, this was much larger than the one outside their rooms; they had space to stand up, facing each other, their noses almost touching.

"Now, elder brother to the cat and the bird," said Zhem, "what do we do?"

Benoni did not answer him but shouted through the window. His voice must have carried down the hall above the crashing of the ram against the door, for all the women whirled and stared down the dark hall.

The Pwez, Lezpet, came running, her rapier held out in front of her. Behind her came a woman holding a torch she had taken from a wallsocket in the anteroom.

"You!" said Lezpet, seeing their faces in the torchlight. "Have you come to kill me, too?"

"No," said Benoni. "We do not know who is trying to kill you. We heard the commotion, figured out what might be happening. But we could not get out through our door, so we left by the window."

Lezpet's eyes became even wider. "You leaped to my window?"

"Yes, let us in."

"You risked your life to help me?" she repeated slowly, as if she could not believe him.

"Can you get those bars off?" said Benoni. "You will need two good fighting men in a minute."

"This may be a trick," said the woman holding the torch. "How do you know that these wild-men haven't been hired by the Greens or the Skego?"

"I don't," said Lezpet. "But if they are assassins, why are they unarmed?"

Benoni knew then that she was not in a panic but was thinking coolly.

"We have risked our lives, Your Excellency," he said. "Do not waste that risk and throw away our lives, and yours."

"I think it is a trick," said the other woman. "Let them stay there. As long as they are on the other side of the bars, they can do nothing to harm us. Even if they do mean to help us, we don't have time or the strength to remove the bars. After all, they're just two wild-men."

"If they leaped from the other wall to help

me," said Lezpet, "they are more than *just* wild-men."

"You don't have much time," said Benoni, pointing down the hallway.

"But we don't have the strength to pull the bars out," said Lezpet.

For answer, Benoni grabbed one of the bars with both hands, and he was quickly imitated by Zhem. With a strength they would never have thought themselves capable of, but doubtless pumped into their muscles by the fear of death, they bent the bar. This time, it was not necessary to pull the bar from its retaining sockets. They managed, with much loss of skin, to squeeze through between the bar and the wall of the window.

Zhem and Benoni pushed past the two women and ran down the hall and into the anteroom. This was a tremendous chamber with a huge fireplace on one wall. On both sides of the fireplace, placed in racks against the wall, were many weapons, trophies of victories.

Benoni took a short bow made of two joined horns from a longhorn bull and picked up a quiver full of arrows. He also strapped a belt and scabbard around his waist, then removed the long sword and stuck a shorter one in it.

"Not enough time or room to swing a broadsword in these quarters," he said.

Zhem, although armed with a bow, arrows, and sword, picked up five javelins in one hand. He laid the weapons down when Benoni ordered him to help in piling furniture just before the door.

The blows outside were having their effect;

a crack suddenly appeared in the bar across the door; the door was already shattered but still hanging together.

"Come with me," said Benoni, and he retreated to the hallway. Here, he and Zhem stood within the dark of the hallway and fitted arrows to their strings.

At Benoni's order, a woman hastened to the other end of the hall to draw the drapes across the window.

"They won't be able to see us in the dark," said Benoni. "Not at first, anyway."

He called to Pwez. "Stand to one side. When the door breaks, and they charge in, throw spears at them."

"You," he said, addressing the woman who had argued against admitting them. "Take that lamp and spread the oil across the floor between the door and the barricade."

He told two others to do the same, and when they had finished, he said, "Just as they come in, throw a torch down on the oil."

There was a loud cheer outside, then a great crash as the ram slammed into the door. Abruptly, the bar snapped in half, and the men carrying the ram, a thick hardwood beam, fell into the room.

At the same time, a woman threw a torch on the oil and flames and smoke shot up around them.

They screamed and leaped to their feet and then jumped to the top of the barricade formed by the piled-up furniture. Some were on fire, their long green cloaks and kilts burning.

Benoni and Zhem shot their first arrows,

aiming as planned by Benoni. He shot at the one on the extreme left; Zhem, at the one on the extreme right. Both arrows struck their mark, driving through the chainmail corselet and into the flesh beneath. Benoni's man fell backward into the fire. Zhem's victim spun around and knocked the man by his side into the flames.

Lezpet threw a javelin and caught a man in the unprotected region of his neck, between helmet and corselet. Two more javelins hit their targets, though one only wounded.

Benoni and Zhem fired again, and they dropped two men in their tracks. Lezpet's rapier darted out like a frog's tongue and thrust into the eye of a man and drove into his brain. He fell, wrenching the rapier from her grasp.

But the men behind the fallen were brave and determined. They charged from the hall and through the fire and threw themselves over the barricade. Benoni and Zhem shot for the third time. Benoni's arrow missed and stuck quivering in the wooden jamb of the door. Zhem's arrow went through chainmail and into the belly of a man.

Then, seeing that they had as much chance to hit one of the women as they did the attackers, Benoni and Zhem dropped their bows, seized a javelin, and ran up at the melee.

Benoni lunged at a man swinging a short sword, and he drove the javelin point into the man's throat. Another man slashed at him; Benoni interposed his javelin; the sword cut through the shaft.

Benoni flung the butt at the man's face, drew his short sword, and chopped down. His blade slid down the other's, was stopped by the hilt. Benoni stepped back and, as he did so, drew the edge of his sharp blade across the man's hand. Tendons cut, the hand dropped the sword. Benoni cut halfway through the man's neck.

Two men leaped at Benoni. Benoni had to retreat. One of the men fell, the red point of a javelin sticking through his chest, the shaft protruding from his back. Benoni had time to see that it was Lezpet who had killed the man. Then, he was trying to defend himself against the big redheaded man who was a master with the blade.

Twice, he suffered cuts, one on the arm, one on the leg. And the man was driving him backwards, hoping to catch him in a corner of the room. Benoni thought he was good with a sword, but this man, bigger, longer armed, and about five or six years older, was his superior.

No man, however, no matter how excellent a swordsman, can do anything against a chair thrown against his back. He was forced forwards, his guard momentarily down from the shock. Benoni brought the edge of his weapon down on the wrist and half severed it. The red-beard whirled to run but did not get to take one step in flight. Zhem's blade drove into his Adam's apple.

Then, the ring of blades ceased. It was over. Over, at least, in this room and for the time being, for the sounds of shouts and steel came from elsewhere in the building.

All the attackers were dead except for two
badly burned men. Three of the women were
dead and one was badly wounded. Nobody
was unwounded.

Lezpet, wrapping a scarf around her arm to
stanch the flow of blood, said "You have
proved yourself, Rider. Guilty or not of
leaving your Eyzonuh companion to die, you
have proven yourself."

Benoni said, wonderingly, "You have not
determined yet? But I thought the Usspika
said . . . ?" and his voice trailed off, for it was
evident that the Pwez was thinking of
something else. She had plenty to think about.
About treachery, how the fight was going in
the palace, about her future even if the
traitors in the palace were killed.

Presently, there was the sound of running
feet and clanking armor, and Lezpet said, "If
those are not my men, and there are many of
them, kill me at once. I will not be taken
prisoner or suffer indignities at their hands."

"I will be too busy killing them to spare a
swordstroke for you, Your Excellency," said
Benoni.

He stood just on the roomward side of the
furniture barricade. The oil had burned out,
and he was wondering if he should pour some
more on the floor. Then, he saw the leader of
the approaching party and breathed easier.
The man was the general of the First Army
and wore a scarlet cloak. Since all the
attackers had worn green cloaks (marking
them as members of the party opposing the
family of Mohso's policies) and since the
members of the Scarlet party wore cloaks to

match their title, this man must be loyal.

Yet, there was no use taking the chance this man might not be a traitor. So Benoni fitted an arrow to the string of a bow and held it on the general until he would declare himself.

The general, a middle-aged grey-haired man, stood in the doorway, glaring about, his bloody sword in hand. Then, seeing the Pwez, his face lit up, and he cried, "Your Excellency! You are safe! Praise to the First!"

"Yes, dear cousin," said Lezpet, "I am. Thanks to these two wild-men and my brave ladies-in-waiting. Tell me, what has been happening?"

"The situation was nip-and-tuck for a while, but we are victors. At least, within the palace we are. I do not know the details, of course, but it looks to me as if the Green Party, or some members of it, anyway, conspired with Skego agents to assassinate you. Some of your own bodyguard were in the plot. They are all dead, the traitors in your bodyguard, that is, but we have taken several of the Green traitors alive and have at least one Skego agent. He will die soon, however, for he is badly wounded."

He paused a moment, and then he said, "I have very bad news. Your uncle and mine, Jiwi, the Usspika, is dead!"

Lezpet gave a cry, and she swayed. But, mastering herself, she said, "Where is he?"

"We found his body within his room, Your Excellency. You will be pleased to hear that, though an old man, he acquitted himself as a Mohso should. He killed a strong young man and badly wounded another. No lion like an

old lion. But they cut off his head and took it
with them. We ran across the desecrators a
few minutes ago, and we took off their heads.
I have already turned over his remains to the
slaves, so that they might prepare him for the
state funeral.

"We will give him a hundred, a thousand,
heads to repay him for the loss of his," said
Lezpet grimly. "But there is no time to think
about a funeral now. I am sure that the filthy
Green took other measures to insure the
success of their treachery. Send out men to
find out what is going on in the city."

The general saluted with his sword,
wheeled, and left, leaving twenty men to
protect the Pwez.

Benoni and Zhem patched up their wounds
and followed the Pwez to the office in which
they had been interviewed the morning
before. Here, Benoni saw what a great leader
the woman was. She became a whirlwind of
energy and quick decisions. If he had any
doubts left about her qualifications as a ruler,
he lost them. Her men, too, seemed to think
the same, for they asked her many questions
and went away satisfied with the answers.

At this time, Joel appeared. He carried a
bloody sword and boasted, loudly, that he had
broken from his room on first hearing the
noise made by the would-be assassins. He had
taken the sword from a fallen soldier and
killed three Greens with it. Now, he was here
to serve the Pwez, to defend her with his life.

Lezpet thanked him, though briefly, and
said that it was her good luck to have had the
three wild-men as guests this night.

Nevertheless, when Joel was out of earshot, she told an officer to investigate his story—after more pressing business was out of the way. Benoni, overhearing her, wondered what she suspected.

But the officer was killed that night, and she must have forgotten about the order.

As the night wore on, the picture of what had happened became clearer. Benoni got a deeper insight into Kaywo politics. He had known something of Kaywo history, that the city had originally been a democracy with a government elected by people who owned more than five acres of land. But only a hundred years ago, the Mohso family had gained a practical monopoly on the presidency and a majority of seats in the House of Speakers, the unicameral legislature. Either a member of the family or of families closely related had been elected president. Meanwhile, the Speakers had raised the requirements of the voter eligibility. Now, a man or woman had to own three hundred acres to be a voter. To qualify for a chance to run for seat in the *Uss a Spika*, he had to own a thousand acres or the equivalent in property.

Some of the lower classes had been agitating for a long time to lower the requirements. The Greens, the aristocratic opponents of the Scarlet or Mohso party, had allied themselves with the commoners. They knew that old Jiwi Mohso wanted to get rid of the electorate system entirely, that he wished to establish a dynastic rule of his family. He had succeeded in suspending the constitution,

the so-called Eternal Agreement Of The
Elders Of Kaywo, during the recent wars with
the Juju and Senglwi. And he had planned on
the coming war with Skego to continue the
suspension and keep his brother as the Pwez.
However, his brother and two sons of the
brother had died during the storming of
Senglwi, under suspicious circumstances.
The Greens rejoiced, for they had a chance to
elect one of their own. The wily old fox had
forestalled them. According to Kaywo law, a
Pwez had the right to name his own successor
in case he died while holding office. The
successor had never been officially named;
the Greens were content to think that Jiwi's
brother had forgotten the matter. Jiwi
produced his late brother's will, witnessed by
the high priest of the First (a Mohso) naming
his daughter as the Pwez.

The Greens had protested violently, saying,
first, that the will was a fraud. Second, that no
woman should be the Pwez. But Jiwi had
pointed out that the ambiguously worded
Eternal Agreement did not specify a male
should hold the office. The Greens, thinking
that when an election did occur, it would be
unlikely that a woman would be elected and
also that she must inevitably shame the
Mohso family through inability, agreed to
accept her.

To their dismay, she proved to be a very
successful ruler. Part of this was because she
leaned heavily on her uncle's advice. But she
was popular, as long as she was successful.

And so, the Greens, rationalizing that a war
with Skego might ruin Kaywo in her

weakened condition and that killing her was their patriotic duty, had conspired with Skego.

That night, a number of Greens and a lesser amount of Skego agents had made the attempt. The Third Army, whose officers and non-coms were largely Greens, had attempted an insurrection. They were fighting the loyal minority of the Third Army. If they won, they would march on the palace and recruit on the way.

There was bloody fighting in the streets and on the housetops that night. Part of the city caught on fire. Before morning, a quarter of the city (the poorer quarter) was burned to the ground. But the city's garrison and part of the First Army, which had hastily moved in from their camping grounds five miles from the city's outer limits, had won.

Benoni and Zhem got in some more fighting that night. Lezpet left her office and led her followers in the street battles. Though she took little part in the actual swinging of a sword, she was close to the front, and she revealed a strategical genius that night. Why not, said her victory-flushed followers? Was she not the grand-daughter of Viyya Mohso, the great general who had decimated the barbarian invaders of Tenziy?

All that next day, instead of resting, Lezpet interrogated prisoners through means of the whip and the fire. She ordered the arrests of all Green speakers and their families. Some of these, understanding what would happen, had already fled northward with their families. Or, in some cases, left them behind. These

poor unfortunates were stripped of their
citizenship and sold as slaves. Their property
was confiscated by the government.

By the evening of the fourth day, Lezpet
held all of Kaywo firmly in her grasp. The
Eternal Agreement had been suspended—only temporarily, of course, during
the emergency—most of the Greens had been
killed, arrested, or had fled. And a group of
enthusiastic commoners and Scarlet *kefl'wiy*
offered her a crown. Pwez, henceforth, was to
mean Emperor.

She, however, refused, saying that the
Eternal Agreement must be restored, that
being a Kaywo citizen must always mean
being free, and so on.

The crowd cheered her enthusiastically and
said that she could not have made a better
Pwez if she were a man.

Benoni marvelled and wondered what
would happen to Kaywo now. If she had been
weakened before, how strong was she now?
Destruction of part of the city, the Third Army
reduced in half, many of her officers slain or
fled the country to fight on Skego's side. If the
Eyzonuh did come to battle for Kaywo, could
they get here before the Skego had come down
from the Northern Seas and put the
inhabitants to the sword and the slave block?

The fifth day, while standing on a corner
after a triumphal parade by the First Army,
he met a strange man. This fellow was tall,
wore a green turban and flowing white robes,
and a veil over the lower part of his face. The
veil was, obviously, only worn for decorative
or religious purposes, for it was too trans-

parent to conceal his features. These consisted of a very dark skin, dark blue eyes, a hooked nose, and thin lips. His beard hung halfway down his chest and was black with a sprinkling of grey hairs. His brown slippers were made of some animal hide and curled up at the ends. Around his neck he wore a string of beads which he constantly fingered.

Benoni had been watching him for some time and soon became aware that the fellow was also watching him. Finally, as the crowd melted away, the man spoke to Benoni. His speech, though fluent Kaywo, contained some odd sounds.

"Stranger and brother," he said, "permit me to introduce myself. I am Hiji Affatu ib Abdu of the land of Khemi, although I sometimes facetiously, sometimes seriously, call myself Aw Hichmakani. Which means 'from nowhere,' if you will allow me a liberal translation. Stranger, would you think me rude if I asked you your name and from what far-off land you come?"

"Not at all," said Benoni, smiling, yet a little ill at ease. "I am Benoni, son of Hozey, and I come from the nation of Fiiniks in the land of Eyzonuh. But tell me, how did you know I wasn't a Kaywo?"

"I overheard you say a few words to that black man just before he left you," said Aflatu ib Abdu. "If you will pardon my seeming immodesty, I do have an extensive knowledge of languages, probably more than any man on earth—no matter what my enemies and some of my friends say—and a keen ear. I could tell instantly that you did not come from this

general area. Although your language is
distantly related to Kaywo."

"It is?" said Benoni. He had surmised that
his speech was descended from the same
parent tongue as Zhem's, but Kaywo was so
foreign that he had not considered it any
relation to Inklich.

"Eyzonuh, heh? Then what I've heard is
true. That two wild-men, if you will pardon
the term, have come a thousand miles or more
from the west, from a terrible desert, a land
of fire-belching mountains and house-
toppling shrugs of the earth?"

"Where is Khemi?" said Benoni.

"Much farther away than your desert, my
friend. Ten times as far in a straight line. And
measuring the path I've followed, forty times
as far. Like a drunken crow. Speaking of
which, would you honor me by allowing me to
buy you a drink?"

"I don't drink," said Benoni, ready to take
offense if the man laughed.

"Ah, it rejoices my heart to meet a camel so
far from the banks of my native river. But I
drink. My religion forbids the consumption of
alcoholic beverages, which is why I consume
all I can get. Come, I will buy a cup of the
disgusting concoction they call coffee."

"I thank you. But I have an appointment
which cannot be broken."

"Too bad. Perhaps, some other time.
Though, in view of the recent events, it is
better not to plan on anything stable in the
future. Our meeting place might be destroyed
or one or both of us might be dead or fleeing
for his life. Too bad. However, tell me, would

it be terribly dangerous to journey to your distant land? I say that laughingly, of course, for I have never made anything but perilous voyages. Ah, to be home again, to see the pyramids and the stone womanlion and the cool waters of the river beside which I first saw the light of Eastern day."

Benoni, though apprehensive about getting to the palace on time for his conference with the Pwez, was overwhelmed with curiosity. This new planet had just swum into his ken, and now it might depart forever, leaving nothing but the ripples of strange names and unsettling reference to distances and lands he had never dreamed of.

"You talk as if you have been even further east than Jinya," he said. "How could that be? Isn't the edge of the world beyond that?"

"I will not laugh at your touchingly innocent remark, friend. I have heard too many like it since I came to this land. And seen too many flushed faces and clenched fists when I expressed surprise at such ignorance. Yes, I've been further east. And no, the edge of the world is not close to Jinya. You see in me, Aflatu ib Adbu, a man who knows. For I am in the process of walking around the world, learning all I can, in order to make a report and, perhaps, to write a book. I was commissioned by the Council of Africa to do so.

"And so, I crossed a sea larger than all your Northern Seas put together, and walked northwards through many countries until I reached the bitter climate of the Skanava, the seafaring terrors of my world. Although they

are not as terrible as the Yagi of Asia. And I
took passage aboard a Skanava ship and
crossed a sea that is the largest in the
world—although I have heard there is one
much larger to the west. And I came down a
river to the Northern Seas and lived in Skego
for a while.

"Then, down the Siy river, a mighty river
indeed, to Senglwi just after the Kaywo
leveled it. And then to this nation.

"I can speak forty languages fluently, know
three dead ones quite well, and any number of
dialects. And I may say, though it hurts me to
do so because I might appear to boast, that I
know more of the world than any man living."

"Around the world?" Benoni dazedly. "I
know that some say the world is round; some,
flat; some, a cube; others, that it has no
beginning or end but merges into the sky, beyond which is heaven. I'm not surprised that
it is round but that it is as big as you say. But I
must be going."

"Wisdom and truth attempt to detain a
man, and he flees," said Aflatu sadly. "Well,
never mind."

"Just one thing," said Benoni. "You have
seen Skego. Do you think that Skego or
Kaywo will win?"

Aflatu quit fingering his beads to throw his
hands up in the air.

"Who knows? Only Awwah knows! I will
say, from a purely statistical viewpoint,
Skego seems to be in the better position. But
Skego has its own problems. All history,
which I surmise you, like all in this land and
most in mine, know little of—history, I say

shows that a young nation may be in worse trouble than Kaywo, yet survive to become the ruler of the known world. Think of Room. You have never heard of Room? I thought not! Well, you will not stay to listen.

"But I will give you on this continent a word, my friend. Forget your wars against each other, band together. For some day, a menace more terrible than you have ever dreamed will sweep across the Lantuk Ocean. The Yagi, who re-discovered the long lost secret of the ancients. Explosives. They threatened the Empire of Africa when I left. They, the Yagi, I mean, were cutting our armies to pieces. For all I know, Khemi may no longer exist when I round the corner of the world and return. I hope not, but it is as Awwa decrees. Or so say those who should know, but often don't."

"If you go west," said Benoni, "look for . . ." And he told him of the strange needle-shaped silvery metal house of the great plains.

At that, Aflatu became excited, and he cried, "The Hairy Men from the Stars!"

Benoni wanted to ask him what he meant, for this was the second time he had heard that phrase. But he knew that he might be late, and the Pwez did not tolerate tardiness.

"I will see you later," he said as he walked away.

"Come back, friend!" shouted the veiled man. "You cannot excite my curiosity so and then leave me! It is against nature, man, and the will of God!"

Benoni hurried to the chamber in which he had first seen the Pwez. Here, he was greeted by Lezpet and the new Usspika, her cousin, the general of the First Army.

"Because of your obvious loyalty to me and the way in which you have fought for me," she said, "I am making you members of my personal bodyguard, the Red Wolves. My beloved cousin will swear you in."

Lezpet Mohso placed a sword on the table and then asked the three to put their right hands on the blade. "Do you three swear by your god or gods and by this sword to obey the Pwez of Kaywo and to give up your life for hers if necessary? Do you swear by your god or gods and this sword to protect her from all harm until you are released from this vow?"

Benoni hesitated, for he wondered why the three should become members of her personal bodyguard only a few weeks before they were due to leave for their native lands. Then, he saw why. She was doing this to make sure that they would not betray her, that they would argue for Kaywo's behalf during the treaty negotiations. And that they would not lead expeditions by their people against her.

Lezpet looked at him strangely. "Why do you not swear?" she said. "Your companions did not think twice."

"I do not give my oath lightly," he said. "Once given, always given."

Surprisingly, she smiled. "That is good," she said. "And have you considered?"

"Yes. I will swear that I will do my best to keep you from harm. As long as I am a member of the Red Wolves. And as long as you are the friend of my people."

Her face became expressionless, and she

said, in a cold voice, "The Pwez is not accustomed to bargain with wild-men. But, since this is a special case, and since we could not reasonably expect you to swear to anything that might endanger your little city-state, we agree. However, we will amend the oath. You will swear to protect me as long as I am not the enemy of your people."

Benoni was a little puzzled by the difference implied in being a friend or a not-friend, but he saw no harm in it. So, he swore.

The woman relaxed somewhat and ordered wine for all of them.

"We will drink a toast to the success of your missions," she said.

Benoni thought for a moment of refusing, but decided that it would be all right to drink. After all, wine and liquor were permissible during religious ceremonies, and this was at least semi-religious.

After they had gulped their wine, the Pwez said, "Perhaps you two Fiiniks wondered why one of you was not judged and executed the day after we had decided to determine who was lying. I will tell you why. My departed uncle told me that he knew which was guilty. He would not tell me how he knew, because he said that I must some day be without his guidance. I would have to find out by myself, although he would give me some clues. He often did this as part of my training as ruler of Kaywo.

"I must confess that I did not know what he knew. I had planned to do some thinking about it early in the morning. But, you know what happened that night. And he was killed.

Luckily for you two. However, I have concluded that it does not matter which of you left the other for dead in that faraway desert. Both have shown your loyalty to me. And I cannot blame you for lying to hurt your enemy. Our god has said that it is good to do so.

"Of course, if I had sworn you in as a Red Wolf and then put the question to you, and you had lied, you would be a traitor. But I am not going to do that now. So, consider yourself lucky."

Benoni was shocked. He had been taught from the day he understood the meaning of a lie that a liar should be condemned under any circumstances. Admittedly, the Eyzonhu did not always realize their ideal in practice, as witness Joel Vahndert. But, at least, his people had that idea, while the Kaywo had just the opposite.

Could the Eyzonuh trust the word of the Kaywo?

During the next two weeks, he did not have much time to think about that. His education proceeded at a rapid pace. And then, one morning, a messenger from the Pwez interrupted a session with a Kaywo historian. He was to leave in two days, at dawn. He and Joel would be accompanied by a hundred cavalrymen and two ambassadors.

"I am to leave that same morning," said Zhem, mournfully.

"Blood-brother, I have a very bad feeling about this. I feel that we are soon to part forever."

"Let us hope not," said Benoni. "But, if it is so, it will be the will of Jehovah."

The night before they were to leave, he and Zhem stayed up late, talking of what had happened and of what might happen. Zhem, near to tears, said "Why don't we leave the city tonight? Go to the east? They say the Iykwa will adopt any runaways into their nation. The Iykwa have a fine life. They live in the forest and the mountains and spend most of their time hunting and fishing. We could each marry one of their red-skinned women and let them till the soil and raise our children while we enjoyed life."

"That sounds fine," said Benoni. "But we have given our word to the Pwez. And the fate of my people depends on my mission. Moreover, I love Debra Awvrez. It is her face that haunts my dreams."

"You have told me that the face of the Pwez sometimes haunts your dreams, too," said Zhem. "What do you make of that?"

"A man is not responsible for his dreams," said Benoni. "And I would be a fool to even think of marrying the Pwez. She thinks of me as a wild-man."

"Yes, you would be a fool. But wild-men can be fools, too."

Zhem drank down half a bottle of wine and soon was asleep. Benoni stayed awake for some time, wondering if he were doing the right thing. Then, deciding that only time would determine that, he, too, fell asleep.

It seemed to him that he had just closed his eyes when he opened them again. A Red Wolf, clad in full armor, was shaking his shoulder and bellowing at him to wake up.

Benoni sat up and said, "It is not even dawn yet."

"Out of your bed and into battle dress!" said the soldier. "You have fifteen minutes to fall in line in front of the palace!"

The soldier hurried out of the room, and Zhem and Benoni hastened to obey the order. When they had put on their armor and fastened their field packs to their backs, the slaves had saddled their horses for them. After inspecting the horses to make sure that their gear was in good shape, they mounted and rode to the Circle of the First, before the palace.

Here, they took their place in the ranks of the Red Wolf Feykhunt.

Presently, the Pwez appeared on her white horse. She, too, was clad in armor, and she was accompanied by her cousin, the Usspika and the general of the First Army cavalry.

Trumpets sounded; drums beat. Lezpet reined in her horse.

"Soldiers of Kaywo!" she said in a loud voice that carried through the ranks. "We must ride at once for the north! Into the forests by the river of L'wan! We have just received a message by carrier pigeon from our agents! I will not tell you now, because every second is important, what the message is. But you will be informed at our first camp. Just trust in me to lead you for a good cause and to promise you hard riding and hard fighting after we get to our destination! The fate of your country depends upon your horse and your sword!"

She wheeled her white stallion and began riding at a gallop down the Avenue of Victory, northwards. Her staff rode after her at the same mad pace. A few seconds later, the Red Wolves followed.

The rest of the night and all that day they rode. Occasionally, they stopped to rest the horses; sometimes, they dismounted and walked at a fast pace while leading the horses. The crack cavalry of the First Army rode behind the Red Wolves. These were composed mainly of the young aristocrats of Kaywo, the best riders in the land who were fanatically devoted to the Pwez.

"They say that the foot-soldiers of the First Army have been given horses and that they are following us as fast as possible," said Zhem. "Did you see the supply wagons? Very light vehicles and drawn by teams of six horses. The wagons hold nothing but food, water, blankets and weapons. Only the essentials. No tents."

"I wonder what the emergency can be?" said Benoni. "It must really be something grave for us to be called along too."

That night, they camped outside a large valley. They had to build their own fires and cook their own meals, for this expedition was not to be slowed down by servants or slaves. Each man was given two extra horses, requisitioned from the villages, towns, and farms they had passed on the road. The riders would get little rest, but it was essential that the horses take turns carrying the men.

After eating, the men collected around a big fire in the center of camp. A platform of logs had been built so that the Pwez could address her troops from a height.

She saw Zhem, Benoni, and Joel in the front

ranks of the Red Wolves, and her eyes widened. She called them before the platform and said, in a low voice, "What are you doing here?"

"We were ordered," said Benoni.

Lezpet bit her lips and said, "In the hurry, it never occurred to me that you might come along. After all, you are members of my body-guard. And I gave orders that all such should assemble immediately. I had thought you three were on your way now with your escort."

"They are riding with us," said Joel. "I saw the officer who was supposed to command our escort."

"It can't be helped," said Lezpet. "Now, it may not matter. If our mission is a success, we won't be in any hurry for you to carry out your command. And, if we fail, which, of course, we won't, then it won't matter."

She sent them back to the ranks. And she said, "Soldiers of Kaywo! Our spies in the forests of L'wan sent a carrier pigeon to the palace with a very urgent message. It said that the people of Pwawwaw, an independent village of wild-men living by the side of the L'wan river, were digging to establish a foundation for new walls around their village. While digging, the Pwawwaw came upon a strange object. This was a great needleshaped building made of a hard silvery metal. It must have been buried under the earth for a thousand years. It must be a fallen ship of the Hairy Men from the Stars!"

There was a murmur from the assembled men. The Pwez held up her hand for silence and continued. "Who knows what that ship may contain? It may hold nothing, for it may have been stripped of everything and have been buried and empty for a millennium. Such a ship was seen recently by one of our Red Wolves, a wild-man from Eyzonuh. He saw it on the great plains. A tribe of wild-men were living in it because it had not been buried by the dust.

"But the ship uncovered by the Pwawwaw may be a different case. It is possible that it made a great hole when it fell and was quickly covered. Or it fell after devastating the area and was soon buried beneath dust blown by the wind. In any event, if it was not stripped, it undoubtedly contains many of the magical devices of the Hairy Men from the Stars! And he who gets his hands on these will control the powers of demons!"

Another murmur arose, and, here and there, shouts. The Pwez again raised her hand, and she said, "The Skego undoubtedly have their spies, and these will have sent reports. So, you may safely bet your pay for the next ten years that the Skego will send soldiers, that they are riding even now to Pwawwaw!

"We must get there first! We must demand that the ship be turned over to Kaywo! If the Pwawwaw refuse, then we take it from them! And, if the Skego arrive, we must defeat them, too!"

The soldiers cheered. Their swords flashed in the firelight as they swore to take the ship or die to the last man while trying. Then, dismissed, they went back to their blankets.

Lezpet motioned to the three wild-men to come to her fire.

"Now," she said to Benoni, "do you understand why my uncle was so excited when he heard you describe that silvery structure on the plains?"

"Yes. Your Hairy Men from the Stars must be the same beings that we Eyzonuh call demons. Our preachers say that, a thousand years ago, they came out of the earth and warred against man. Man drove them back into the bowels of the earth. Sometimes, Seytuh struggles to get free, and that is why the earth quakes and mountains belch fire."

Lezpet laughed, and she said, "We have our stories, too, very integral parts of our religion, as I suppose yours are of your religion. I will tell you ours.

"Once, the people of Earth were a very wise and powerful people. They covered the earth with their millions then and were not just a handful here and there, as we now are. They were very happy, too, for they could control the weather, grow as much food as they wanted, and had such mastery they even subjected the sun god and the demons of the earth. But the sun god and the demons, who were enemies, chafed at being enslaved and were angered at man's arrogance. So, despite their enemity, they banded together. The demons went to the faraway stars on a vehicle provided by the sun god. And the demons made a treaty with their brothers who lived on a star or stars. These demons were half-devil, half-human.

"One day, the half-demons, who looked like

hairy men with pointed furry ears, appeared over earth in their ships. They told the people of Earth a lie. They said their world was burning up and they had no place to live. The sun god was angry at them and was destroying their world. Would Earth give them living space?

"But Earth said no. Man did not have enough space for himself. In those days, each man and woman lived a thousand years and bred many children, who also lived a thousand years. So, the Hairy Men from the Stars said that they would make space. And they had a war with men. It was the most horrible war that earth has ever suffered. At its end, all the Hairy Men from the Stars were killed. But the price of victory for humanity was great. Only one in every hundred thousand survived. And the survivors forgot their magic, forgot everything in their battle for survival. They became savages, unhappy fierce men. And only in the last two hundred years has humanity become numerous enough and wise to begin building civilization again."

"That is not quite the way I heard it," said Benoni cautiously. He did not wish to get involved in a religious discussion. "We have never heard of the Hairy Men from the Stars. According to what our preachers say, the demons of earth tried to master men. They did call in the demons of the air to help them, but most of these were captured and also buried with Seytuh under the earth."

Lezpet laughed again. She said, "That story, and the one told in my country, is good

enough for the common people, children, and
fools. They need something they can understand. But I think otherwise. I think that the
Hairy Men were people something like us.
They lived on a planet like ours, and it
revolved around a star, which was a sun to
their planet. Something drove them to leave
their world; perhaps, their sun got too hot. In
any event, they did come to Earth in their
vehicles. They asked to be allowed to live on
Earth. Man turned down their request, for
what reason, I do not know. A war did ensue,
and civilization was smashed.

"But I do not believe in any sun god or earth
demon. I do not believe that there is a First
God, nor do I believe that Kaywo was founded
by the two-headed son of a two-headed bitch
wolf.

"Of course, if you were to repeat this, I
would have to deny saying such, and I would
have you burned as blasphemers. The best
thing to do is to subscribe publicly to the
belief. After all, it keeps the people in order.
It's a useful lie, decorative rubbish."

Benoni was shocked. He did not believe in a
sun god, either. But he did believe in earth
demons. Had he not felt the earth quake and
the land break open in fire as Seytuh
struggled with his chains deep beneath the
crust of the earth?

"You look shaken," said Lezpet. "Don't.
Haven't you found out that many things you
believed were so, while you lived behind your
desert mountains, just aren't so? And you will
find many other things untrue also."

Benoni went back to his campfire a very

troubled youth. During the next four days, he had time to think. He was busy, but most of what he did was automatic and his brain was free. Could what Lepzet had said be true? That both their religions were false? After all, if, say, Jehovah were the real god, then why was his worship known only in the valley of the Sun? Why not all over the world?

But Jehovah had once been only known to a very small group, the Hebrews. And they, a desert people, had carried their worship into the land of Canaan and from there all over the world. So, why not the Eyzonuh? Perhaps, it was as the preachers said. Jehovah always preserved a nucleus of faithful. The Eyzonuh had inherited the torch of the true religion from the Hebrews, who must have perished, for no one he had ever met outside the Valley had heard of them. Or could they be in the land from which that gabby veiled man, Aflatu ib Abdu, had come?

Anyway, the preachers said that the Eyzonuh alone knew the true god. All other peoples worshipped Seytuh. For instance, the Navahos and the Mek.

But, Benoni told himself, why hadn't I ever thought of that before? I know very well that the Navahos have never heard of Seytuh, and the Mek worship a god called Thiys. I never thought of that before.

By the time they had reached Senglwi, he had decided to quit thinking. For the time being, at least. It was easier to live for the moment alone and think only of the fighting ahead.

They slept that night on the ground outside

the breached walls of the conquered city. At
dawn, they and their horses boarded a fleet of
long low swift galleys. Word had been sent
ahead by drum and by heliograph to prepare
the boats. Using an extraordinarily large crew
of rowers, working day and night shifts, the
galleys could make even better time than the
horses. They did not have to stop to rest.

Benoni slept most of that day, for he was
tired. But the next day he took his turn at
rowing. Slave's work, true, but the Pwez had
so ordered. If the slaves could rest while the
freemen broke their backs for several hours,
the slaves could row just that much harder
when their turn came. And the timer could
keep his gavel hammering out the full-speed
beat.

They forged against the current of the
broad and muddy Siy River, the Father of
Waters, running close to the shore where the
current was weakest. Then, they turned right
into the mouth of the L'wan river and rowed
northward. They left the civilized area and
began to pass little villages inhabited by the
wild-men of L'wan. Day and night they rowed,
working the oars, eating, and sleeping in
shifts. Not once did they stop, for they carried
all they needed. And the wild-men, seeing this
great fleet approach up the river, did not
bother. The wild-men either shut the gates of
their wooden fortress-villages or else fled into
the forests.

One morning, two hours after dawn, they
saw a band of horsemen standing on the left
bank. These wore shining armor, and the
standard-bearer at their head carried a long
pole on which was mounted two wolf-heads.

Lezpet gave the order, and her galley swung into the bank.

Their leader, a young lieutenant, clenched his fist to his chest. He said, "Your Excellency! You are only ten miles from Pwawwaw! You may proceed safely on your boats the rest of the way. We control the river at this point."

"What has happened so far?" said Lezpet.

"We did what was ordered. So far, things have turned out as planned. On receiving your message from Kaywo, the Second Army boarded galleys, leaving just enough behind for your forces to use. Part of the army went by land, because we did not have enough craft. We rendezvoused just below Pwawwaw. Part of us attacked Pwawwaw. We forced them into the fort but did not have enough men to storm it. The rest proceeded up the L'wan on the galleys. And a good thing we did.

"We ran headlong at night into a fleet of Skego soldiers. There was a battle. Every Kaywo fought without thought of surrender. We sank their galleys and killed every soldier and slave. At a terrible cost, for they fought like demons. We lost every boat but one and all our soldiers except thirty. I, a lieutenant, was the highest left in command.

"We came back to the besiegers around Pwawwaw and waited for you. But our spies tell us that another Skego fleet is coming fast, is about forty miles up river. And about two thousand Skego cavalry on a forest road not thirty miles away. Twenty miles behind them, a great army."

"How many of the Second are besieging

Pwawwaw?''

"Eight hundred and fifty."

"There are fifty of you, and a thousand
warriors on these boats. A thousand and nine
hundred in all. How many Pwawwaw men?''

"I would estimate about a thousand. But
their women will fight by their sides, and they
are all excellent archers."

"And they will all fight like furies to defend
their children," said Lezpet. "And will be
shooting from behind walls. Well, we haven't
time to starve them out. Pwawwaw will have
to be stormed inside an hour or two after we
begin the attack. We have to get to the vessel
of the Hairy Men, take what is valuable, and
leave at once. Then, it'll be a race back to
Senglwi.''

She ordered soldiers aboard, and the
galleys raced towards the north. A pigeon was
released; it shot off to the southwest, toward
its home in Senglwi. The message it carried
ordered the garrison to march at once toward
the confluence of the Siy and L'wan. There, if
the Skego galleys did pursue the Kaywo, they
could be ambushed and the fleeing Kaywo
galleys could turn and fight.

Every man aboard took a turn at the oars,
rowing with all his strength. The blue L'wan
waters turned white before the prows; in an
hour, the lookout on the lead ship saw the
reflection of the sun on the armor of the
Second.

Pwawwaw was the largest village of the
L'wan wild-men. It lay next to a river on the
left bank and was surrounded by a wall of
earth on top of which was another wall of

heavy logs. The inhabitants lived within the walls in square log cabins. However, on the big bluff just behind the village was a large log fort, almost a wooden castle. Here, the Pwawwaw had retreated upon first seeing the Kaywo galleys of the Second. The Kaywo had landed and burned the village to the ground. They had also stationed troops near the two gates of the fort on the bluff, just beyond arrow range.

"If the Pwawwaw had any sense," said Lezpet, "they would have come out from behind their walls and fought the besiegers. They outnumbered us until now."

"The L'wan fear us ever since the Third Army, ten years ago, made a punitive campaign up and down the river valley and burned many villages and took many captives," said the Usspika. "They learned that undisciplined and unarmored savages cannot stand against Kaywo."

"According to the report, the vessel is buried within the site of the fort," said Lezpet. "Too bad it wasn't in the village, instead. But that can't be helped."

She gave orders to have all the slaves chained to their benches on the galleys. They were to be provided with food and water so they did not suffer while the fighting went on. But she had the oars removed from the galley, since she did not want to see the slaves rowing away. Leaving only a few soldiers to watch over the slaves, she led her bodyguard and the cavalry of the First Army up the bluff.

Within a few minutes, she found that tall siege-ladders had been built from wood cut from the trees of the neighboring forest. And many wooden walls on wheels had been built so that the Kaywo might advance behind them close to the fort and be protected from arrow fire.

After complimenting the commander on his foresight, the Pwez turned her horse to face the assembled soldiers.

"Sons of the two-headed wolf! The fate of Kaywo lies in your hands! The Skego are coming swiftly in great numbers! We must conquer the Pwawwaw within the next two hours if we are to succeed! This means that we cannot count our costs and that no man must turn back, even to gather his strength for another attack! Once the charge trumpet is blown, we must go forward without pause! Sons of the wolf, you must be wolves!"

A trumpet blew the long call to action. The soldiers, chanting "Kaywo! Kaywo!" began to push the tall and thick log shields on wheels before them. Behind the pushers came files of man carrying the long and heavy siege-ladders.

Benoni, with Joel and Zhem, was not among the attackers. He was stationed about fifty yards behind them with a group of three hundred cavalry. Lezpet at their head, they waited until the time was ripe.

As soon as the mobile walls came within arrow range of the Pwawwaw, a cloud of feathered shafts rose from the many towers and from behind the sharp points of the walls of the fort. Most of these thudded into the Kaywo shields; a few found targets among those who had dropped too far behind their shelters. After two volleys, the Pwawwaw, seeing that they were wasting arrows, ceased fire. But a powerful drumming rose from the fort, and the wild-men shrieked in their strange tongue at the attackers.

When the wheeled walls had gotten within fifty yards of the Pwawwaw ramparts, they stopped. Now, half of the men behind the mobiles fitted arrows to their bows. The others gripped the ladders and waited. The Pwawwaw, unable to hold themselves any longer, began to shoot. The disciplined Kaywo did not retaliate, despite some losses; they waited until their commander gave the signal.

He, looking through a peephole in the mobile, chose a time between the volleys. Then, he lowered his hand, a trumpeter gave the assault call, and the soldiers ran out from behind their shelters.

The archers quickly marshalled themselves into ranks of four deep. At the orders of their sergeants, they began to fire in volleys, rank by rank. And the men carrying the ladders rushed forward to the foot of the twenty-five foot high walls of the fort. Now, the arrows of the Pwawwaw began to find their flesh. Kaywo dropped, several ladders fell to the ground and were not picked up again; so many of their carriers were dead or wounded.

But the archers of the Kaywo were finding their marks, too. Many a Pwawwaw head projecting over the edge of the pointed logs dropped with an arrow in it or in the chest below the head. And the Pwawwaw suddenly quit sending over concerted fire and resorted to individual initiative.

The Kaywo gave a loud shout and raised their ladders high and planted the feet on the ground and let the upper part fall against the walls. The Kaywo bowmen now aimed at the areas where the ladders were. When a brave Pwawwaw jumped up from behind his walls to push the ladders back, he suddenly bristled with shafts.

Lezpet turned on her saddle and motioned to a wagon behind this. This had been especially fitted with a giant log mounted on top and lashed to the frame. The wagon faced backwards, and a team of twelve horses had been hitched to the specially prepared tongue. The back wheels of the wagon were on a rotatable axle; the axle could be turned several degrees to the right or left by means of cables and a huge wheel fixed to the top of the wagon. A soldier crouched on a chair and turned the wheel; he peered through a hole set in the middle of a heavy log shield and was protected by a roof. Since the ramming-log took up most of the space on top of the wagon, the pilot's shelter and the wheel within were set to one side. Braces had been built on the side of the wagon to support the half of the pilot's shelter which projected.

The Pwez rode up to the ram-wagon and spoke a few words to the soldier crouched behind the steering wheel. Then she rode to a position a few yards behind the team that was to push the ram-wagon. Behind her, the three hundred cavalry arranged themselves in ranks of four abreast.

A trumpeter, at a signal from Lezpet, blew the charge call. Lezpet and some of the

officers began striking the flanks of the
wagon team with whips and shouted at them.
At first, the horses were reluctant to gallop,
as if they were afraid of this strange arrange-
ment of pushing, instead of pulling, the
wagon. But, under the sting of the lash, they
began to pick up speed. Long before the
wagon reached the gates of the fort, it was
traveling at maximum speed.

Benoni, in the front rank of the cavalry,
could see Lezpet just ahead of him, but the
huge bulk of the wagon and the log it carried
blocked out much of his view. So it was that
he did not, at first, see that some quick-
thinking and daring Pwawwaw were opening
the gates. Their intention was to swing them
open just enough to allow the wagon to come
speeding through, and perhaps, a few of the
cavalry. Then the gates would be swung shut,
and the Kaywo would have lost their only
immediate chance to burst the gates apart.

Lezpet, however, saw at once what the
Pwawwaw were planning. She spurred her
stallion to race around the team and drew up
alongside the wagon. Despite the rumble
made by the wagon's wheels, she managed to
shout out an order. And she dropped back.

The pilot turned the front wheels just in
time; the wagon veered; the great butt of the
log, projecting six feet ahead of the wagon,
crashed into the edge of the right gate and
flung it back against the wall, sending the
Pwawwaw who were holding it rolling over
and over.

The ram struck the gate and the wall behind
it with an impact that tore the gate from its

hinges and bent the logs of the wall backwards.

The horses driving the wagon piled into the
rear of the wagon as their traces broke, and
they became a kicking, screaming tangle. The
pilot house itself was ripped loose and
smashed against the gate, killing the pilot.

But the ramming had not only opened the
way to the cavalry; the impact had knocked
off the archers on that side of the gate, sent
them tumbling to the ground. And reduced
the effective fire against the horsemen
pouring through the gateway.

The next ten minutes was a melee. Benoni
found himself engulfed in a swirling mob, but
the Pwawwaw were all on foot, and he could
strike downwards. His sword rose and fell,
rose and fell. Kaywo around him went down
as arrows fired from the wall struck them or
their horses: or Pwawwaw leaped up from the
ground and dragged them off their saddles.

But, by then, many of the Kaywo on the
siege-ladders had successfully climbed up the
ladders, over the walls, and onto the
platforms behind the walls. After clearing
some areas of the defenders, they fought
others while archers began shooting at the
Pwawwaw on the ground within the
enclosure.

One of the arrows went through the belly of
the chief of the Pwawwaw. The chief, standing
on a platform and directing the fighting,
toppled off into the swirling mob around him.
Another Pwawwaw, a subchief, picked up the
fallen standard, a pole with a wild boar's head
at its end. Benoni, his horse shoved against

the platform by the weight of the crowd, struck out with his sword and half-severed the subchief's leg. The standard fell within reach of Benoni; he picked it up, rose in his stirrups the better to be seen by all, and waved the standard.

The Kaywo cheered and began to press around Benoni to defend him against the Pwawwaw struggling to regain it. Some of the heart seemed to go out of many of the barbarians. Perhaps, in their belief, the standard contained the strength of the Pwawwaw, and he who possessed it possessed their strength.

Whatever the explanation, the battle went speedily in the Kaywo's favor. A few minutes later, the Kaywo burst into the big longhouse in the middle of the fort. Here, they found the children and many of the women huddled, expecting to be slaughtered or captured for slavery. But Lezpet had ordered that they be dispossessed as quickly as possible; if the Pwawwaw men saw that they were not harmed, they might not fight so desperately.

Lezpet shouted orders; the Kaywo managed to form themselves into two lines. Between the avenue made by the lines, the women and children fled for the gates. Many fell and were crushed beneath the panicky crowd, but the majority managed to get outside. From there, they fled towards the woods. Then, the Kaywo regrouped and fought towards the other end of the fort. After reaching it, they unbarred the other gate and admitted the Kaywo outside it.

From then on, it was slaughter and flight.

The Pwawwaw men, finding that the Kaywo
were making no effort to keep them from
leaving through the gates, broke and ran.

The Kaywo had no difficulty finding the
vessel of the Hairy Men from the Stars. It lay
in a huge excavation beside the northern wall.

Benoni, reining in his horse beside Lezpet,
said, "It looks just like the one I saw on the
plains!"

Lezpet slid from her horse, ran down the
steps into the excavation, and stopped before
the towering bulk. The vessel was only partly
uncovered; over-two-thirds of it was still
buried under dirt. But a ramp of earth led up
to a window, and she could see within.

Benoni stood by her, for the window was a
circle ten feet across, and also looked. The
glass or metal was clear. The sun was at the
correct angle to flood the interior. They had
no trouble making out details.

There were many things that looked alien;
they were incomprehensible to him. That was
to be expected. Beings that controlled such
power would use devices beyond his understanding.

One thing he did understand. The skeletons
on the floor of the chamber within the ship.
The Hairy Men from the Stars, who had died
when their ship fell. There were six of them,
lying here and there. The skull of one was
broken open, doubtless from the impact so
many hundreds of years ago.

The skulls and skeletons seemed to
resemble those of human beings. From this
distance, Benoni could detect only two out-
standing differences. Every skull had very

prominent cheekbones. And every hand had six fingers.

Lezpet stepped back and said, "How do we get in? There don't seem to be any doors."

She ordered a Pwawwaw prisoner, a wounded man, brought to her. The fellow spoke only his native language, but one of her officers, a specialist in Pwawwaw, translated.

"Have any of you entered this?" she said.

The officer directed the question; the fellow spewed forth some gibberish.

"He says that they have tried to get in. But that, so far, they have found nothing that even looks like a door. Moreover, the metal has resisted all their efforts. They pounded two days on the window and didn't even make a dent. Broke all the tools."

Lezpet bit her lip, and she said, "The First would laugh at us if we sacrificed so many then had to leave empty-handed. Perhaps, there may be an entrance farther back on the ship. But we've no time to dig away all that dirt."

Benoni left the ramp and walked along the curving silvery bulk of the vessel. He searched on both sides and returned to the Pwez.

"The skin of the vessel is absolutely smooth," he said. "Except for six slight indentations. These are arranged in a circle, not as wide as my hand."

"Perhaps, they mean something," said Lezpet. "But what?"

Benoni looked again inside the room. Would they have to leave the ship as they found her? Go away with the mysteries, and possible treasuries of the Hairy Men forever unknown?

"At least, Your Excellency," he said, "If we can't get in, neither can the Skego."

"The Skego will have all the time they need to uncover the rest of the ship," she said, furiously. "And time to study means for getting in. No, we have to find its secret now! Within the next few hours!"

Benoni looked at the skeletons again. Six fingers on each hand. He tried to imagine what those hands looked like when clothed with flesh.

Then, abruptly, he spun around and raced down the ramp of earth.

"What is it?" said the Pwez, but he did not bother to answer. He ran along the side of the vessel until just before the rear half plunged into the wall of the excavation. Then, he extended one hand with the five fingers and the other hand with one finger extended. And he pressed down on the six indentations forming a circle.

Immediately, a great circular crack appeared in the smooth skin.

Benoni shouted, and Lezpet came running. "What is it?"

She had no need for an explanation. A section of the skin was sinking inwards. Within a minute, the circular portion had sunk a half-foot, then begun sliding to the left into the skin itself.

Benoni told her what he had done. She, forgetting her dignity for a second, squealed with joy. "First above! It took a wild-man to solve it! You have shamed us Kaywo!"

She motioned to the soldiers to bring the Pwawwaw prisoner. Through the interpreter, she said, "You are lying to me. Did none of your people press down on those indentations?"

The prisoner's eyes were wide at the sight of the sliding door. He said, "Yes, some of us did. But nothing happened."

Now that they could see within, they hung back. The interior was dark and silent, dark and silent with a thousand years and the dangers of beings from a star so distant it made the head reel to think about it.

Lezpet looked about her, looked at the awe they made no effort to disguise. Then, turning, she stepped into the entrance. If she was as reluctant as they, she did not show it.

Benoni took a torch from a man and followed her. The torch showed a small chamber with nothing in it except some buttons and a metal bulb on the wall. Beyond was a corridor; it joined another at right angles that seemed to run the length of the ship.

Lezpet stopped and said, "I will go forward with three men to the room that we saw through the window. You, Rider, will go to the rear with three more. Colonel, you send two men each to each chamber. Pick up everything that can be carried and bring it outside. Look for anything that might be a weapon. But, for the sake of the First, do not do anything but carry it outside. We do not want to be releasing unknown powers."

Benoni led his men down the main corridor to the rear. At the end of the corridor was a

huge room. The walls were lined with great
metal boxes, twice as tall as himself. On the
sides of these were little windows of glass and
needles pointing to strange symbols. He did
not know the use of the boxes, but it was
useless to examine them. They were stuck to
the floor. In any event, they were too large to
carry in a wagon or galley.

He directed each man to enter one of the
rear chambers. He went into another. This
was a large room with many chairs and tables
bolted to the metal floor. A narrow platform
ran along one wall, and a white sheet of metal
above the platform covered the wall.

On a metal table in the middle of the room
was a large metal box. This was bolted to the
table. It had several buttons on the side and a
circular metal window at one end. The
window pointed towards the white metal
sheet on the wall.

Benoni looked into the window but could
see nothing except blackness. What could this
strange device have been used for? Perhaps, if
he pressed one of the buttons on the side, the
device might be activated, just as pressing the
indentations on the side of the vessel had
activated the door.

But Pwez, with good reason, had forbidden
them to experiment.

Benoni did not see how this box could be a
weapon. In the first place, the chairs and
tables, and the scattered debris, showed that
this might have been some sort of lounge. Or,
perhaps, a lecture room. The lecturer could
have stood on the platform.

Unable to resist, Benoni pushed in on one of

the buttons, then sprang back. Nothing happened.

Shakily, he extended his hand and pressed on another button. And sprang back. Nothing.

There was a third button. Almost, he decided to forget about it and continue his search in another room. But he had taken no more than two steps before he turned back to the box. This time, when he pressed the last button, he got a response that almost sent him running out of the doorway.

A light shot from the eye in the box, and a square of brightness appeared on the white metal sheet against the wall.

Benoni froze, his finger over the button. If this were some horrible weapon, if the wall started to melt, he had to stop it.

But the brightness was suddenly changed, and it became a configuration of shadows.

For a moment, because he had never seen such a thing, he did not make any pattern, any sense, out of the shadows on the wall. Then, as if somebody had pressed a button within him, he saw that the shadows were moving pictures!

And what pictures! Great buildings that made even the giant structures of Kaywo look like ant heaps. Men and women in strange clothes. And the Hairy Men bestial looking with the shaggy reddish fur, the pointed ears, and monstrously prominent cheeks.

The pictures seemed to be of fighting in the streets. Evidently, they had been made during the taking of a city by the Hairy Men. There were many types of devices that made the fronts of stone buildings go up in dust. But

the one that interested him most was a hand
weapon. The Hairy Men pointed it at their
enemies, and the enemies disappeared in a
cloud of smoke.

Hearing voices down the hall, Benoni
hastily pressed on the button that had
activated the picture box. The pictures on the
wall continued moving. He pressed down on
another button; the pictures speeded up in
their action, became a blur.

Sweating, in an agony because he might be
detected in disobedience, he pressed the third
button. The light blinked out, and the pictures
disappeared.

Benoni went out into the corridor and
asked the lieutenant he found there if he had
discovered anything of value. The lieutenant
shrugged and said they had found many
portable objects. Who knew if they were of
value? Doubtless, they must have been to the
Hairy Men, but they would have to be
evaluated after they were taken to Kaywo.

Benoni located the three men he had sent to
search and questioned them. One took him to
a large room which was obviously a store-
room. Here, in a bin, Benoni found about two
hundred of the handweapons he had seen in
the moving pictures. And, in a bin next to the
first, thousands of metal cylinders. These, he
knew from the pictures, were placed in the
weapons and discharged.

Benoni stood before the bins for several
moments in an agony of indecision. A few
Kaywo, equipped with these, could defeat an
army. If the Skego showed up in force at this
moment, they could be blasted apart. If the

weapons were taken back to Kaywo, the wise men might be able to analyze their workings and even manufacture more like them. Which would mean that Kaywo would soon conquer the entire land. They would not need the Eyzonuh. In fact, it was inevitable that his people would be defeated and enslaved.

Yet, he had sworn to be loyal to Pwez, to save her from harm if it meant giving up his own life.

If he kept his oath, he would be betraying his people. If he carried out his duty to them, he broke his oath.

Finally, he saw his way clear. For the moment, at least. There was nothing he could do to prevent the weapons being taken to Kaywo. But he could put off the moment of knowledge about the weapons by keeping silent. Sooner or later, the Kaywo would know. Every moment of ignorance on their part, however, meant another moment of survival and hope for his people.

If he took a weapon and the cylinders back to Eyzonuh, they might be duplicated there. That would give the Eyzonuh a fighting chance against the Kaywo. His loyalty to the Pwez went only as far as the literal words of the oath. He would fight for her against Skego or any enemies that arose during their return to her country. And, if he must, he would give his life to protect hers.

But no-one, not even Jehovah, could expect him to betray his own people. And, first chance he got, he would finally renounce the oath. That was the only way out.

On the pretext that he wanted to bring

others into the room to start carrying out the
artifacts, he sent the Kaywo out to get them.
As soon as the man stepped into the hall,
Benoni dropped two of the weapons and
several hundred or so of the cylinders into his
knapsack. He returned to the room with the
picture box and inspected the box. At its rear
was a door that swung open when he pulled
on its handle. Inside was a smaller aperture; a
handle protruded from its middle. He pulled
on the handle, and a little black box came out.
At the front of the box were two short metal
prongs; these had fitted into two receptacles
at the far end of the chamber into which the
little box fitted.

Benoni planned to drop the box some place
where the Skego would not find it. He did not
know its purpose, but he hoped that the larger
box would not operate without it. To test, he
pressed on the starter push-button, and the
box did not project any pictures.

Quickly, he searched the room, found a
locker full of small boxes with two prongs
and just the size of the one he had removed.
He stepped out into the hall and ordered two
soldiers to remove these. Now, the Skego
would not know how to operate the
handweapons even if they should succeed in
capturing them.

The ship was looted of all detachable
objects, and the objects were transferred to
three wagons. Just as the last load was being
taken out of the vessel, an officer rode up the
hill and reported to the Pwez.

"We have just sighted an immense fleet of
galleys coming around the bend," he said.

"They are only a few miles away. And the first of the Skego cavalry have appeared out of the forest road. If we don't hurry, we will be cut off from the valley."

Lezpet rode to the top of the bluff to see for herself, Benoni behind her. The officer's report was true. Over a hundred galleys filled the river, their long oars rising and dipping in a frenzy. Also, the first of a long line of horsemen were racing towards the beached galleys of the Kaywo, only a mile away.

"There will be a very large force between us and the galleys before we can get down there," said Lezpet. "Enough to delay until the Skego gallies have arrived. We could never make it."

She turned to her cousin, the Usspika. "We'll have to escape by land. We'll take that forest road you were telling me about, the one that leads along the bluffs for a while, then dips down to the river road."

"We can't make any time if we carry our wounded along," said the Usspika.

"I hate to do this to men who have fought so bravely for me and for Kaywo," said Lezpet. "But we can't lose everything they fought for. Kill all those who are too wounded to ride. Tell them their names will be inscribed forever on the Column of Heroes, and their families will never have to go hungry or be without a roof over their heads."

The Usspika saluted and rode off. Tears appeared in Lezpet's eyes. Seeing Benoni look at her, she wiped them away and shook her head angrily.

"Kaywo comes first," she said. "Those men

will die with the name of their motherland on
their lips and blessing me."

She rode to the head of the hastily
assembling column. Of the nineteen hundred
who had ridden up the bluff to the Pwawwaw
fort, less than half could now sit a horse.

"A high cost," she said. "But it will be worth
it."

An officer reined in his horse before her.
"The Skego are already beginning to climb
the bluff! Do you want some of us to attack, to
hold them and give you more time?"

"You could not hold them very long," she
said. "It would not be worth it. Your swords
will be more valuable later on."

She looked around to make sure that the
bloody business of dispatching the wounded
was done. Then, she gave the signal to ride.
And she spurred her horse into a breakneck
gallop. Behind came the cavalry and the three
wagons, piled high with the artifacts from the
ship.

The road was a dirt track, hemmed in by the
thick growth of trees, wide enough for two
horses abreast. It wound in and out over the
bluff for three miles, then suddenly went
down the bluff and toward the river. At the
crest of the hill, Lezpet stopped her horse and
looked northwards. Far down below and to
the north was a long line of horsemen
galloping on the dirt road that followed the
river.

"We are about three miles ahead of them,"
she said. "And our horses must be much
fresher than theirs. I think we have more than
a good chance."

They rode down the bluff slowly, for the road was steep. From the foot of the bluff, the road angled off towards the river road. Two miles of dirt, and they reached the river. Here, the track lay between the bluffs to their right and the river to their left. They could not see the pursuing horsemen, but they could see the first of the galleys, still churning water.

"If we took to the woods, we might lose them," said Lezpet. "But we could never get the wagons through the forest. No, we'll keep on running until we find a good place to make a stand. Perhaps . . . well, never mind. Forward!"

At one of the stops they made to give their horses a short but absolutely necessary rest, Benoni slipped into the woods. Here, he opened the back of the handweapon as he had seen with Hairy Men do in the moving pictures. The cylinders, which tapered slightly at one end, he slid one at a time into the twenty receptacles of the revolving chamber inside the weapon. He closed the lid and then sighted along the barrel of the weapon. There was a little projection near its far end; this, he supposed, was to aid in aiming. A button on the inside of the butt in his hand must, he reasoned, be pressed to activate the weapon. It was the only external projection. He would have liked to test the weapon, but he was afraid that the result would alarm the Kaywo. If they found out he he was concealing knowledge. . . .

He rejoined the column and mounted his horse. The Kaywo resumed the march with a canter; there was no use running the horses until they foundered.

After two miles, they came to a point where the road swung to the right and entered a narrow valley formed by two steep cliffs. The makers of this rough road had been forced to take this path, for the bluff on the left abutted the riverbank.

Lezpet stopped her horse. "This would be a good place to leave a holding force," she said.

The Usspika said, "What will keep the Skego from going around, on the other side of this bluff?"

"Nothing will keep them from trying," she said. "But they will have to go through very dense forest and take a long time getting around. I think they will try fighting their way through this valley before they try that. By then, we will have the wagons miles away, and they will never catch up."

A scout galloped down the length of the column and reined his horse sharply before the Pwez.

"The Skego galleys are less than half a mile away!"

"They must be working their slaves until they foam at the mouth," said Lezpet. "If we can keep ahead of them long enough, we can tire them out."

She called for volunteers to station themselves at the entrance to the valley. Every man raised his sword to indicate his willingness. Benoni was among them. Not that he was so willing to fight what would have had to be a fatal battle—under ordinary circumstances—but that he felt that he could fight his way out with the Hairy Men's weapon and then, having been left behind by the Pwez, desert with a good conscience.

But she did not pick him among the two hundred she chose as a Leonidean force.

A hundred and fifty stationed themselves behind rocks piled across the face of the entrance. Another fifty climbed to the top of both sides of the valley, there to shoot arrows and roll rocks down upon the Skego. The Pwez, after saluting the valiants who would stay behind, led the rest through the valley. This ran for three miles between ever narrowing and steeper cliffs. Their progress was slowed down because of the muddy and slippery soil. Suddenly, the bluffs fell away, and the open road and the river were before them.

Also before them were Skego. On foot.

The Pwez halted her horse. "The galleys got here first," she said. "Some, anyway. We'll have to charge, try to break through them."

Benoni, calculating their chances, saw that they would not be able to present a broad front to the Skego. Coming out of the narrow valley, they had no chance to spread out before running into the Skego. And archers were climbing the sides of the hills and up trees.

Benoni, hoping that no one would notice him because they were all eyeing the Skego, pulled one of the weapons out of the knapsack. He put it in his left hand and held his sword in the other. When they charged, he would exchange the two.

The Usspika said, "You must go back to the middle of the column, Your Excellency.

Almost all of those in the front are bound to die. We cannot take a chance that you will be killed. Or worse, taken prisoner. The heart would go out of the men. And the Skego might then capture the treasure of the Hairy Men."

Lezpet hesitated a moment. Then she said, "I do not like to act like a cowardly woman, cousin. But, for the good of Kaywo, I will do as you say."

Benoni, Joel, and Zhem, as part of her bodyguard, rode back with her to the middle of the column. Benoni was pleased. Being surrounded by so many people, all intent on the Skego, would make it easier to use the weapon.

The trumpeter blew the signal to charge. Screaming, "Kaywo! Kaywo!" the column lurched forward, then began to pick up speed. By the time the first of the Kaywo left the valley, the entire force was at a gallop.

The Skego stood massed just outside the entrance, a solid body of bristling spears. And others were hurrying from the river to join them as swiftly as the late-arriving galleys could be beached and their soldiers could leap overboard.

The first of the Kaywo went down, arrows sticking from their bodies or the flesh of their horses. Those behind leaped over them or also went down as their horses were caught in the flailing legs of the fallen. Then, the Kaywo had rammed into the spears of the Skego, fallen transfixed on the front ranks. Behind them came the swinging swords of their fellows, and the Skego were falling, too.

Just before getting to the mouth of the

valley, Benoni urged his horse to one side and
slowed it. He transferred his sword to his left;
the hand weapon, to his right. He raised the
device, sighted along its barrel at a group of
Skego running up from the bank. And pressed
on the button.

The weapon recoiled slightly. A cloud of
smoke and a loud noise came from the group
at which he had aimed.

Heads and arms and broken bodies hurled
out of the smoke. When the smoke cleared,
there were at least twenty torn bodies. And
the men near them were standing as if
paralyzed, not knowing what had happened.

Benoni was awed at the results and somewhat scared, too. However, he aimed again,
this time at the edge of the melee, where a
number of Skego were trying to get close
enough to use their spears. Another cloud of
smoke and a bang like a giant clapping his
hands. A dozen torn-apart bodies.

The noises had had one unfortunate effect.
It had frightened the horses close to the
explosion so that they reared and upset many
of their riders. That could not be helped. Any
more than it could be helped when he fired a
third time and blew apart some of the Kaywo
along with a much larger number of Skego.

Now, he aimed over the heads of the group
at a galley that had just beached and was
disgorging its cargo of fifty soldiers. The
explosion took place too far from the boat to
do anything but scare the soldiers. He
lowered the sights a trifle and pressed the
button again. This time, the front half of the
boat blew apart. He turned his attention to

the rocks and the trees concealing the Skego
archers. He held the button down and saw one
cloud after another appear, and rocks, bodies,
and trees fly apart. And the archers, throwing
down their bows, ran as if Seytuh himself
were after them.

When he had released pressure on the
button, it was only because the handweapon
had ceased functioning. It was the work of
less than a minute to open the lid and place
twenty more cylinders within the revolving
chamber. There was no sign of the spent
cylinders; he supposed that they had been
self-immolated when they did their work.

He put his sword in its scabbard and urged
his horse into a full gallop. By then, the Skego
had retreated, and the survivors of the Kaywo
were riding down the road, the three wagons
among them. When Benoni came out of the
valley, the others were far ahead of him. The
Skego, seeing a lone rider, ran to intercept
him.

Two shots killed a dozen of the foremost;
the others turned and ran in the opposite
direction as swiftly as they had come towards
him. And he was away from them.

It did not take him long to catch up. The
Kaywo had stopped and were staring at a
barricade of logs on the road ahead of them.

"You got away!" said Zhem exultantly. "I
thought you were killed."

"Who threw that up?" said Benoni, pointing
at the barricade.

"Wild-men. L'wan from some of the villages
around here. But they wouldn't have done it
on their own. We've seen some men in helmets

with red horsehair plumes. Skego agents."

Benoni urged his horse closer to the Pwez, and he said to Zhem, "Why don't we charge them?"

"The wild-men outnumber us two to one. Must be over a thousand."

Benoni pointed at the river and said, "Here come some more Skego gallies."

The Pwez was talking to a colonel, second-in-command now that the Usspika had fallen. "I do not know what caused those explosions," she was saying. "Perhaps they were lightning bolts thrown by the First to help us, as you say. But, if they were, why doesn't the First destroy that barricade? And, with it, the savages?"

"Perhaps he will, when we charge," said the colonel.

"There must be some other explanation," said Lezpet. Maybe they had a new weapon, but it wasn't tested sufficiently, and it exploded before it was supposed to."

"We have to go through the L'wan or around them," said the colonel. "The Skego will be beaching their gallies soon."

"It'd be suicide to go through the forest. There must be a L'wan behind every tree. No, it's through them."

The bugler was dead, and no one had picked up his horn. So, the Pwez gave the signal, and the five hundred charged. Benoni, riding just behind the Pwez, fired past her. The logs of the barricade flew out of the smoke. With them, pieces of bodies.

The deafening blasts, however, frightened the horses, and they stopped and reared or

bolted off into the forest. The horses that kept
running straight ahead smashed into those
that had stopped. Then, if the L'wan had
charged, they would have caught the Kaywo
in a very bad situation. But the L'wan were
too busy running for their lives into the
forest.

By the time the horses had been settled
down and order restored, seven Skego gallies
had beached.

"Take the boats!" screamed Lezpet. "If we
can capture some gallies, we'll have a better
chance of getting away! No more ambushes!"

She spurred her horse towards the men
jumping from the boats into the shallow
water. The others followed her. All except
Benoni.

He rode to the river's edge and aimed at the
five gallies just coming up to help the others
already beached. Now, he kept the button
pressed and corrected his aim according to
the gouts of water from the misses. Three of
the boats blew up before he had to reload.
Two of the survivors rammed their prows
into the soft mud of the bank, and the Skego
climbed out. Benoni finished reloading, sank
the third, and then blasted the group
assembling for battle array. There were a
hundred of them when he started shooting.
After the smoke cleared, fifty were
permanently out of action. The rest were
running towards the forest.

He emptied the weapon at them to
stimulate their panic, then reloaded and
replaced it in his knapsack. With sword in
hand, he steered his horse into the melee.

It was bloody work for five minutes before

the surviving Skego broke. They tried to shove their galleys back into the river; two boats did get away and began floating downstream with only a few aboard. The other boats were saved; the would-be refugees were cut down in the shallow waters alongside their craft.

"It's too late, Your Excellency!" said the colonel. He was pale, clutching a fountaining gash on his right arm, and swaying on the saddle. "See! They'll be on us before we can get a good start!"

Lezpet looked at the twenty galleys speeding towards them, and she frowned. What the colonel said was true. They could get aboard the captured boats. But, by the time they could start rowing, their avenue of escape would be cut off.

"It's too bad we lost so much time and so many men trying to take these," she said. "So be it. Perhaps the First will intercede some more to save us."

Benoni hesitated for a minute. Should he tell her the truth? If he did, the Kaywo could unload the weapons from the wagons, charge the weapons with the cylinders, and sink all twenty of the Skego craft. But then Kaywo would be the inevitable conquerer of Eyzonuh. And Lezpet would execute him for not having told her when he first found out the weapon's use.

No, better to wait and see what would happen.

"Let's ride the river road," said Lezpet. "Perhaps, the First will not run out of thunderbolts."

"Why not trust the First to sink those ships for us?" said the colonel.

Lezpet opened her mouth to answer but gasped instead. The colonel had fainted and fallen off his horse.

A soldier dismounted to examine him. He looked up and said, "I think he broke his neck, Your Excellency. He's dead."

They rode off at a canter, for their horses were tiring. No L'wan or Skego agents appeared to bar their way. Benoni, suddenly seeing how they could escape, pulled his horse to a stop. He got off and pretended to be examining the hoof of his horse, as if it were injured. Apparently, his ruse worked, for the others rode by. Zhem had not noticed that he had stopped; he was riding with the others, close to Lezpet.

As soon as the last of the column had disappeared around a bend in the road, Benoni led his horse into the woods. Near the bank, he tied the animal to a bush and then walked to a tree close to the bank. The Skego galleys came opposite him just as he reached the tree, and they were not twenty yards from him. He knelt by the tree, steadied the weapon against the trunk, and pressed the button.

One after the other, the galleys blew up. He reloaded and re-emptied the weapon until the last of the boats broke in half and sank.

Benoni paused a moment before placing more cylinders in the revolving chamber. His plan had worked out so far. Now, he could catch up with the others and tell them that the First had sunk the remaining boats. They could return and board the galleys they had left on the bank. Unless something unforeseen happened, nothing would bar them from rowing down the L'wan and to the Siy.

He looked at the last of the boats as its stern turned over before sinking and at the hundreds of men struggling in the swift current. Most of them would drown, for they wore armor. Owning this weapon, he thought, was almost like being a god. Twenty boats and a thousand men destroyed in less than sixty seconds!

But, what kind of a world would it be if everyone had a weapon like this? Then, a great warrior would be less than a man, for a half-grown woman could destroy him merely by pressing a button. Would it not be best if the weapons were to disappear forever?

Still, this moment could never be taken away from him. He was if not a god . . .

For a second, he could not understand what had happened. The shock drained away, and he knew that that was a spear with its head half-buried in the tree and the shaft vibrating. It had come so close that the head had burned his arm yet not drawn blood.

He leaped to his feet, whirling as he did so, the weapon coming up in his hand, pointing at the unknown enemy.

Unknown no longer, Joel Vahndert stood not less than fifty yards away. He was drawing his arm back for another try with a second javelin.

Benoni pointed the weapon and pressed on the button. Nothing happened. He cursed as he realized that he had not reloaded the weapon. Joel threw the javelin. Benoni threw himself to one side, and the javelin whizzed through the space where he had been. Joel, drawing his sword from his scabbard, was running towards him.

Benoni opened the little door in the back of the weapon, fumbled in his knapsack, found two cylinders, but dropped them as he tried to place both at the same time in the revolving chamber.

There was a shout from behind Joel. Zhem appeared from the bushes. Joel whirled, saw Zhem, and kept on spinning. Evidently, he had decided that Benoni was the more dangerous. He must have seen Benoni use the weapon and must realize that, if Benoni were to load it, he was dead.

Benoni rose and hurled the weapon at Joel's face, striking him over the nose. Joel's head flew back, and blood appeared over his face. But he kept on running. Benoni had time to draw his sword; Joel was like a whirlwind, striking with great force; he drove Benoni backwards.

Benoni's foot slipped on the mud at the edge of the bank, and he fell backwards five feet into the water. Joel poised to leap into the water after him and to strike him down before he could get up. But a dark form soared through the air and leaped on his back. Both tumbled forward into the water, went under, and came up apart.

Benoni got to his feet and found himself waist-deep. He waded towards Joel, who still had his sword in his hand. Zhem, coming up two seconds later, was only a few feet from the much bigger man. Yet, weaponless, he leaped at him. And was caught on the ribs with the edge of Joel's blade.

Benoni, screaming, came up behind Joel, grabbed him around the neck with one arm, and punched with his fist into the small of his back.

Joel's breath whoofed out of him, and he tried to strike backwards, over his shoulder, at Benoni. The flat of the blade struck Benoni on the back and hurt him, but he refused to let go. Filled with the strength of his hate at Joel and with fury because he thought Zhem was dead, he reached around with his left hand. Found the open mouth, plunged his fist into the mouth, deep, deep, and closed upon the tongue.

Joel choked, waved his arms, dropped the sword, and tried to close his mouth upon the fist. He was helpless. Strong as he was, he was in the grip of a man temporarily given superhuman force by his rage and grief.

Benoni jerked once with a savage cry. Joel threw his hands up and fell backwards into the water as Benoni released him. He did not try to rise but floated a few feet, then sank. A great stain of blood spread out from where he had gone down. Benoni was left standing in the water, staring at the thing, so like a headless fish, in his hand.

Finally, Benoni opened his hand and dropped the tongue into the river. He waded to Zhem, who was leaning against the bank. Zhem's eyes were open, but they were fast becoming glazed.

"You got him? Good," he whispered. He slumped down and would have gone under the surface if Benoni had not caught and held him.

"Listen," he murmured. "You . . . tell my people . . . I died like a . . . man?"

"I'll do that if I get a chance," said Benoni. "But you aren't dead yet."

"My debt . . . paid. So lo . . ."

He slumped forward, and his heart quit beating.

Benoni, though suddenly drained of his strength, managed to get Zhem up on the bank. He sat there, panting, wondering what to do next. Only when he heard the hooves of horses on the underbrush and the scrape of branches against armor, did he realize that all was not yet over.

He rose to see the Pwez approaching on horseback. Behind her, the rest of Kaywo.

Without thinking he stepped forward, picked up the fallen weapon, and reloaded it. He placed it in his belt.

"We wondered why you three wild-men suddenly dropped out of sight," she said. "I would not have bothered coming after you, but when I heard the explosions I got to thinking. Could the so-called intervention of the First have been you, using one of the devices we took from the Hairy Men's ship? It did not seem likely that a simple savage could have discovered something we haven't. However, you are not simple. After all, you were the one who found out how to enter the vessel."

Her face contorted and became an ugly red. "You traitor!" she screamed. "You found out how to use that thing at your belt! And you did not tell me! You were planning on taking it to the Eyzonuh!"

"That is true," said Benoni. "But I am no traitor. I was going to see that you got back to your country safely."

"Traitor! Ugly stinking wild-man!"

She pointed at him with a shaking finger and shrilled, "Kill him! Kill him!"

Benoni felt tired, very tired. He had had enough of blood to last him for a lifetime. And, these men were brave men, great warriors. They should not have to die, here, in this alien forest, far from their homes. Especially, since they had fought so well and were so close to success.

But he did not want to die. So, he must do what he had to do.

He emptied the weapon and reloaded it, taking his time now and not fumbling. He fired half of it the second time, then waited for the smoke to clear. And for the few survivors, their courage broken, to flee on foot or on horse.

Lezpet had not run away. At the first explosion, her horse had reared violently and thrown her to the ground. She did not get her senses back until it was all over. When she looked around and saw the carnage, she wept.

Benoni pulled her to her feet, turned her around, and tied her hands behind her with a rope taken from the saddle on a dead horse. Docile, the fight taken from her, she submitted without a word. After tying the end of the rope to a tree, Benoni mounted his horse and went after a horse for her. It took about five minutes for him to find one of the animals that had bolted and to rope it. He returned, loosed her from the tree, and lifted her into the saddle. Holding the reins of her horse in one hand, he saw the three wagons waiting by the roadside. The drivers and about twenty soldiers were standing by them.

Seeing their ruler with her hands tied behind her, they raised a cry and began to mount their horses. Benoni did not want any witnesses left, so, reluctantly but carefully, he shot.

Not carefully enough, for one of his shots, the force, or whatever it was that was projected by the weapon, must have struck one of the wagons. And the wagon must have contained a powerful explosive of some sort. Perhaps, the cylinders stored there all went off at once.

Whatever was responsible, a tremendous cloud of smoke with a pillar of fire blossomed, and a blast roared down the road and knocked over Benoni's horse and Lezpet's.

Luckily, neither was hurt, beyond some bruises and deafness, and the horses managed to get back away and reveal a crater thirty feet wide on the side of the road. Of the three wagons, the teams of horses, and their riders, there was no sign.

If he had not been so stunned, he would have wept. All his dreams of burying the artifacts of the Hairy Men and of returning some day with the Eyzonuh and digging them up, all his dreams were gone. He was left with two handweapons and perhaps fifty cylinders.

"I hope you are satisfied," said Lezpet. "Now, why don't you kill me and complete your bloody work?"

"I have sworn an oath not to harm you," said Benoni.

Lezpet began laughing shrilly and uncontrollably. Benoni did not find it difficult to understand her behavior; his statement seemed foolish to himself. But he had kept the literal terms of his word. He had protected her from others, and he had no intention of harming her. Besides, when she ordered her men to kill him, she had released him from his vow—as far as he was concerned.

Finally, Lezpet quit laughing. She stared at him with her great blue eyes, reddened with tears and smoke, and she said, "What do you intend to do, wild-man?"

"I can't take you back to Kaywo," he said. "They would kill me. So, I will take you to Fiiniks. I think that my people can use you as a hostage, a lever with which to pry some sort of treaty out of the Kaywo."

"The journey will take many months," she said. "I will get loose, and I will kill you."

"No, you won't," he said. "I promise."

He was as good as his word. Three months later, just as spring was beginning to melt the snows, he and Lezpet paused on the line where the plains left off and the desert began. They were on a high hill which gave them a view for miles ahead. Benoni was examining the group of horsemen about half a mile away at the bottom of the hill. From time to time, he shifted his gaze to the great cloud of dust rising some miles beyond the horsemen.

Finally, he smiled, and he said, "Those are not enemies. They are Fiiniks. Look at the flag! A scarlet fiiniks on a blue field!"

Shouting with joy, he spurred his horse down the hillside. The men below looked up alarmedly. Seeing only one man, and he without a sword in his hand, they reined in their animals to wait for him.

One of the group suddenly recognized Benoni, for he rode toward him. Benoni burst into tears. His father!

There was much confusion, shouting, and crying after that. The others crowded around him and all tried to question him at once. When order and comparative quiet was restored, his father said, "It makes me happier than I can say to see you alive, Benoni, for I had thought you were dead! But where is the scalp you were to bring back?"

Benoni flinched as if he had been struck on the cheek, but he said, "You would think I was mad, father, if I told you I have killed over a thousand men. I would not blame you. But I have a witness to that."

There was more clamor. Finally, Benoni managed to tell them something of what had occurred. And he learned why his father was here and what the cloud of dust in the distance meant. The Eyzonuh had left their valley after a new volcano had begun forming only two miles from the city. This was a scouting party; the dust behind them was being raised by the main body: women, children, mules, horses, wagons.

"We are looking for a new land," said Benoni's father.

"There are many," replied Benoni. "You will have to fight to take one and fight to hold it."

He paused and then he said, "Tell me about Debra Awvrez. Is she back there?"

His father tightened his lips and hesitated. "Like the rest of us, she thought you were dead. She married Baw Chonz, one of the boys who went out on the warpath with you. She is carrying his child."

He watched his son closely, waiting for the explosion. Then, he smiled as he saw Benoni shrug and heard him say, "It was to be expected. Now, I do not care. I would not have wanted her."

His father asked for an explanation. Benoni said he would give it later. As of now, he wanted to ride back to the main group and see his mother, brothers, and sisters.

Four days later, Benoni entered the tent that had been given to Lezpet as her own. She looked coldly at him and said, "What do you want?"

"I wanted to tell you that I have been made a member of the Council of Kelbek," he said. "It is a great honor. Never before has one my age been so honored. The Council feels that, in view of my knowledge of the land and of my experience, and also of my possession of the Hairy Men's weapon, I should be a leader."

"So?" she said.

"Lezpet, I know you hate me. But, I do not hate you. On the contrary, having known you, I could never be satisfied to marry a lesser woman. I intend to make you my wife. I will not force you. You will come to me willingly."

She spat in his face. Eyes wide and blazing, she said, "I will kill myself first! Marry you, a wild-man and a traitor! You disgust me!"

"I have sworn an oath to marry no woman but you," he said. "You and I will some day rule the Kaywo and the Eyzonuh; they will become one nation."

He patted the weapon stuck in his belt. "I have sworn by Jehovah and by this weapon that I will marry you. And, as you know, I have never broken my oath."

He left the tent but stood outside for a moment, listening to her rage within. Never in all his life had he felt so strongly that the world would some day be his. And that she, part of the world, would also be his.

RASTIGNAC THE DEVIL

I

After the Apocalyptic War, the decimated remnants of the French huddled in the Loire Valley were gradually squeezed between two new and growing nations. The Colossus to the north was unfriendly and obviously intended to absorb the little New France. The Colossus to the south was friendly and offered to take the weak state into its confederation of republics as a full partner.

A number of proud and independent French citizens feared that even the latter alternative meant the eventual transmutation of their tongue, religion, and nationality into those of their southern neighbor. Seeking a way of salvation, they built six huge space-ships that would hold thirty thousand people, most of whom would be in deep freeze until they reached their destination. The six vessels then set off into interstellar space to find a planet that would be as much like Earth as possible.

That was in the 22nd Century. Over three hundred and fifty years passed before Earth heard of them again. However, we are not here concerned with the home world but with the story of a man of that pioneer group who wanted to leave the New Gaul and sail again to *the stars . . .*

Rastignac had no Skin. He was, nevertheless, happier than he had been since the age of five.

He was as happy as a man can be who lives deep under the ground. Underground organizations are often under the ground. They are formed into cells. Cell Number One usually contains the leader of the underground.

Jean-Jacques Rastignac, chief of the Legal Underground of the Kingdom of L'Bawpfey, was literally in a cell beneath the surface of the earth. He was in jail.

For a dungeon, it wasn't bad. He had two cells. One was deep inside the building proper, built into the wall so that he could sit in it when he wanted to retreat from the sun or the rain. The adjoining cell was at the bottom of a well whose top was covered with a grille of thin steel bars. Here, he spent most of his waking hours. Forced to look upwards if he wanted to see the sky or the stars, Rastignac suffered from a chronic stiff neck.

Several times during the day, he had visitors. They were allowed to bend over the grille and talk down to him. A guard, one of the King's mucketeers,* stood by as a censor.

When night came, Rastignac ate the meal let down by ropes on a platform. Then another of the King's mucketeers stood by with drawn epee until he had finished eating.

---

*Mucketeer is the best translation of the 26th century French noun *foutriquet*, pronounced *vfeutwikey*.

When the tray was pulled back up and the grille lowered and locked, the mucketeer marched off with the turnkey.

Rastignac sharpened his wit by calling a few choice insults to the night guard, then went into the cell inside the wall and lay down to take a nap. Later, he would rise and pace back and forth like a caged tiger. Now and then he would stop and look forwards, scan the stars, hunch his shoulders and resume his savage circuit of the cell. But the time would come when he would stand statue-still. Nothing moved except his head, which turned slowly.

"Some day I'll ride to the stars with you."

He said it as he watched the Six Flying Stars speed across the night sky—six glowing stars that moved in a direction opposite to the march of the other stars. Bright as Sirius seen from Earth, strung out one behind the other like jewels on a velvet string, they hurtled across the heavens.

They were the six ships on which the original Loire Valley Frenchmen had sailed out into space, seeking a home on a new planet. They had been put into an orbit around New Gaul and left there while their thirty thousand passengers had descended to the surface in chemical-fuel rockets. Mankind, once on the fair and fresh earth of the new planet, had never again ascended to revisit the great ships.

For three hundred years, the six ships had circled the planet known as New Gaul, nightly beacons and glowing reminders to Man that he was a stranger on this planet.

When the Earthmen landed on the new

planet they had called the new land *Le Beau
Pays*, or, as it was now pronounced,
L'Bawpfey—The Beautiful Country. They had
been delighted, entranced with the fresh new
land. After the burned, war-racked Earth they
had left, it was like coming to Heaven.

They found two intelligent species living on
the planet, and they found that the species
lived in peace and that they had no conception
of war or of poverty. And they were quite
willing to receive the Terrans into their
society.

Provided, that is, they became integrated,
or—as they phrased it—natural. The Frenchmen from Earth had been given their choice.
They were told:

"You can live with the people of the
Beautiful Land on our terms or else war with
us or leave to seek another planet."

The Terrans conferred. Half of them
decided to stay; the other half decided to
remain only long enough to mine uranium
and make chemicals. Then, they would voyage
onwards.

But nobody from that group of Earthmen
ever again stepped into the ferry-rockets and
soared up to the six ion-beam ships circling
about Le Beau Pays. All succumbed to the
Philosophy of the Natural. Within a few
generations, a stranger landing upon the
planet would not have known without
previous information that the Terrans were
not aboriginal.

He would have found three species. Two
were warm-blooded egglayers who had
evolved directly from reptiles without

becoming mammals—the Ssassarors and the Amphibs. Somewhere in their dim past—like all happy nations, they had no history—they had set up their society and been very satisfied with it since.

It was a peaceful quiet world, largely peasant, where nobody had to scratch for a living and where a superb manipulation of biological forces ensured very long lives, no disease, and a social lubrication that left little to desire—from their viewpoint, anyway.

The government was, nominally, a monarchy. The Kings were a different species than the group each ruled. Ssassaror ruled Human, and vise versa, each assisted by foster-brothers and sisters of the race over which they reigned. These were the so-called Dukes and Duchesses.

The Chamber of Deputies—*L'Syawp t' Tapfuti*—was half Human and half Ssassaror. The so-called Kings took turns presiding over the Chamber for forty day intervals. The Deputies were elected for ten-year terms by constituents who could not be deceived about their representatives' purposes because of the sensitive skins which allowed them to determine their true feelings and worth.

In one custom alone did the ex-Terrans differ from their neighbors. This was in carrying arms. In the beginning, the Ssassaror had allowed the Men to wear their short rapiers, so they would feel safe even though in the midst of aliens.

As time went on, only the King's mucketeers—and members of the official underground—were allowed to carry epees.

These men were the congenital adventurers, men who needed to swashbuckle and revel in the name of individualist.

Like the egg-stealers, they needed an institution in which they could work off anti-social steam.

From the beginning, the Amphibians had been a little separate from the Ssassaror, and when the Earthmen came they did not get any more neighborly. Nevertheless, they preserved excellent relations—for a long time—and they, too, participated in the Changeling-custom.

This Changeling-custom was another social device set up millenia ago to keep a mutual understanding between all species on the planet. It was a peculiar institution, one that the Earthmen had found hard to understand and even more difficult to adopt. Nevertheless, once the Skins had been accepted, they had changed their attitude, forgot their speculations about its origin, and thrown themselves into the custom of stealing babies—or eggs—from another race and raising the children as their own.

You rob my cradle; I'll rob yours. Such was their motto, and it worked.

A Guild of Egg Stealers was formed. The Human branch of it guaranteed, for a price, to bring you a Ssassaror child to replace the one that had been stolen from you. Or, if you lived on the seashore, and an Amphibian had crept into your nursery and taken your baby—always under two years old, according to the rules—then the Guildsman would bring you an Amphib or, perhaps, the child of a

Human Changeling reared by the Seafolk.

You raised it and loved it as your own. How could you help loving it? Your Skin told you that it was small and helpless and needed you and was, despite appearances, as Human as any of your babies. Nor did you need to worry about the one that had been abducted. It was getting just as good care as you were giving this one.

It had never occurred to anyone to quit the stealing and voluntary exchange of babies. Perhaps, that was because it would strain even the loving nature of the Skin-wearers to give away their own flesh and blood. But, once the transfer had taken place, they could adapt.

Or, perhaps, the custom was kept because tradition is stronger than law in a peasant-monarchy society and also because egg-and-baby stealing gave the more naturally aggressive and daring citizens a chance to work off anti-social behavior.

Nobody but a historian would have known, and there were no historians in The Beautiful Land.

Long ago, the Ssassaror had discovered that if they lived meatless, they had a much easier time curbing their belligerency, obeying the Skins and remaining cooperative. So, they induced the Earthmen to put a taboo on eating flesh. The only drawback to the meatless diet was that both Ssassaror and Man became as stunted in stature as they did in aggressiveness, the former so much so that they barely came to the chins of the Humans. These, in turn, would have seemed short to a

Western European.

But Rastignac, an Earthman, and his good friend, Mapfarity, the Ssassaror Giant, became taboo-breakers when they were children and played together on the beach where they first ate seafood out of curiosity, then continued because they liked it. And, due to their protein diet, the Terran had grown well over six feet in height and the Ssassaror seemed to have touched off a rocket of expansion in his body. Those Ssassarors who shared his guilt—became meateaters— became ostracized and eventually moved off to live by themselves. They were called Ssassaror-Giants and were pointed to as an object lesson to the young of the normal Ssassarors and Humans on the land.

If a stranger had landed shortly before Rastignac was born, however, he would have noticed that all was not as serene as it was supposed to be among the different species. The cause for the flaw in the former Eden might have puzzled him if he had not known the previous history of *L'Bawpfey* and the fact that the situation had not changed for the worst until the introduction of Human Changelings among the Amphibians.

Then it had been that blood-drinking began among them, that Amphibians began seducing Humans to come live with them by their tales of easy immortality, and that they started the system of leaving savage little carnivores in the Human nurseries.

When the Land-dwellers protested, the Amphibs replied that these things were carried out by unnaturals or outlaws, and that the Sea-King could not be held responsible. Permission was given to Chalice those caught in such behavior.

Nevertheless, the suspicion remained that the Amphib monarch had given his unofficial official blessing and that he was preparing even more disgusting and outrageous and unnatural moves. Through his control of the populace by the Master Skin, he would be able to do as he pleased with their minds.

It was the skins that had made the universal peace possible on the planet of New Gaul. And it would be the custom of the Skins that would make possible the change from peace to conflict among the populace.

Through the artificial Skins that were put on all babies at birth—and which grew with them, attached to their body, feeding from their bloodstreams, their nervous systems—the Skins, controlled by a huge Master Skin that floated in a chemical vat in the palace of the rulers, fed, indoctrinated and attended day and night by a crew of the most brilliant scientists of the planet, gave the Kings complete control of the minds and emotions of the inhabitants of the planet.

Originally, the rulers of New Gaul had desired only that the populace live in peace and enjoy the good things of their planet equally. But the change that had been coming gradually—the growth of conflict between the Kings of the different species for control of the whole populace—was beginning to be generally felt. Uneasiness, distrust of each other was growing among the people. Hence

the legalizing of the Underground, the
Philosophy of Violence by the government, an
effort to control the revolt that was brewing.

Yet, the Land-dwellers had managed to take
no action at all and to ignore the growing
number of vicious acts.

But not all were content to drowse. One
man was aroused. He was Rastignac.

They were Rastignac's hope, those Six
Stars, the gods to which he prayed. When they
passed quickly out of his sight, he would
continue his pacing, meditating for the
twenty-thousandth time on a means for
reaching one of those ships and using it to
visit the stars. The end of his fantasies was
always a curse because of the futility of such
hopes. He was doomed! Mankind was
doomed!

And it was all the more maddening because
Man would not admit that he was through.
Ended, that is, as a human being.

Man was changing into something not quite
homo sapiens. It might be a desirable change,
but it would mean the finish of his climb
upwards. So it seemed to Rastignac. And he,
being the man he was, had decided to do
something about it even if it meant violence.

That was why he was now in the well-
dungeon. He was an advocator of violence
against the status quo.

II

There was another cell next to his. It was also
at the bottom of a well and was separated

from his by a thin wall of cement. A window had been set into it so that the prisoners could talk to each other. Rastignac did not care for the woman who had been let down into the adjoining cell, but she was somebody to talk to.

"Amphib-changelings" was the name given to those human beings who had been stolen from their cradles and raised among the non-humanoid Amphibians as their own. The girl in the adjoining cell, Lusine, was such. It was not her fault that she was a blood-drinking Amphib. Yet, he could not help disliking her for what she had done and for the things she stood for.

She was in prison because she had been caught in the act of stealing a Man child from its cradle. This was no legal crime, but she had left in the cradle, under the covers, a savage and blood-thirsty little monster that had leaped up and slashed the throat of the unsuspecting baby's mother.

Her cell was lit by a cageful of glowworms. Rastignac, peering through the grille, could see her shadowy shape in the inner cell inside the wall. She rose langorously and stepped into the dim orange light cast by the insects.

"*B'zhu, m'fweh,*" she greeted him.

It annoyed him that she called him her brother, and it annoyed him even more to know that she knew it. It was true that she had some excuse for thus addressing him. She did resemble him. Like him, she had straight glossy blue-black hair, thick bracket-shaped eyebrows, brown eyes, a straight nose and a prominent chin. And where his build was superbly masculine, hers was magnificently feminine.

Nevertheless, this was not her reason for so speaking to him. She knew the disgust the Land-walker had for the Amphib-changeling, and she took a perverted delight in baiting him.

He was proud that he seldom allowed her to see that she annoyed him. "*B'zhu, fam tey zafeep,* " he said. "Good evening, woman of the Amphibians."

Mockingly, she said, "Have you been watching the Six Flying Stars, Jean-Jacques?"

"Vi. I do so every time they come over."

"Why do you eat your heart out because you cannot fly up to them and then voyage among the stars on one of them?"

He refused to give her the satisfaction of knowing his real reason. He did not want her to realize how little he thought of Mankind and its chances for surviving—as humanity—upon the face of this planet, L'Bawpfey.

"I look at them because they remind me that Man was once captain of his soul."

"Then you admit that the Land-walker is weak?"

"I think he is on the way to becoming non-human, which is to say that he is weak, yes. But what I say about Landman goes for Seaman, too. You Changelings are becoming more Amphibian every day and less Human. Through the Skins, the Amphibis are gradually changing you. Soon you will be completely sea-people."

She laughed scornfully, exposing perfect

white teeth as she did so.

"The Sea will win out against the Land. It launches itself against the shore and shakes it with the crash of its body. It eats away the rock and the dirt and absorbs it into its own self. It can't be worn away nor caught and held in a net. It is elusive and all-powerful and never-tiring."

Lusine paused for breath. He said, "This is a very pretty analogy, but it doesn't apply. You Seafolk are as much flesh and blood as we Landfolk. What hurts us hurts you."

She put a hand around one bar. The glow-light fell upon it in such a way that it showed plainly the webbing of skin between her fingers. He glanced at it with a faint repulsion under which was a countercurrent of attraction. This was the hand that had, indirectly, shed blood.

She glanced at him sidewise, challenged him in trembling tones. "You are not one to throw stones, Jean-Jacques. I have heard that you eat meat."

"Fish, not meat. That is part of my Philosophy of Violence," he retorted. "I maintain that one of the reasons man is losing his power and strength is that he has so long been upon a vegetable diet. He is as cowed and submissive as the grass-eating beast of the fields."

Lusine put her face against the bars.

"That is interesting," she said. "But how did you happen to begin eating fish? I thought we Amphibs alone did that."

What Lusine had just said angered him. He had no reply.

Rastignac knew he should not be talking to a Sea-changeling. They were glib and seductive and always searching for ways to twist your thoughts. But, being Rastignac, he had to talk. Moreover, it was so difficult to find anybody who would listen to his ideas that he could not resist the temptation.

"I was given fish by the Ssassaror, Mapfarity, when I was a child. We lived along the seashore. Mapfarity was a child, too, and we played together. 'Don't eat fish!' my parents said. To me that meant 'Eat it!' So, despite my distaste at the idea, and my squeamish stomach, I did eat fish. And I liked it. And, as I grew to manhood, I adopted the Philosphy of Violence and I continued to eat fish although I am not a Changeling."

"What did your Skin do when it detected you?" Lusine asked. Her eyes were wide and luminous with wonder and a sort of glee as if she relished the confession of his sins. Also, he knew, she was taunting him about the futility of his ideas of violence so long as he was a prisoner of the Skin.

He frowned in annoyance at the reminder of the Skin. Much thought had he given, in a weak way, to the possibility of life without the Skin.

Ashamed now of his weak resistance to the Skin, he blustered a bit in front of the teasing Amphib girl.

"Mapfarity and I discovered something that most people don't know," he answered boastfully. "We found that if you can stand the shocks your Skin gives you when you do something wrong, the Skin gets tired and quits after a while. Of course, your Skin recharges itself and the next time you eat fish it shocks you again. But, after very many shocks, it becomes accustomed, forgets its conditioning, and leaves you alone."

Lusine laughed and said in a low conspiratorial tone, "So your Ssassaror pal and you adopted the Philosophy of Violence because you remained fish and meat eaters?"

"Yes, we did. When Mapfarity reached puberty he became a Giant and went off to live in a castle in the forest. But we have remained friends through our connection in the underground."

"Your parents must have suspected that you were a fish eater when you first proposed your Philosophy of Violence?" she said.

"Suspicion isn't proof," he answered. "But I shouldn't be telling you all this, Lusine. I feel it is safe for me to do so only because you will never have a chance to tell on me. You will soon be taken to Chalice and there you will stay until you have been cured."

She shivered and said, "This Chalice? What is it?"

"It is a place far to the north where both Terrans and Ssassarors send their incorrigibles. It is an extinct volcano whose step-sided interior makes an inescapable prison. There those who have persisted in unnatural behavior are given special treatment."

"They are bled?" she asked, her eyes widening as her tongue flicked over her lips again hungrily.

"No. A special breed of Skin is given them

to wear. These Skins shock them more powerfully than the ordinary ones, and the shocks
are associated with the habit they are trying
to cure. The shocks effect a cure. Also, these
special Skins are used to detect hidden
unnatural emotions. They recondition the
deviate. The result is that when the Chaliced
Man is judged able to go out and take his
place in society again, he is thoroughly
reconditioned. Then, his regular Skin is given
back to him, and it has no trouble keeping him
in line from then on. The Chaliced Man is a
very good citizen."

"And what if a revolter doesn't become
Chaliced?"

"Then, he stays in Chalice until he decides
to become so."

Her voice rose sharply as she said, "But if I
go there, and I am not fed the diet of the
Amphibs, I will grow old and die!"

"No. The government will feed you the diet
you need until you are reconditioned.
Except . . ." He paused.

"Except I won't get blood," she wailed.
Then, realizing she was acting undignified
before a Landman, she firmed her voice.

"The King of the Amphibians will not allow
them to do this to me," she said. "When he
hears of it, he will demand my return. And, if
the King of Men refuses, my King will use
violence to get me back."

Rastignac smiled and said, "I hope he does.
Then, perhaps, my people will wake up and
get rid of their Skins and make war upon your
people."

"So that is what you Philosophers of

Violence want, is it? Well, you will not get it. My father, the Amphib King, will not be so stupid as to declare a war."

"I suppose not," replied Rastignac. "He will send a band to rescue you. If they're caught, they'll claim to be criminals and say they are *not* under the King's orders."

Lusine looked upwards to see if a guard was hanging over the well's mouth listening. Perceiving no one, she nodded and said, "You have guessed it correctly. And that is why we laugh so much at you stupid Humans. You know as well as we do what's going on, but you are afraid to tell us so. You keep clinging to the idea that your turn-the-other-cheek policy will soften us and insure peace."

"Not I," said Rastignac. "I know perfectly well there is only one solution to man's problems. That is—"

"That is Violence," she finished for him. "That is what you have been preaching. And that is why you are in this cell, waiting for trial."

"You don't understand," he said. "Men are not put into the Chalice for *proposing* new philosophies. As long as they behave naturally, they may say what they wish. They may even petition the King that the new philosophy be made a law. The King passes it on to the Chamber of Deputies. They consider it and put it up to the people. If the people like it, it becomes a law. The only trouble with that procedure is that it may take ten years before the law is considered by the Chamber of Deputies."

"And in those ten years," she mocked, "the

Amphibs and the Amphibian-changelings will have won the planet."

"That is true," he said.

"The King of the Humans is a Ssassaror and the King of the Ssassarors is a Man," said Lusine. "Our King can't see any reason for changing the status quo. After all, it is the Ssassaror who are responsible for the Skins and for Man's position in the sentient society of this planet. Why should he be favorable to a policy of Violence? The Ssassarors loathe violence."

"And so you have preached Violence without waiting for it to become a law? And for that you are now in this cell?"

"Not exactly. The Ssassarors have long known that to suppress too much of Man's naturally belligerent nature only results in an explosion. So they have legalized illegality—up to a point. Thus, the King socially made me the Chief of the Underground and gave me a state license to preach—but not practice—Violence. I am even allowed to advocate overthrow of the present system of government—as long as I take no action that is too productive of results.

"I am in jail now because the Minister of Ill-Will put me here. He had my Skin examined, and it was found to be 'unhealthy.' He thought I'd be better off locked up until it became 'healthy' again. But the King . . ."

III

Lusine's laughter was like the call of a silver-bell bird. Whatever her unhuman appetites, she had a beautiful voice. She said, "How comical! And how do you, with your brave ideas, like being regarded as a harmless figure of fun, or as a sick man?"

"I like it as well as you would," he growled.

She gripped the bars of her window until the tendons on the back of her long thin hands stood out and the membranes between her fingers stretched like windblown tents. Face twisted, she spat at him, "Coward! Why don't you kill somebody and break out of this ridiculous mold—that Skin that the Ssassarors have poured you into?"

Rastignac was silent. That was a good question. Why didn't he? Killing was the logical result of his philosophy. But the Skin kept him docile. Yes, he could vaguely see that he had purposely shut his eyes to the destination towards which his ideas were slowly but inevitably traveling.

And there was another facet to the answer to her question—if he had to kill, he would not kill a Man. His philosophy was directed towards the Amphibians and the Sea-changelings.

He said, "Violence doesn't necessarily mean the shedding of blood, Lusine. My philosophy urges that we take a more vigorous action, that we overthrow some of the biosocial institutions which have imprisoned Man and stripped him of his dignity as an individual."

"Yes, I have heard that you want Man to stop wearing the Skin. That is what has horrified your people, isn't it?"

"Yes," he said. "And I understand it has had the same effect among the Amphibians."

She bridled, her brown eyes flashing in the feeble glowworms' light. "Why shouldn't it? What would we be without our Skins?"

"What, indeed?" he said, laughing derisively afterwards.

Earnestly, she said, "You don't understand. We Amphibians—our Skins are not like yours. We do not wear them for the same reason you do. You are imprisoned by your Skins—they tell you how to feel, what to think. Above all, they keep you from getting ideas about noncooperation or nonintegration with Nature as a whole.

"That, to us individualistic Amphibians, is false. The purpose of our Skins is to make sure that our King's subjects understand what he wants so that we may all act as one unit and thus further the progress of the Seafolk."

The first time Rastignac had heard this statement, he had howled with laughter. Now, however, knowing that she could not see the fallacy, he did not try to argue the point. The Amphibs were, in their way, as hidebound—no pun intended—as the Landwalkers.

"Look, Lusine," he said, "there are only three places where a Man may take off his Skin. One is in his own home, when he may hang it upon the halltree. Two is when he is, like us, in jail and therefore may not harm anybody. The third is when a man is King. Now, you and I have been without our Skins for a week. We have gone longer without them than anybody, except the King. Tell me true, don't you feel free for the first time in your life?

"Don't you feel as if you belong to nobody but yourself, that you are accountable to no one but yourself, and that you love that feeling? And don't you dread the day we will be let out of prison and made to wear our Skins again? That day which, curiously enough, will be the very day that we will lose our freedom."

Lusine looked as if she didn't know what he was talking about.

"You'll see what I mean when we are freed and the Skins are put back upon us," he said. Immediately after, he was embarrassed. He remembered that she would go to the Chalice where one of the heavy and powerful Skins used for unnaturals would be fastened to her shoulders.

Lusine did not notice. She was considering the last but most telling point in her argument. "You cannot win against us," she said, watching him narrowly for the effect of her words. "We have a weapon that is irresistible. We have immortality."

His face did not lose its imperturbability.

She continued, "And what is more, we can give immortality to anyone who casts off his Skin and adopts ours. Don't think that your people don't know this. For instance, during the last year more than two thousand Humans living along the beaches deserted and went over to us, the Amphibs."

He was a little shocked to hear this, but he did not doubt her. He remembered the mysterious case of the schooner *Le Pauvre Pierre* which had been found drifting and crewless, and he remembered a conversation he had had with a fisherman in his home port of Marrec.

He put his hands behind his back and began pacing. Lusine continued staring at him through the bars. Despite the fact that her face was in the shadows, he could see—or feel—her smile. He had humiliated her, but she had won in the end.

Rastignac quit his limited roving and called up to the guard.

"*Shoo l'footyay, kal v ay tee?*"

The guard leaned over the grille. His large hat with its tall wings sticking from the peak was green in the daytime. But now, illuminated only by a far off torchlight and by a glowworm coiled around the band, it was black.

"*Ah, shoo Zhaw-Zhawk W'stenyek,*" he said, loudly. "What time is it? What do you care what time it is?" And he concluded with the stock phrase of the jailer, unchanged through millenia and over light-years. "You're not going any place, are you?"

Rastignac threw his head back to howl at the guard but stopped to wince at the sudden pain in his neck. After uttering, *"Sek Ploo!"* and *"S'pweestee!"* both of which were close enough to the old Terran French so that a language specialist might have recognized them, he said, more calmly, "If you would let me out on the ground, *monsier le foutriquet*, and give me a good *epee*. I would show you where I am going. Or, at least, where my sword is going. I am thinking of a nice sheath for it."

Tonight, he had a special reason for keeping the attention of the King's mucketeer directed towards himself. So, when the guard grew tired of returning insults—mainly because his limited imagination could invent no new ones—Rastignac began telling jokes aimed at the mucketeer's narrow intellect.

"Then," said Rastignac, "there was the itinerant salesman whose *s'fel* threw a shoe. He knocked on the door of the hut of the nearest peasant and said . . ." What was said by the salesman was never known.

A strangled gasp had come from above.

IV

Rastignac saw something enormous blot out the smaller shadow of the guard. Then, both figures disappeared. A moment later, a silhouette cut across the lines of the grille. Unoiled hinges screeched; the bars lifted. A rope uncoiled from above to fall at Rastignac's feet. He seized it and felt himself being drawn powerfully upwards.

When he came over the edge of the well, he saw that his rescuer was a giant Ssassaror. The light from the glowworm on the guard's hat lit up feebly his face, which was orthagnathous and had quite humanoid eyes and lips. Large canine teeth stuck out from the mouth, and its huge ears were tipped with feathery tufts. The forehead down to the eyebrows looked as if it needed a shave, but Rastignac knew that more light would show the blue-black shade came from many small feathers, not stubbled hair.

"Mapfarity!" Rastignac said. "It's good to see you after all these years!"

The Ssassaror giant put his hand on his friend's shoulder. Clenched, it was almost as big as Rastignac's head. He spoke with a voice like a lion coughing at the bottom of a deep well.

"It is good to see you again, my friend."

"What are you doing here?" said Rastignac, tears running down his face as he stroked the great fingers on his shoulder.

Mapfarity's huge ears quivered like the wings of a bat tied to a rock and unable to fly off. The tufts of feathers at their ends grew stiff and suddenly crackled with tiny sparks.

The electrical display was his equivalent of the human's weeping. Both creatures discharged emotion; their bodies chose different avenues and manifestations. Nevertheless, the sight of the other's joy affected each deeply.

"I have come to rescue you," said Mapfarity. "I caught Archambaud here,"—he indicated the other man—"stealing eggs from my golden goose. And . . ."

Raoul Archambaud—pronounced Wawl Shebvo—interrupted excitedly, "I showed him my license to steal eggs from Giants who were raising counterfeit geese, but he was going to lock me up anyway. He was going to take my Skin off and feed me on meat . . ."

"Meat!" said Rastignac, astonished and revolted despite himself. "Mapfarity, what have you been doing in that castle of yours?"

Mapfarity lowered his voice to match the distant roar of a cataract. "I haven't been very active these last few years," he said, "because I am so big that it hurts my feet if I walk very much. So I've had much time to think. And I, being logical, decided that the next step after eating fish was eating meat. It couldn't make me any larger. So, I ate meat. And while doing so, I came to the same conclusion that you, apparently, have done independently. That is, the Philosophy of . . ."

"Of Violence," interrupted Archambaud. "Ah, Jean-Jacques, there must be some mystic bond that brings two of such different backgrounds as yours and the Ssassaror together, giving you both the same philosophy. When I explained what you had been doing and that you were in jail because you had advocated getting rid of the Skins, Mapfarity petitioned . . ."

"The King to make an official jail-break," said Mapfarity with an impatient glance at the rolypoly egg-stealer. "And . . ."

"The King agreed," broke in Archambaud, "provided Mapfarity would turn in his counterfeit goose and provided you would agree to say no more about abandoning Skins, but . . ."

The Giant's basso profundo-redundo pushed the eggstealer's high pitch aside. "If this squeaker will quit interrupting, perhaps we can get on with the rescue. We'll talk later, if you don't mind."

At that moment, Lusine's voice floated up from the bottom of her cell. "Jean-Jacques, my love, my brave, my own, would you abandon me to the Chalice? Please take me with you! You will need somebody to hide you when the Minister of Ill-Will sends his mucketeers after you. I can hide you where no one will ever find you." Her voice was mocking, but there was an undercurrent of anxiety to it.

Mapfarity muttered, "She will hide us, yes, at the bottom of a sea-cave where we will eat strange food and suffer a change. Never . . ."

"Trust an Amphib," finished Archambaud for him.

Mapfarity forgot to whisper. "*Bey-t'cul, vu nu fez vey! Fe'm sa!*" he roared.

A shocked hush covered the courtyard. Only Mapfarity's wrathful breathing could be heard. Then, disembodied, Lusine's voice floated from the well.

"Jean-Jacques, do not forget that I am the foster-daughter of the King of the Amphibians! If you were to take me with you, I could assure you of safety and a warm welcome in the halls of the Sea-King's Palace!"

"Pah!" said Mapfarity. "That web-footed witch!"

Rastignac did not reply to her. He took the broad silk belt and the sheathed epee from Archambaud and buckled them around his waist. Mapfarity handed him a mucketeer's hat; he clapped that on firmly. Last of all, he took the Skin that the fat egg-stealer had been holding out to him.

For the first time, he hesitated. It was his Skin, the one he had been wearing since he was six. It had grown with him, fed off his blood for twenty-two years, clung to him as clothing, censor, and castigator, and parted from him only when he was inside the walls of his own house, went swimming, or, as during the last seven days, when he lay in jail.

A week ago, after they had removed his second Skin, he had felt naked and helpless and cut off from his fellow creatures. But that was a week ago. Since then, as he had remarked to Lusine, he had experienced the birth of a strange feeling. It was, at first, frightening. It made him cling to the bars as if they were the only stable thing in the center of a whirling universe.

Later, when that first giddiness had passed, it was succeeded by another intoxication—the joy of being an individual, the knowledge that he was separate, not a part of a multitude. Without the Skin, he could think as he pleased. He did not have a censor.

Now, he was on level ground again, out of the cell. But as soon as he put that prison-shaft behind him, he was faced with the old second Skin.

Archambaud held it out like a cloak in his hands. It looked much like a ragged garment. It was pale and limp and roughly rectangular with four extensions at each corner. When Rastignac put it on his back, it would sink four tiny hollow teeth into his veins and the suckers on the inner surface of its flat body would cling to him. Its long upper extensions

would wrap themselves around his shoulders
and over his chest; the lower, around his loins
and thighs. Soon it would lose its paleness
and flaccidity, become pink and slightly
convex, pulsing with Rastignac's blood.

V

Rastignac hesitated for a few seconds. Then,
he allowed the habit of a lifetime to take over.
Sighing, he turned his back. In a moment, he
felt the cold flesh descend over his shoulders
and the little bite of the four teeth as they
attached the Skin to his shoulders. Then, as
his blood poured into the creature he felt it
grow warm and strong. It spread out and
followed the passages it had long ago been
conditioned to follow, wrapped him warmly
and lovingly and comfortably. And he knew,
though he couldn't feel it, that it was pushing
nerves into the grooves along the teeth.
Nerves to connect with his.

A minute later, he experienced the first of
the expected *rapport*. It was nothing that you
could put a mental finger on. It was just a
diffused tingling and then the sudden consciousness of how the others around him *felt*.

They were ghosts in the background of his
mind. Yet, pale and ectoplasmic as they were,
they were easily identifiable. Mapfarity
loomed above the others, a transparent
Colossus radiating streamers of confidence in
his clumsy strength. A meat-eater, uncertain
about the future, with a hope and trust in
Rastignac to show him the right way. And

with a strong current of anger against the conqueror who had inflicted the Skin upon him.

Archambaud was a shorter phantom, roly-poly even in his psychic manifestations, emitting bursts of impatience because other people did not talk fast enough to suit him, his mind leaping on ahead of their tongues, his fingers wriggling to wrap themselves around something valuable—preferably the eggs of the golden goose—and a general eagerness to be up and about and onwards. He was one round fidget on two legs yet a good man for any project requiring action.

Faintly, Rastignac detected the slumbering guard as if he were the tendrils of some plant at the sea-bottom, floating in the green twilight, at peace and unconscious.

Another radiation dipped into the general picture and out. A wild glowworm had swooped over them and disturbed the smooth reflection built up by the Skins.

This was the way the Skins worked. They penetrated into you and found out what you were feeling and emoting, and then they broadcast it to other closeby Skins, which then projected their hosts' psychosomatic responses. The whole was then integrated so that each Skin-wearer could detect the group-feeling and at the same time, though in a much duller manner, the feeling of the individuals of the *gestalt*.

That wasn't the only function of the Skin. The parasite, created in the bio-factories, had several other social and biological uses.

Rastignac almost fell into a reverie at that

point. It was nothing unusual. The effect of the Skins was a slowing-down one. The wearer thought more slowly, acted more leisurely, and was much more contented.

But now, by a deliberate wrenching of himself from the feeling-pattern, Rastignac woke up. There were things to do, and standing around and eating the lotus of the group-rapport was not one of them.

He gestured at the prostrate form of the mucketeer. "You didn't hurt him?"

The Ssassaror rumbled, "No. I scratched him with a little venom of the dream-snake. He will sleep for an hour or so. Besides, I would not be allowed to hurt him. You forget that all this is carefully staged by the King's Official Jail-breaker."

"*Me'dt!*" swore Rastignac.

Alarmed, Archambaud said, "What's the matter, Jean-Jacques?"

"Can't we do anything on our own? Must the King meddle in everything?"

"You wouldn't want us to take a chance and have to shed blood, would you?" breathed Archambaud.

"What are you carrying those swords for? As a decoration?" Rastignac snarled.

"*Seelahs, m'fweh,*" warned Mapfarity. "If you alarm the other guards, you will embarrass them. They will be forced to do their duty and recapture you. And the Jail-breaker would be reprimanded because he had fallen down on his job. He might even get a demotion."

Rastignac was so upset that his Skin, reacting to the negative fields racing over the

Skin and the hormone imbalance of his blood, writhed away from his back.

"What are we, a bunch of children playing war?"

Mapfarity growled, "We are all God's children, and we mustn't hurt anyone if we can help it."

"Mapfarity, you eat meat!"

"*Voo zavf w'zaw m'fweh*," admitted the Giant. "But it is the flesh of unintelligent creatures. I have not yet shed the blood of any being that can talk."

Rastignac snorted and said, "If you stick with me you will some day do that, *m'fweh* Mapfarity. There is no other course. It is inevitable."

"Nature spare me the day! But if it comes it will find Mapfarity unafraid. They do not call me Giant for nothing."

Rastignac sighed and walked ahead. Sometimes he wondered if the members of his underground—or anybody else for that matter—ever realized the grim conclusions formed by the Philosophy of Violence.

The Amphibians, he was sure, did. And they were doing something positive about it. But it was the Amphibians who had driven Rastignac to adopt a Philosophy of Violence.

"*Law*," he said again, "Let's go."

The three of them walked out of the huge courtyard and through the open gate. Nearby stood a short man whose Skin gleamed black-red in the light shed by the two glowworms attached to his shoulders. The Skin was oversized and hung to the ground.

The King's man, however, did not think he

was a comic figure. He sputtered, and the red of his face matched the color of the skin on his back.

"You took long enough," he said accusingly, and then, when Rastignac opened his mouth to protest, the Jail-breaker said, "Never mind, never mind. *Sa n'apawt*. The thing is that we get you away fast. The Minister of Ill-will has doubtless by now received word that an official jail-break is planned for tonight. He will send in advance of his mucketeers to intercept you. By coming in advance of the appointed time we shall have time to escape before the official rescue party arrives."

"How much time do we have?" asked Rastignac.

The King's man said, "Let's see. After I escort you through the rooms of the Duke, the King's foster-brother—he is most favorable to the Violent Philosophy, you know, and has petitioned the King to become your official patron, which petition will be considered at the next meeting of the Chamber of Deputies in three months—let's see, where was I? Ah, yes, I escort you through the rooms of the King's brother. You will be disguised as His Majesty's mucketeers, ostensibly looking for the escaped prisoners. From the rooms of the Duke, you will be let out through a small door in the wall of the palace itself. A car will be waiting.

"From then on it will be up to you. I suggest, however, that you make a dash for Mapfarity's castle. Follow the *Rue des Nues*; that is your best chance. The mucketeers have been pulled off that boulevard. However, it is

possible that Auverpin, the Ill-Will Mini
may see that order and will rescind it,
realizing what it means. If he does, I suppose I
will see you back in your cell, Rastignac."

He bowed to the Ssassaror and
Archambaud and said, "And you two
gentlemen will then be with him."

"And then what?" rumbled Mapfarity.

"According to the law, you will be allowed
one more jail-break. Any more after that will,
of course, be illegal. That is, unthinkable."

Rastignac unsheathed his epee and slashed
it at the air. "Let the mucketeers stand in my
way," he said fiercely. "I will cut them down
with this!"

The Jail-breaker staggered back, hands out-
thrust.

"Please, Monsieur Rastignac! Please! Don't
even talk about it! You know that your
philosophy is, as yet, illegal. The shedding of
blood is an act that will be regarded with
horror throughout the sentient planet.
People would think you are an Amphibian!"

"The Amphibians know what they're doing
far better than we do," answered Rastignac.
"Why do you think they're winning against us
Humans?"

Suddenly, before anybody could answer,
the sound of blaring horns came from somewhere on the rampants. Shouts went up;
drums began to beat, calling the mucketeers
to alert.

"*M'plew*!" said the Jail-breaker. "The
Minister of Ill-Will has warned the guards! Or
something else, equally disastrous, has
happened!"

Lusine's voice, shrill but powerful, soared out of the well.

"Jean-Jacques, will you take me with you? You must!"

"No!" shouted Rastignac. "Never! Nothing would make me help a bloodsucker!"

"Ah, Jean-Jacques, but you do not know what I know. Something I would never have told you if I did not have to tell in order to get free!"

"Shut up, Lusine! You cannot influence me!"

"But I can. I have a secret! A secret that will enable you to escape from this planet, to fly to the stars!"

Rastignac almost dropped his sword. But, before he could run to the lip of the well, Mapfarity had leaned his huge head over the mouth and rumbled something to the prisoner below.

Rastignac could not hear what Lusine answered, but he did not have to. The giant Ssassaror straightened up, and he bellowed, "She says that an Earthship has landed in the sea! And the pilot of the ship is in the hands of the Amphibians!"

Surprisingly, Mapfarity began laughing. Finally, choking, the sparks crackling from the tips of his ears, he said, "You can leave her in the well. Her news is no news; I know her so-called secret. But I didn't say anything to you because I didn't think that now was the time."

As the meaning of the words seeped into Rastignac's consciousness, he made a sudden violent movement—and began to tear the Skin from his body!

VI

Rastignac ran down the steps, out into the courtyard. He seized the Jail-breaker's arm and demanded the key to the grilles. Dazed, the white-faced official meekly and silently handed it to him. Without his Skin, Rastignac was no longer fearfully inhibited. If you were forceful enough and did not behave according to the normal pattern, you could get just about anything you wanted. The average Man or Ssassaror did not know how to react to his violence. By the time they had recovered from their confusion, he could be miles away.

Such a thought flashed through his head as he ran towards the prison wells. At the same time he heard the horn-blasts of the king's mucketeers and knew that he shortly would have a different type of Man to deal with. The mucketeers, closest approach to soldiers in this pacifistic land, wore Skins that conditioned them to be more belligerent than the common citizen. They carried epees and, while it was true that their points were dull and their wielders had never engaged in serious swordsmanship, the mucketeers could be dangerous because of numbers alone.

Mapfarity bellowed, "Jean-Jacques, what are you doing?"

He called back over his shoulder, "I'm taking Lusine with us! She can help us get the Earthman from the Amphibians!"

The Giant lumbered up behind him, threw a rope down to the eager hands of Lusine, and pulled her up without effort to the top of the well. A second later, Rastignac leaped upon Mapfarity's back, dug his hands under the upper fringe of the huge Skin and, ignoring its electrical blasts, ripped downwards.

Mapfarity cried out with shock and surprise as his skin flopped on the stones like a devilfish on dry land.

Archambaud ran up then and, without bothering to explain, the Ssassaror and the Man seized him and peeled off *his* artificial hide.

"Now we're all free men!" panted Rastignac. "And the mucketeers have no way of locating us if we hide, nor can they punish us with shocks."

He put the Giant on his right side, Lusine on his left, and the egg-stealer behind him. He removed the Jail-breaker's rapier from his sheath. The official was too astonished to protest.

"*Law, m'zawfa!*" cried Rastignac, parodying in his grotesque French the old Gallic war cry of "*Allons, mes enfants!*"

The King's official came to life and screamed orders at the group of mucketeers who had poured into the courtyard. They halted in confusion. They could not hear him above the roar of horns and thunder of drums and the people sticking their heads out of windows and shouting.

Rastignac scooped up with his epee one of the abandoned Skins flopping on the floor and threw it at the foremost guard. It descended upon the man's head, knocking off his hat and wrapping itself around the head and shoulders. The guard dropped his sword and staggered backwards into the group. At the same time, the escapees charged and bowled over their feeble opposition.

It was here that Rastignac drew first blood. The tip of his epee drove past a bewildered mucketeer's blade and entered the fellow's throat just below the chin. It did not penetrate very far because of the dullness of the point. Nevertheless, when Rastignac withdrew his sword, he saw blood spurt.

It was the first flower of violence, this scarlet blossom set against the whiteness of a Man's skin.

It would, if he had worn his Skin, have sickened him. Now, he exulted with a shout of triumph.

Lusine swooped up from behind him, bent over the fallen man. Her fingers dipped into the blood and went to her mouth. Greedily, she sucked her fingers.

Rastignac struck her cheek hard with the flat of his hand. She staggered back, her eyes narrow, but she laughed.

The next moments were busy as they entered the castle, knocked down two mucketeers who tried to prevent their passage to the Duke's rooms, then filed across the long suite.

The Duke rose from his writing-desk to greet them. Rastignac, determined to sever all ties and impress the government with the fact that he meant a real violence, snarled at his benefactor, "*Va t'feh fout!*"

The Duke was disconcerted at this harsh command, so obviously impossible to carry out. He blinked and said nothing. The escapees hurried past him to the door that gave exit to the outside. They pushed it open and stepped out into the car that waited for them. A chauffeur leaned against its thin wooden body.

Mapfarity pushed him aside and climbed in. The others followed. Rastignac was the last to get in. He examined in a glance the vehicle they were supposed to make their flight in.

It was as good a car as you could find in the realm. A Renault of the large class, it had a long boat-shaped scarlet body. There wasn't a scratch on it. It had seats for six. And that it had the power to outrun most anything was indicated by the two extra pairs of legs sticking out from the bottom. There were twelve pairs of legs, equine in form and shod with the best steel. It was the kind of vehicle you wanted when you might have to take off across the country. Wheeled cars could go faster on the highway, but this Renault would not be daunted by water, plowed fields, or steep hillsides.

Rastignac climbed into the driver's seat, seized the wheel, and pressed his foot down on the accelerator. The nerve-spot beneath the pedal sent a message to the muscles hidden beneath the hood and the legs projecting from the body. The Renault lurched forward, steadied, and began to pick up speed. It entered a broad paved highway. Hooves drummed; sparks shot out from the steel shoes.

Rastignac guided the brainless, blind creature concealed within the body. He was helped by the somatically-generated radar it employed to steer it past obstacles. When he came to the *Rue des Nues*, he slowed it down to a trot. There was no use tiring it out. Halfway up the gentle slope of the boulevard, however, a Ford galloped out from a side-street. Its seats bristled with tall peaked hats with outspread glowworm wings and with drawn epees.

Rastignac shoved the accelerator to the floor. The Renault broke into a gallop. The Ford turned so that it would present its broad side. As there was a fencework of tall shrubbery growing along the boulevard, the Ford was thus able to block most of the passage.

But, just before his vehicle reached the Ford, Rastignac pressed the Jump button. Few cars had this; only sportsmen or the royalty could afford to have such a neural circuit installed. And it did not allow for gradations in leaping. It was an all-or-none reaction; the legs spurned the ground in perfect unison and with every bit of the power in them. There was no holding back.

The nose lifted, the Renault soared into the air. There was a shout, a slight swaying as the trailing hooves struck the heads of mucketeers who had been stupid enough not to duck, and the vehicle landed with a screeching lurch, upright, on the other side of the Ford. Nor did it pause.

Half an hour later Rastignac reined in the car under a large tree whose shadow protected them. "We're well out in the country," he said.

"What do we do now?" asked impatient Archambaud.

"First we must know more about this Earthman," Rastignac answered. "Then we can decide."

VII

Dawn broke through night's guard and spilled a crimson swath on the hills to the East, and the Six Flying Stars faded from sight like a necklace of glowing jewels dipped into an ink bottle.

Rastignac halted the weary Renault on the top of a hill, looked down over the landscape spread out for miles below him. Mapfarity's castle—a tall rose-colored tower of flying buttresses—flashed in the rising sun. It stood on another hill by the sea shore. The country around was a madman's dream of color. Yet to Rastignac every hue sickened the eye. That bright green, for instance, was poisonous; that flaming scarlet was bloody; that pale yellow, rheumy; that velvet black, funereal; that pure white, maggotty.

"Rastignac!" It was Mapfarity's bass, strumming irritation deep in his chest.

"What?"

"What do we do now?"

Jean-Jacques was silent. Archambaud spoke plaintively.

"I'm not used to going without my Skin. There are things I miss. For one thing, I don't know what you're thinking, Jean-Jacques. I don't know whether you're angry at me or love me or are indifferent to me. I don't know where other people *are*. I don't feel the joy of the little animals playing, the freedom of the flight of the birds, the ghostly plucking of the growing grass, the sweet stab of the mating lust of the wild-horned apigator, the humming of bees working to build a hive, and the sleepy stupid arrogance of the giant cabbage-eating *duexnez*. I can feel nothing without the Skin I have worn so long. I feel alone."

Rastignac replied, "You are not alone. I am with you."

Lusine spoke in a low voice, her large brown eyes upon his.

"I, too, feel alone. My Skin is gone, the Skin by which I knew how to act according to the wisdom of my father, the Amphib King. Now that it is gone and I cannot hear his voice the vibrating tympanum, I do not know what to do."

"At present," replied Rastignac, "you will do as I tell you."

Mapfarity repeated, "What now?"

Rastignac became brisk. He said, "We go to your castle, Giant. We use your smithy to put sharp points on our swords, points to slide through a man's body from front to back. Don't pale! That is what we must do. And then we pick up your goose that lays the golden eggs, for we must have money if we are to act efficiently. After that, we buy—or steal—a boat and we go to wherever the Earthman is held captive. And we rescue him."

"And then?" said Lusine, her eyes shining.

"What you do then will be up to you. But I am going to leave this planet and voyage with the Earthman to other worlds."

Silence. Then Mapfarity said, "Why leave here?"

"Because there is no hope for this land. Nobody will give up his Skin. *Le Beau Pays* is doomed to a lotus-life. And that is not for me."

Archambaud jerked a thumb at the Amphib girl. "What about her people?"

"They may win, the water-people. What's the difference? It will be just the exchange of one Skin for another. Before I heard of the landing of the Earthman I was going to fight no matter what the cost to me or inevitable defeat. But not now."

Mapfarity's rumble was angry. "Ah, Jean-Jacques, this is not my comrade talking. Are you sure you haven't swallowed your Skin? You talk as if you were inside-out. What is the matter with your brain? Can't you see that it will indeed make a difference if the Amphibs get the upper hand? Can't you see *who* is making the Amphibs behave the way they have been?"

Rastignac urged the Renault towards the rose-colored lacy castle high upon a hill. The vehicle trotted tiredly along the rough and narrow forest path.

"What do you mean?" he said.

"I mean the Amphibs got along fine with the Ssassaror until a new element entered their lives—the Earthmen. Then the antagonizing began. What is this new element? It's the Changelings—the mixture of Earthmen and Amphibs or Ssassaror and Terran. Add it up.

Turn it around. Look at it from any angle. It is the Changelings who are behind this restlessness—the Human element.

"Another thing. The Amphibs have always had Skins different from ours. Our factories create our Skins to set up an affinity and communication between their wearers and all of Nature. They are designed to make it easier for every Man to love his neighbor.

"Now, the strange thing about the Amphibs' Skin is that they, too, were once designed to do such things. But in the past thirty or forty years new Skins have been created for one primary purpose—to establish a communication between the Sea-King and his subjects. Not only that, the Skins can be operated at long distances so that the King may punish any disobedient subject. And they are set so that they establish affinity only among the Waterfolk, not between them and all of Nature."

"I had gathered some of that during my conversations with Lusine," said Rastignac. "But I did not know it had gone to such lengths."

"Yes, and you may safely bet that the Changelings are behind it."

"Then it is the human element that is corrupting?"

"What else?"

Rastignac said, "Lusine, what do you say to this?"

"I think it is best that you leave this world. Or else turn Changeling-Amphib."

"Why should I join you Amphibians?"

"A man like you could become a Sea-King."

"And drink blood?"

"I would rather drink blood than mate with a Man. Almost, that is. But I would make an exception with you, Jean-Jacques."

If it had been a Land-woman who made such a blunt proposal he would have listened with equanimity. There was no modesty, false or otherwise, in the country of the Skin-wearers. But to hear such a thing from a woman whose mouth had drunk the blood of a living man filled him with disgust.

Yet, he had to admit Lusine was beautiful. If she had not been a blood-drinker . . .

Though he lacked his receptive Skin, Mapparity seemed to sense Rastignac's emotions. He said, "You must not blame her too much, Jean-Jacques. Sea-changelings are conditioned from babyhood to love blood. And for a very definite purpose, too, unnatural though it is. When the time comes for hordes of Changelings to sweep out of the sea and overwhelm the Landfolk, they will have no compunctions about cutting the throats of their fellow-creatures."

Lusine laughed. The rest of them shifted uneasily but did not comment. Rastignac changed the subject.

"How did you find out about the Earthman, Mapparity?" he said.

The Ssassaror smiled. Two long yellow canines shone wetly; the nose, which had nostrils set in the sides, gaped open; blue sparks shot out from it; at the same time, the feathered ears stiffened and crackled with red-and-blue sparks.

"I have been doing something besides breeding geese to lay golden eggs," he said. "I have set traps for Waterfolk, and I have caught two. These I caged in a dungeon in my castle, and I experimented with them. I removed their Skins and put them on me, and I found out many interesting facts."

He leered at Lusine, who was no longer laughing, and he said, "For instance, I discovered that the Sea-king can locate, talk to, and punish any of his subjects anywhere in the sea or along the coast. He has booster Skins planted all over his realm so that any message he sends will reach the receiver, no matter how far away he is. Moreover, he has conditioned each and every Skin so that, by uttering a certain codeword to which only one particular Skin will respond, he may stimulate it to shock or even to kill its carrier."

Mapfarity continued, "I analyzed those two Skins in my lab and then, using them as models, made a number of duplicates in my fleshforge. They lacked only the nerves that would enable the Sea-King to shock us."

Rastignac smiled his appreciation of this coup. Mapfarity's ears crackled blue sparks of joy, his equivalent of blushing.

"Ah, then you have doubtless listened in to many broadcasts. And you know where the Earthman is located?"

"Yes," said the Giant. "He is in the palace of the Amphib King, upon the island of Kata-proimnoin. That is only thirty miles out to the sea."

Rastignac did not know what he would do, but he had two advantages in the Amphibs' Skins and in Lusine. And he burned to get off

this doomed planet, this land of men too sunk
in false happiness, sloth, and stupidity to see
that soon death would come from the water.

He had two possible avenues of escape. One
was to use the newly arrived Earthman's
knowledge so that the fuels necessary to
propel the ferry-rockets could be
manufactured. The rockets themselves still
stood in a museum. Rastignac had not
planned to use them because neither he nor
any one else on this planet knew how to make
fuel for them. Such secrets had long ago been
forgotten.

But now that science was available through
the newcomer from Earth, the rockets could
be equipped and taken up to one of the Six
Flying Stars. The Earthman could study the
rocket, determine what was needed in the way
of supplies, then it could be outfitted for the
long voyage.

An alternative was the Terran's vessel.
Perhaps he might invite him to come along in
it . . .

The huge gateway to Mapfarity's castle
interrupted his thoughts.

VIII

He halted the Renault, told Archambaud to
find the Giant's servant and have him feed
their vehicle, rub its legs down with liniment,
and examine the hooves for defective shoes.

Archambaud was glad to look up Mapfabvisheen, the Giant's servant, because he had
not seen him for a long time. The little

Ssassaror had been an active member of the
Egg-stealer's Guild until the night three years
ago when he had tried to creep into
Mapfarity's strongroom. The crafty guildsman had avoided the Giant's traps and there
found the two geese squatting upon their bed
of minerals.

These fabulous geese made no sound when
he picked them up with lead-lined gloves and
put them in his bag, also lined with lead-leaf.
They were not even aware of him. Laboratory-
bred, retort-shaped, their protoplasm a blend
of silicon-carbon, unconscious even that they
lived, they munched upon lead and other
elements, ruminated, gastrated, transmuted,
and every month, regular as the clockwork
march of stars or whirl of electrons, each laid
an octagonal egg of pure gold.

Mapfabvisheen had trodden softly from the
strongroom and thought himself safe. And
then, amazingly, frighteningly, and totally
unethically, from his viewpoint, the geese had
begun honking loudly!

He had run but not fast enough. The Giant
had come stumbling from his bed in response
to the wild clamor and had caught him. And,
according to the contract drawn up between
the Guild of Egg-stealers and the League of
Giants, a guildsman seized within the precints
of a castle must serve the goose's owner for
two years. Mapfabvisheen had been greedy;
he had tried to take both geese. Therefore, he
must wait upon the Giant for a double term.

Afterwards, he found out how he'd been
trapped. The egg-layers themselves hadn't
been honking. Mouthless, they were utterly

incapable of that. Mapfarity had fastened a so-called "goose-tracker" to the strongroom's doorway. This device clicked loudly whenever a goose was nearby. It could smell out one even through a lead-leaf-lined bag. When Mapfabvisheen passed underneath it, its clicks woke up a small Skin beside it. The Skin, mostly lung-sac and voice organs, honked its warning. And the dwarf, Mapfabvisheen, began his servitude to the Giant, Mapfarity.

Rastignac knew the story. He also knew that Mapfarity had infected the fellow with the philosophy of Violence and that he was now a good member of his Underground. He was eager to tell him his servitor days were over, that he could now take his place in their band as an equal. Subject, of course, to Rastignac's order.

Mapfabvisheen was stretched out upon the floor and snoring a sour breath. A grey-haired man was slumped on a nearby table. His head, turned to one side, exhibited the same slack-jawed look that the Ssassaror's had, and he flung the ill-smelling gauntlet of his breath at the visitors. He held an empty bottle in one loose hand. Two other bottles lay on the stone floor, one shattered.

Besides the bottles lay the men's Skins. Rastignac wondered why they had not crawled to the halltree and hung themselves up.

"What ails them? What is that smell?" said Mapfarity.

"I don't know," replied Archambaud, "but I know the visitor. He is Father Jules, priest of the Guild of Egg-stealers."

Rastignac raised his bracket-shaped eyebrows, picked up a bottle in which there remained a slight residue, and drank.

"Mon Dieu, it is the sacrament wine!" he cried.

Mapfarity said, "Why would they be drinking that?"

"I don't know. Wake Mapfabvisheen up, but let the good father sleep. He seems tired after his spiritual labors and doubtless deserves a rest."

Doused with a bucket of cold water the little Ssassaror staggered to his feet. Seeing Archambaud, he embraced him. "Ah, Archambaud, old baby-abductor, my sweet goose-bagger, my ears tingle to see you again!"

They did. Red and blue sparks flew off his ear-feathers.

"What is the meaning of this?" sternly interrupted Mapfarity. He pointed at the dirt swept into the corners.

Mapfabvisheen drew himself up to his full dignity, which wasn't much. "Good Father Jules was making his circuits," he said. "You know he travels around the country and hears confession and sings Mass for us poor egg-stealers who have been unlucky enough to fall into the clutches of some rich and greedy and anti-social Giant who is too stingy to hire servants, but captures them instead, and who won't allow us to leave the premises until our servitude is over . . ."

"Cut it!" thundered Mapfarity. "I can't stand around all day, listening to the likes of

you. My feet hurt too much. Anyway, you
know I've allowed you to go into town every
week-end. Why don't you see a priest then?"

Mapfabvisheen said, "You know very well
the closest town is ten kilometers away and
it's full of Pantheists. There's not a priest to
be found there."

Rastignac groaned inwardly. Always, it was
thus. You could never hurry these people or
get them to regard anything seriously.

Take the case they were wasting their
breath on now. Everybody knew the Church
had been outlawed a long time ago because it
opposed the use of the Skins and certain other
practices that went along with it. So, no
sooner had that been done than the
Ssassarors, anxious to establish their check-
and-balance system, had made arrangements
through the Minister of Ill-Will to give the
Church unofficial legal recognizance.

Then, though the aborigines had belonged
to that pantheistical organization known as
the Sons of Good And Old Mother Nature,
they had all joined the Church of the Terrans.
They operated under the theory that the best
way to make an institution innocuous was for
everybody to sign up for it. Never persecute.
That makes it thrive.

Much to the Church's chagrin, the theory
worked. How can you fight an enemy who
insists on joining you and who will also agree
to everything you teach him and then still
worship at the other service? Supposedly
driven underground, the Church counted
almost every Landsman among its supporters
from the Kings down.

Every now and then a priest would forget to wear his Skin out-of-doors and be arrested, then released later in an official jail-break. Those who refused to cooperate were forcibly kidnapped, taken to another town and there let loose. Nor did it do the priest any good to proclaim boldly who he was. Everybody pretended not to know he was a fugitive from justice. They insisted on calling him by his official pseudonym.

However, few priests were such martyrs. Generations of Skin-wearing had sapped the ecclesiastical vigor.

The thing that puzzled Rastignac about Father Jules was the sacrament wine. Neither he nor anybody else in L'Bawpfey, as far as he knew, had ever tasted the liquid outside of the ceremony. Indeed, except for certain of the priests, nobody even knew how to make wine.

He shook the priest awake, said, "What's the matter, Father?"

Father Jules burst into tears. "Ah, my boy, you have caught me in my sin. I am a drunkard."

Everybody looked blank. "What does that word *drunkard* mean?"

"It means a man who's damned enough to fill his Skin with alcohol, my boy, fill it until he's no longer a man but a beast."

"Alcohol? What is that?"

"The stuff that's in the wine, my boy. You don't know what I'm talking about because the knowledge was long ago forbidden except to us of the cloth. Cloth, he says! Bah! We go around like everybody, naked except for these extra-dermal monstrosities which reveal rather than conceal, which not only serve us as clothing but as mentors, parents, censors, interpreters, and, yes, even as priests. Where's a bottle that's not empty? I'm thirsty."

Rastignac stuck to the subject. "Why was the making of this alcohol forbidden?"

"How should I know?" said Father Jules. "I'm old, but not so ancient that I came with the Six Flying Stars . . . Where is that bottle?"

Rastignac was not offended by his crossness. Priests were notorious for being the most ill-tempered, obstreperous, and unstable of men. They were not at all like the clerics of Earth, whom everybody knew from legend had been sweet-tempered, meek, humble, and obedient to authority. But on L'Bawpfey these men of the Church had reason to be out of sorts. Everybody attended Mass, paid their tithes, went to confession, and did not fall asleep during sermons. Everybody believed what the priests told them and were as good as it was possible for human beings to be. So, the priests had no real incentive to work, no evil to fight.

Then why the prohibition against alcohol?

"*Sacre Bleu!*" groaned Father Jules. "Drink as much as I did last night, and you'll find out. Never again, I say. Ah, there's another bottle, hidden by a providential fate under my traveling robe. Where's the corkscrew?"

Father Jules swallowed half of the bottle, smacked his lips, picked up his Skin from the floor, brushed off the dirt and said, "I must be going, my sons. I've a noon appointment with the bishop, and I've a good twelve kilometers to travel. Perhaps, one of you gentlemen has a car?"

Rastignac shook his head and said he was sorry, but their car was tired and had, besides, thrown a shoe. Father Jules shrugged philosophically, put on his Skin and reached out again for the bottle.

Rastignac said, "Sorry, Father. I'm keeping this bottle."

"For what?" asked Father Jules.

"Never mind. Say I'm keeping you from temptation."

"Bless you, my son, and may you have a big enough hangover to show you the wickedness of your ways."

Smiling, Rastignac watched the Father walk out. He was not disappointed. The priest had no sooner reached the huge door than his Skin fell off and lay motionless upon the stone.

"Ah," breathed Rastignac. "The same thing happened to Mapfabvisheen when he put his on. There must be something about the wine that deadens the Skins, makes them fall off."

After the padre had left, Rastignac handed the bottle to Mapfarity. "We're dedicated to breaking the law most illegally, brother. So I'm asking you to analyze this wine and find out how to make it."

"Why not ask Father Jules?"

"Because priests are pledged never to reveal the secret. That was one of the original agreements whereby the Church was allowed to remain on L'Bawpfey. Or, at least that's what my parish priest told me. He said it was a good thing, as it removed an evil from man's temptation. He never did say why it was so evil. Maybe he didn't know.

"That doesn't matter. What does matter is that the Church has inadvertently given us a weapon whereby we may free Man from his bondage to the Skins and it has also given itself once again a chance to be really persecuted and to flourish on the blood of its martyrs."

"Blood?" said Lusine, licking her lips. "The Churchmen drink blood?"

Rastignac did not explain. He could be wrong. If so, he'd feel less like a fool if they didn't know what he thought.

Meanwhile, there were the first steps to be taken for the unskinning of an entire planet.

IX

Later that day, the mucketeers surrounded the castle, but they made no effort to storm it. The following day one of them knocked on the huge front door and presented Mapfarity with a summons requiring them to surrender. The Giant laughed, put the document in his mouth, and ate it. The server fainted and had to be revived with a bucket of cold water before he could stagger back to report this tradition-shattering reception.

Rastignac set up his underground so it could be expanded in a hurry. He didn't worry about the blockade because, as was well known, Giants' castles had all sorts of subterranean tunnels and secret exits. He contacted a small number of priests who were

willing to work for him. These were
congenital rebels who became quite
enthusiastic when he told them their
activities would result in a fierce persecution
of the Church.

The majority, however, clung to their Skins
and said they would have nothing to do with
this extradermal-less devil. They took pride
and comfort in that term. The vulgar phrase
for the man who refused to wear his Skin was
"devil," and, by law and logic, the Church
could not be associated with a devil. As everybody knew, the priests have always been on
the side of the angels.

Meanwhile, the Devil's band slipped out of
the tunnels and made raids. Their targets
were Giants' castles and government
treasuries; their loot, the geese. So many
raids did they make that the president of the
League of Giants and the Business Agent for
the Guild of Egg-stealers came to plead with
them. And remained to denounce. Rastignac
was delighted with their complaints, and,
after listening for a while, threw them out.

Rastignac had, like all other Skin-wearers,
always accepted the monetary system as a
thing of reason and balance. But, without his
Skin, he was able to think objectively, and he
saw its weaknesses.

For some cause buried far in history, the
Giants had always had control of the means
for making the hexagonal golden coins called
oeufs. But the Kings, wishing to get control of
the golden eggs, had set up that elite branch of
the Guild which specialized in abducting the
half-living 'geese.' Whenever a thief was

successful, he turned the goose over to his King. The monarch, in turn, sent a note to the robbed Giant informing him that the government intended to keep the goose to make its own currency. But even though the Giant was making counterfeit geese, the King, in his generosity, would ship to the Giant one out of every thirty eggs laid by the kidnappee.

The note was a polite and well-recognized lie. The Giants made the only genuine gold-egg-laying geese on the planet because the Giants' League alone knew the secret. And the King gave back one-thirtieth of his loot so the Giant could accumulate enough money to buy the materials to create another goose. Which would, possibly, be stolen later on.

Rastignac, by his illegal rape of geese, was making money scarce. Peasants were hanging on to their produce and waiting to sell until prices were at their highest. The government, merchants, the league, the guild, all saw themselves impoverished.

Futhermore, the Amphibs, taking note of the situation, were making raids on their own and blaming them on Rastignac.

He did not care. He was intent on trying to find a way to reach Kataproimnoin and rescue the Earthman so he could take off in the spaceship floating in the harbor. But he knew that he would have to take things slowly, to scout out the land and plan accordingly.

Furthermore, Mapfarity had made him promise he would do his best to set up the Landsmen so they would be able to resist the Waterfolk when the day for war came.

Rastignac made his biggest raid when he and his band stole one moonless night into the capital itself to rob the big Goose House, only an egg's throw away from the Palace and the Ministry of Ill-Will. They put the Goose House guards to sleep with little arrows smeared with dream-snake venom, filled their lead-leaf-lined bags with gold eggs, and sneaked out the back door.

As they left, Rastignac saw a cloaked figure slinking from the back door of the Ministry. On impulse, he tackled the figure. It was an Amphib-changeling. Rastignac struck the Amphib with a venomous arrow before the Water-human could cry out or stab back.

Mapfarity grabbed up the limp Amphib and they raced for the safety of the castle.

They questioned the Amphib, Pierre Pusi-premnoos, in the castle. At first silent, he later began talking freely when Mapfarity got a heavy Skin from his flesh-forge and put it on the fellow. It was a Skin modeled after those worn by the Water-people, but it differed in that the Giant could control, through another Skin, the powerful neural shocks.

After a few shocks, Pierre admitted he was the foster-son of the Amphibian King and that, incidentally, Lusine was his foster-sister. He further stated he was a messenger between the Amphib King and the Ssarraror's Ill-Will Minister.

More shocks extracted the fact that the Minister of Ill-Will, Auverpin, was an Amphib-changeling who was passing himself off as a born Landsman. Not only that, the Human hostages among the Amphibs were about to

stage a carefully planned revolt against the
born Amphibs. It would kill off about half of
them. The rest would then be brought under
control of the Master Skin.

When the two stepped from the lab, they
were attacked by Lusine, knife in hand. She
gashed Rastignac in the arm before he
knocked her out with an uppercut. Later,
while Mapfarity applied a little jelly-like
creature called a *scar-jester* to the wound,
Rastignac complained:

"I don't know if I can endure much more of
this. I thought the way of Violence would not
be hard to follow because I hated the Skins
and the Amphibs so much. But it is easier to
attack a faceless, hypothetical enemy, or
torture him, than the individual enemy. Much
easier."

"My brother," boomed the Giant, "if you
continue to dwell upon the philosophical
implications of your actions, you will end up
as helpless and confused as the leg-counting
centipede. Better not think. Warriors are not
supposed to. They lose their keen fighting
edge when they think. And you need all of that
now."

"I would suppose that thought would
sharpen them."

"When issues are simple, yes. But you must
remember that the system on this planet is
anything but uncomplicated. It was set up to
confuse, to keep one always off balance. Just
try to keep one thing in mind—the Skins are
far more of an impediment to Man than they
are a help. Also, that if the Skins don't come
off, the Amphibs will soon be cutting our

throats. The only way to save ourselves is to kill them first. Right?"

"I suppose so," said Rastignac. He stooped and put his hands under the unconscious Lusine's armpits. "Help me put her in a room. We'll keep her locked up until she cools off. Then we'll use her to guide us when we get to Kataproimnoin. Which reminds me—how many gallons of wine have you made so far?"

X

A week later Rastignac summoned Lusine. She came in frowning and with her lower lip protruding in a pretty pout.

He said, "Day after tomorrow is the day on which the new Kings are crowned, isn't it?"

Tonelessly, she said, "Supposedly. Actually, the present Kings will be crowned again."

Rastignac smiled. "I know. Peculiar, isn't it, how the 'people' always vote the same Kings back into power? However, that isn't what I'm getting at. If I remember correctly, the Amphibs give their King exotic and amusing gifts on coronation day. What do you think would happen if I took a big shipload of bottles of wine and passed it out among the population just before the Amphibs begin their surprise massacre?"

Lusine had seen Mapfarity and Rastignac experimenting with the wine, and she had been frightened by the results. Nevertheless, she made a brave, attempt to hide her fear now. She spit at him and said, "You mud-footed fool! There are priests who will know what it is! They will be in the coronation crowd."

"Ah, not so! In the first place, you Amphibs are almost entirely Aggressive Pantheists. You have only a few priests, and you will now pay for that omission of wine-tasters. Second, Mapfarity's concoction tastes not at all vinous and is twice as strong."

She spat at him again and spun on her heel and walked out.

That night Rastignac's band and Lusine went through a tunnel which brought them up through a hollow tree about two miles west of the castle. There they hopped into the Renault, which had been kept in a camouflaged garage, and drove to the little port of Marrec. Archambaud had paved their way here with golden eggs and a sloop was waiting for them.

Rastignac took the boat's wheel. Lusine stood beside him, ready to answer the challenge of any Amphib patrol that tried to stop them. As the Amphib-King's foster-daughter, she could get the boat through to the Amphib island without any trouble at all.

Archambaud stood behind her, a knife under his cloak, to make sure she did not try to betray them. Lusine had sworn she could be trusted. Rastignac had answered that he was sure she could be, too, as long as the knife point pricked her back to remind her.

Nobody stopped them. An hour before dawn they anchored in the harbor of Kata-proimnoin. Lusine was tied hand and foot inside the cabin. Before Rastignac could scratch her with dream-snake venom, she pleaded. "You could not do this to me, Jean-Jacques, if you loved me."

"Who said anything about loving you?"

"Well, I like that! You said so, you cheat!"

"Oh, *then*! Well, Lusine, you've had enough experience to know that such protestations of tenderness and affection are only inevitable accompaniments of the moment's passion."

For the first time since he had known her, he saw Lusine's lower lip tremble and tears come in her eyes. "Do you mean you were only using me?" she sobbed.

"You forget I had good reason to think you were just using *me*. Remember, you're an Amphib, Lusine. Your people can't be trusted. You blood-drinkers are as savage as the little sea-monsters you leave in Human cradles."

"Jean-Jacques, take me with you! I'll do anything you say! I'll even cut my foster-father's throat for you!"

He laughed. Unheeding, she swept on. "I want to be with you, Jean-Jacques! Look, with me to guide you in my homeland—with my prestige as the Amphib-King's daughter—you can become King yourself after the rebellion. I'd get rid of the Amphib-King for you so there'll be nobody in your way!"

She felt no more guilt than a tigress. She was naive and terrible, innocent and disgusting.

"No, thanks, Lusine." He scratched her with the dream-snake needle. As her eyes closed, he said, "You don't understand. All I want to do is voyage to the stars. Being King means nothing to me. The only person I'd trade places with would be the Earthman the

Amphibs hold prisoner."

He left her sleeping in the locked cabin.

Noon found them loafing on the great square in front of the Palace of the Two Kings of The Sea and The Islands. All were disguised as Waterfolk. Before they'd left the castle, they had grafted webs between their fingers and toes—just as Amphib-changelings who weren't born with them, did—and they wore the special Amphib Skins that Mapfarity had grown in his fleshforge. These were able to tune in on the Amphibs' wavelengths, but they lacked their shock mechanism.

Rastignac had to locate the Earthman, rescue him, and get him to the spaceship that lay anchored between two wharfs, its sharp nose pointing outwards. A wooden bridge had been built from one of the wharfs to a place halfway up its towering side.

Rastignac could not make out any breaks in the smooth metal that would indicate a port, but reason told him there must be some sort of entrance to the ship at that point.

A guard of twenty Amphibs repulsed any attempt on the crowd's part to get on the bridge.

Rastignac had contacted the harbor-master and made arrangements for workmen to unload his cargo of wine. His freehandedness with the gold eggs got him immediate service even on this general holiday. Once in the square, he and his men uncrated the wine but left the two heavy chests on the wagon which was hitched to a powerful little six-legged Jeep.

They stacked the bottles of wine in a huge

pile while the curious crowd in the square encircled them to watch. Rastignac then stood on a chest to survey the scene, so that he could best judge the time to start. There were perhaps seven or eight thousand of all three races there—the Ssassarors, the Amphibs, the Humans—with an unequal portioning of each.

Rastignac, looking for just such a thing, noticed that every non-human Amphib had at least two Humans tagging at his heels.

It would take two Humans to handle an Amphib or a Ssassaror. The Amphibs stood upon their seal-like hind flippers at least six and a half feet tall and weighed about three hundred pounds. The Giant Ssassarors, being fisheaters, had reached the same enormous height as Mapfarity. The Giants were in the minority, as the Amphibs had always preferred stealing Human babies from the Terrans. The Ssassaror-changelings were marked for death also.

Rastignac watched for signs of uneasiness or hostility between the three groups. Soon, he saw the signs. They were not plentiful, but they were enough to indicate an uneasy undercurrent. Three times, the guards had to intervene to break up quarrels. The Humans eyed the non-human quarrelers, but made no move to help their Amphib fellows against the Giants. Not only that, they took them aside afterwards and seemed to be reprimanding them. Evidently, the order was that everyone was to be on his behavior until the time to revolt.

Rastignac glanced at the great tower-clock. "It's an hour before the ceremonies begin," he said to his men. "Let's go."

XI

Mapfarity, who had been loitering in the crowd some distance away, caught Archambaud's signal and slowly, as befit a Giant whose feet hurt, limped towards them. He stopped, scrutinized the pile of bottles, then, in his lion's-roar-at-the-bottom-of-a-well voice said, "Say, what's in these bottles?"

Rastignac shouted back, "A drink which the new Kings will enjoy very much."

"What's that?" replied Mapfarity. "Seawater?"

The crowd laughed.

"No, it's not water," Rastignac said, "as anybody but a lumbering Giant should know. It is a delicious drink that brings a rare ecstacy upon the drinker. I got the formula for it from an old witch who lives on the shores of far off Apfelabvidanahyew. He told me it had been in his family since the coming of Man to L'Bawpfey. He parted with it on condition I make it only for the Kings."

"Will only Their Majesties get to taste this exquisite drink?" bellowed Mapfarity.

"That depends upon whether it pleases Their Majesties to give some to their subjects to celebrate the result of the elections."

Archambaud, also planted in the crowd, shrilled, "I suppose if they do, the big-paunched Amphibs and Giants will get twice as much as us Humans. They always do it, it seems."

There was a mutter from the crowd; approbation from the Amphibs, protest from the others.

"That will make no difference," said Rastignac, smiling. "The fascinating thing about this is that an Amphib can drink no more than a Human. That may be why the old man who revealed his secret to me called the drink Old Equalizer."

"Ah, you're skinless," scoffed Mapfarity, throwing the most deadly insult known. "I can out-drink, out-eat, and out-swim any Human here. Here, Amphib, give me a bottle, and we'll see if I'm bragging."

An Amphib captain pushed himself through the throng, waddling clumsily on his flippers like an upright seal.

"No, you don't!" he barked. "Those bottles are intended for the Kings. No commander touches them, least of all a Human and a Giant."

Rastignac mentally hugged himself. He couldn't have planned a better intervention himself! "Why can't I?" he replied. "Until I make an official presentation, these bottles are mine, not the Kings'. I'll do what I want with them."

"Yeah," said the Amphibs. "That's telling him!"

The Amphibs's big brown eyes narrowed, and his animal-like face wrinkled, but he couldn't think of a retort. Rastignac at once handed a bottle apiece to each of his comrades. They uncorked and drank and then assumed an ecstatic expression which was a tribute to their acting, for these three bottles held only fruit juice.

"Look here, captain," said Rastignac, "why don't you try a swig yourself? Go ahead. There's plenty. And I'm sure Their Majesties would be pleased to contribute some of it on this joyous occasion. Besides, I can always make more for the Kings.

"As a matter of fact," he added, winking, "I expect to get a pension from the courts as the Kings' Old Equalizer-maker."

The crowd laughed. The Amphib, afraid of losing face, took the bottle—which contained wine rather than fruit juice. After a few long swallows, the Amphib's eyes became red and a silly grin curved his thin, black-edged lips. Finally, in a thickening voice, he asked for another bottle.

Rastignac, in a sudden burst of generosity, not only gave him one, but began passing out bottles to the many eager reaching hands. Mapfarity and the two egg-thieves helped him. In a short time, the pile of bottles had dwindled to a fourth of its former height. When a mixed group of guards strode up and demanded to know what the commotion was about, Rastignac gave them some of the bottles.

Within a minute, the square had erupted into a fighting mob. Staggering, red-eyed, slur-tongued, their long-repressed hostility against each other released by the liquor which their bodies were unaccustomed to, Human, Ssassaror and Amphib fell to with the utmost will, slashing, slugging, fighting with everything they had.

None of them noticed that every one who had drunk from the bottles had lost his Skin. The Skins had fallen off one by one and lay motionless on the pavement where they were kicked or stepped upon. Not one Skin tried to crawl back to its owner because they were all nerve-numbed by the wine.

Rastignac, seated behind the wheel of the Jeep, began driving as best he could through the battling mob. After frequent stops, he halted before the broad marble steps that ran like a stairway to heaven, up and up before it ended on the Porpoise Porch of the Palace. He and his gang were about to take the two heavy chests off the wagon when they were transfixed by a scene before them.

A score of dead Humans and Amphibs lay on the steps, evidence of the fierce struggle that had taken place between the guards of the two monarchs. Evidently, the King had heard of the riot and hastened outside. There the Amphib-changelings King had apparently realized that the rebellion was way ahead of schedule, but he had attacked the Amphib King anyway.

And he had won, for his guardsmen held the struggling flipper-footed Amphib ruler down while two others bent his head back over a step. The Changeling-King himself, still clad in the coronation robes, was about to draw his long ceremonial knife across the exposed and palpitating throat of the Amphib King.

This in itself was enough to freeze the onlookers. But the sight of Lusine running up the stairway towards the rulers added to their paralysis. She had a knife in her hand and was holding it high as she ran toward her foster-father, the Amphib King.

Mapfarity groaned, but Rastignac said, "It doesn't matter that she has escaped. We'll go ahead with our original plan."

They began unloading the chests while Rastignac kept an eye on Lusine. He saw her run up, stop, say a few words to the Amphib King, then kneel and stab him, burying the knife in his jugular vein. Then, before anybody could stop her, she had applied her mouth to the cut in his neck.

The Human-King kicked her in the ribs and sent her rolling down the steps. Rastignac saw correctly that it was not her murderous deed that caused his reaction. It was because she had dared to commit it without his permission and had also drunk the royal blood first.

He further noted with grim satisfaction that when Lusine recovered from the blow and ran back up to talk to the King, he ignored her. She pointed at the group around the wagon but he dismissed her with a wave of his hand. He was too busy gloating over his vanquished rival lying at his feet.

The plotters hoisted the two chests and staggered up the steps. The King passed them as he went down with no more than a curious glance. Gifts had been coming up those steps all day for the King, so he undoubtedly thought of them only as more gifts. So Rastignac and his men walked past the knives of the guards as if they had nothing to fear.

Lusine stood alone at the top of the steps. She was in a half-crouch, knife ready. "I'll kill the King, and I'll drink from his throat!" she cried hoarsly. "No man kicks me except for love. Has he forgotten that I am the foster-daughter of the Amphib King?"

Rastignac felt revulsion but he had learned by now that those who deal in violence and rebellion must march with strange steppers.

"Bear a hand here," he said, ignoring her threat.

Meekly she grabbed hold of a chest's corner. To his further questioning, she replied that the Earthman who had landed in the ship was held in a suite of rooms in the west wing. Their trip thereafter was fast and direct. Unopposed, they carted the chests to the huge room where the Master Skin was kept.

There they found ten frantic biotechnicians excitedly trying to determine why the great extraderm—the Master Skin through which all individual Skins were controlled—was not broadcasting properly. They had no way as yet of knowing that it was operating perfectly but that the little Skins upon the Amphibs and their hostage Humans were not shocking them into submission because they were lying in a wine-stupor on the ground. No one had told them that the Skins, which fed off the bloodstream of their hosts, had become anesthetized from the alcohol and failed any longer to react to their Master Skin.

That, of course, applied only to those Skins in the square that were drunk from the wine. Elsewhere all over the kingdom, Amphibs writhed in agony and Ssassarors and Terrans were taking advantage of their helplessness to

cut their throats. But not here, where the crux
of the matter was.

XII

The Landsmen rushed the techs and pushed
them into the great chemical vat in which the
twenty-five hundred foot square Master Skin
floated. Then they uncrated the lead-leaf-lined
bags filled with stolen geese and emptied
them into the nutrient fluid. According to
Mapfarity's calculations, the radio-activity
from the silicon-carbon geese should kill the
big Skin within a few days. When a new one
was grown, that, too, would die. Unless the
Amphib guessed what was wrong and located
the geese on the bottom of the ten-foot deep
tank, they would not be able to stop the
process. That did not seem likely.

In either case, it was necessary that the
Master Skin be put out of temporary
commission, at least, so the Amphibs over the
Kingdom could have a fighting chance.
Mapfarity plunged a hollow harpoon into the
isle of floating protoplasm and through a tube
connected to that poured into the Skin three
gallons of the dream-snake venom. That was
enough to knock it out for an hour or two.
Meanwhile, if the Amphibs had any sense at
all, they'd have rid themselves of their
extraderms.

They left the lab and entered the west wing.
As they trotted up the long winding corridors
Lusine said, "Jean-Jacques, what do you plan
on doing now? Will you try to make yourself

King of the Terrans and fight us Amphib-changelings?" When he said nothing, she went on. "Why don't you kill the Amphib-changeling King and take over here? I could help you do that. You could then have all of L'Bawpfey in your power."

He shot her a look of contempt and cried, "Lusine, can't you get it through that thick little head of yours that everything I've done has been done so that I can win one goal: reach the Flying Stars? If I can get the Earthman to his ship I'll leave with him and not set foot again for years on this planet. Maybe never again."

She looked stricken. "But what about the war here?" she asked.

"There are a few men among the Landfolk who are capable of leading in wartime. It will take strong men, and there are very few like me, I admit, but—oh, oh, opposition!" He broke off at sight of the six guards who stood before the Earthman's suite.

Lusine helped, and within a minute they had slain three and chased away the others. Then they burst through the door—and Rastignac received another shock.

The occupant of the apartment was a tiny and exquisitely formed redhead with large blue eyes and very unmasculine curves!

"I thought you said Earth*man*?" protested Rastignac to the Giant who came lumbering along behind them.

"Oh, I used that in the generic sense," Mapfarity replied. "You didn't expect me to pay any attention to sex, did you? I'm not interested in the gender of you Humans, you know."

There was no time for reproach. Rastignac tried to explain to the Earthwoman who he was, but she did not understand him. However, she did seem to catch on to what he wanted and seemed reassured by his gestures. She picked up a large book from a table and, hugging it to her small, high, and rounded bosom, went with him out the door.

They raced from the palace and descended onto the square. Here, they found the surviving Amphibs clustered into a solid phalanx and fighting, bloody step by step, towards the street that led to the harbor.

Rastignac's little group skirted the battle and started down the steep avenue toward the harbor. Halfway down, he glanced back and saw that nobody as yet was paying any attention to them. Nor was there anybody on the street to bother them, though the pavement was strewn with Skins and bodies. Apparently, those who'd lived through the first savage melee had gone to the square.

They ran onto the wharf. The Earthwoman motioned to Rastignac that she knew how to open the spaceship, but the Amphibs didn't. Moreover, if they did get in, they wouldn't know how to operate it. She had the directions for so doing in the book hugged so desperately to her chest. Rastignac surmised she hadn't told the Amphibs about that. Apparently they hadn't, as yet, tried to torture the information from her.

Therefore, her telling him about the book indicated she trusted him.

Lusine said, "Now what, Jean-Jacques? Are

you still going to abandon this planet?"

"Of course," he snapped.

"Will you take me with you?"

He had spent most of his life under the tutelage of his Skin, which ensured that others would know when he was lying. It did not come easy to hide his true feelings. So a habit of a lifetime won out.

"I will not take you," he said. "In the first place, though you may have some admirable virtues, I've failed to detect one. In the second place, I could not stand your blood-drinking nor your murderous and totally immoral ways."

"But, Jean-Jacques, I will give them up for you!"

"Can the shark stop eating fish?"

"You would leave Lusine, who loves you as no Earthwoman could, and go with that—that pale little doll I could break with my hands?"

"Be quiet," he said. "I have dreamed of this moment all my life. Nothing can stop me now."

They were on the wharf beside the bridge that ran up the smooth side of the starship. The guard was no longer there, though bodies showed that there had been reluctance on the part of some to leave.

They let the Earthwoman precede them up the bridge.

Lusine suddenly ran ahead of him, crying, "If you won't have me, you won't have her, either! Nor the stars!"

Her knife sank twice into the Earthwoman's back. Then, before anybody could reach her, she had leaped off the bridge and into the harbor.

Rastignac knelt beside the Earthwoman. She held out the book to him, then she died. He caught the volume before it struck the wharf.

"My God! My God!" moaned Rastignac, stunned with grief and shock and sorrow. Sorrow for the woman and shock at the loss of the ship and the end of his plans for freedom.

Mapfarity ran up then and took the book from his nerveless hand. "She indicated that this is a manual for running the ship," he said. "All is not lost."

"It will be in a language we don't know," Rastignac whispered.

Archambaud came running up, shrilled, "The Amphibs have broken through and are coming down the street! Let's get to our boat before the whole bloodthirsty mob gets here!"

Mapfarity paid him no attention. He thumbed through the book, then reached down and lifted Rastignac from his crouching position by the corpse.

"There's hope yet, Jean-Jacques," he growled. "This book is printed with the same characters as those I saw in a book owned by a priest I knew. He said it was in Hebrew, and that it was the Holy Book in the original Earth language. This woman must be a citizen of the Republic of Israeli, which I understand was rising to be a great power on Earth at the time you French left.

They walked to the wharf's end and climbed down a ladder to a platform where a dory was tied up. As they rowed out to their sloop Mapfarity said:

"Look, Rastignac, things aren't as bad as they seem. If you haven't the ship nobody else has, either. And you alone have the key to its entrance and operation. For that you can thank the Church, which has preserved the ancient wisdom for emergencies which it couldn't forsee, such as this. Just as it kept the secret of wine, which will eventually be the greatest means for delivering our people from their bondage to the Skins and, thus enable them to fight the Amphibs back instead of being slaughtered.

"Meanwhile, we've a battle to wage. You will have to lead it. Nobody else but the Skinless Devil has the prestige to make the people gather around him. Once we accuse the Minister of Ill-Will of treason and jail him, without an official Breaker to release him, we'll demand a general election. You'll be made King of the Ssassaror; I, of the Terrans. That is inevitable, for we are the only skinless men and, therefore, irresistible. After the war is won, we'll leave for the stars. How do you like that?"

Rastignac smiled. It was weak, but it was a smile. His bracket-shaped eyebrows bent into their old sign of determination.

"You are right," he replied. "I have given it much thought. A man has no right to leave his native land until he's settled his problems here. Even if Lusine hadn't killed the Earthwoman and I had sailed away, my conscience wouldn't have given me any rest. I would have known I had abandoned the fight in the middle of it. But now that I have stripped myself of my Skin—which was a substitute for a conscience—and now that I am being forced to develop my own inward conscience, I must admit that immediate flight to the stars would have been the wrong thing."

The pleased Mapfarity said, "And you must also admit, Rastignac, that things so far have had a way of working out for the best. Even Lusine, evil as she was, has helped towards the general good by keeping you on this planet. And the Church, though it has released once again the old evil of alcohol, has done more good by so doing than . . ."

But here Rastignac interrupted to say he did not believe in this particular school of thought, and so, while the howls of savage warriors drifted from the wharfs, while the structure of their world crashed around them, they plunged into the most violent and circular of all whirlpools—the Discussion Philosophical.

THEY TWINKLED LIKE
JEWELS

I

Jack Crane lay all morning in the vacant lot.
Now and then, he moved a little to quiet the
protest of cramped muscles and stagnant
blood, but most of the time he was as
motionless as the heap of rags he resembled.
Not once did he hear or see a Bohas agent, or,
for that matter, anyone. The predawn
darkness had hidden his panting flight from
the transie jungle, his dodging across
backyards while whistles shrilled and voices
shouted, and his crawling on hands and knees
down an alley into the high grass and bushes
which fringed a hidden garden.

For a while, his heart had knocked so loudly
that he had been sure he would not be able to
hear his pursuers if they did get close. It
seemed inevitable that they would track him
down. A buddy had told him that a new camp
had just been built at a place only three hours
drive away from the town. This meant that
Bohas would be thick as hornets in the
neighborhood. But no black uniforms had so
far appeared. And then, lying there while the
passionate and untiring sun mounted the sky,
the bang-bang of his heart was replaced by a
noiseless but painful movement in his

stomach.

He munched a candy bar and two dried
rolls which a housewife had given him the
evening before. The tiger in his belly quit
pacing back and forth; it crouched and licked
its chops, but its tail was stuck up in his
throat. Jack could feel the dry fur swabbing
his pharynx and mouth. He suffered, but he
was used to that. Night would come as surely
as anything did. He'd get a drink then to
quench his thirst.

Boredom began to sit on his eyelids. Just as
he was about to accept some much needed
sleep, he moved a leaf with an accidental jerk
of his hand and uncovered a caterpillar. It
was dark except for a row of yellow spots
along the central line of some of its segments.
As soon as it was exposed, it began slowly
shimmying away. Before it had gone two feet,
it was crossed by a moving shadow. Guiding
the shadow was a black wasp with an orange
ring around the abdomen. It closed the gap
between itself and the worm with a swift,
smooth movement and straddled the dark
body.

Before the wasp could grasp the thick neck
with its mandibles, the intended victim began
rapidly rolling and unrolling and flinging
itself from side to side. For a minute, the
delicate dancer above it could not succeed in
clenching the neck. Its sharp jaws slid off the
frenziedly jerking skin until the tiring
creature paused for the chip of a second.

Seizing opportunity and larva at the same
time, the wasp stood high on its legs and
pulled the worm's front end from the ground,

exposing the yellowed band of the underpart. The attacker's abdomen curved beneath its own body; the stinger jabbed between two segments of the prey's jointed length. Instantly, the writhing stilled. A shudder, and the caterpillar became as inert as if it were dead.

Jack had watched with an eye not completely clinical, feeling the sympathy of the hunted and the hounded for a fellow. His own struggles of the past few months had been as desperate, though not as hopeless, and . . .

He stopped thinking. He heart again took up the rib-thudding. Out of the corner of his left eye he had seen a shadow that fell across the garden. When he slowly turned his head to follow the stain upon the sun-splashed soil, he saw that it clung to a pair of shining black boots.

Jack did not say anything. What was the use? He put his hands against the weeds and pushed his body up. He looked into the silent mouth of a .38 automatic. It told him his running days were over. You didn't talk back to a mouth like that.

II

Jack was lucky. As one of the last to be herded into the truck, which had been once used for hauling cattle, he had more room to breathe than most of the others. He faced the rear bars. The vehicle was heading into the sun. Its rays were not as hard on him as on some of those who were so jam-packed they could not turn to get the hot yellow splotch out of their eyes.

He looked through lowered lids at the youths on either side of him. For the last three days in the transie jungle, the one standing on his left had given signs of what was coming upon him, what had come upon so many of the transies. The muttering, the indifference to food, not hearing you when you talked to him. And now the shock of being caught in the raid had speeded up what everybody had foreseen. He was hardened, like a concrete statue, into a half-crouch. His arms were held in front of him like a praying mantis', and his hands clutched a bar. Not even the pressure of the crowd could break his posture.

The man on Jack's right murmured something, but the roaring of motor and clashing of gears shifting on a hill squashed his voice. He spoke louder,

"*Cerea flexibilitas*. Extreme catatonic state. The fate of all of us."

"You're nuts," said Jack. "Not me. I'm no schizo, and I'm not going to become one."

As there was no reply, Jack decided he had not moved his lips enough to be heard clearly. Lately, even when it was quiet, people seemed to have trouble making out what he was saying. It made him mildly angry.

He shouted. It did not matter if he were overheard. That any of the prisoners were agents of the Bureau of Health and Sanity didn't seem likely. Anyway, he didn't care. They wouldn't do anything to him they hadn't planned before this.

"Got any idea where we're going?"

"Sure. F.M.R.C. 3. Federal Male Rehabilitation Camp No. 3. I spent two weeks in the hills spying on it."

Jack looked the speaker over. Like all those in the truck, he wore a frayed shirt, a stained and torn coat, and greasy, dirty trousers. The black bristles on his face were long; the back of his neck was covered by thick curls. The brim of his dusty hat was pulled down low. Beneath its shadow, his eyes roamed from side to side with the same fear that Jack knew was in his own eyes.

Hunger and sleepless nights had knobbed his cheekbones and honed his chin to a sharp point. An almost visible air clung to him, a hot aura that seemed to result from veins full of lava and eyeballs spilling out a heat that could not be held within him. He had the face of every transie, the face of a man who was either burning with fever or who had seen a vision.

Jack looked away to stare miserably at the dust boiling up behind the wheels, as if he could see projected against its yellow-brown screen his retreating past.

He spoke out of the side of his mouth. "What's happened to us? We should be happy and working at good jobs and sure about the future. We shouldn't be just bums, hobos, walkers of the streets, rod-hoppers, beggars, and thieves."

His friend shrugged and looked uneasily from the corners of his eyes. He was probably expecting the question they all asked sooner of later: *Why are you on the road?* They asked, but none replied with words that meant anything. They lied, and they didn't seem to take any pleasure in their lying. When they asked questions themselves, they knew they would not get the truth. But something forced them to keep on trying anyway.

Jack's buddy evaded also. He said, "I read a magazine article by a Dr. Vespa, the head of the Bureau of Health and Sanity. He'd written the article just after the President created the Bureau. He viewed, quote, with alarm and apprehension, unquote, the fact that six percent of those between the ages of twelve and twenty-five are schizophrenics who need institutionalizing. And he was, quote, appalled and horrified, unquote, that five percent of the nation are homeless unemployed and that three point seven percent of those are between the ages of fourteen and thirty. He said that if this schizophrenia kept on progressing, half the world would be in rehabilitation camps. But if that occurred, the sane half would go to pot. Back to the stone age. And the schizos would die."

He licked his lips as if he were tasting the figures and found them bitter.

"I was very interested by Vespa's reply to a mother who had written him," he went on. "Her daughter ended up in a Bohas camp for schizos, and her son had left his wonderful home and brilliant future to become a bum. She wanted to know why. Vespa took six long paragraphs to give six explanations, all equally valid and all advanced by equally distinguished sociologists. He himself favored the mass hysteria theory. But if you looked at his gobbledegook closely, you could reduce it to one phrase, *We don't know*.

"He did say this—though you won't like it—that the schizos and the transies were just two sides of the same coin. Both were infected with the same disease, whatever it was. And the transies usually ended up as schizos anyway. It just took them longer."

Gears shifted. The floor slanted. Jack was shoved hard against the rear boards by the weight of the other men. He didn't answer until the pressure had eased and his ribs were free to work for more than mere survival.

He said, "You're way off, schizo. My hitting the road has nothing to do with those splitheads. Nothing, you understand? There's nothing foggy or dreamy about me. I wouldn't be here with you guys if I hadn't been so interested in a wasp catching a caterpillar that I never saw the Bohas sneaking up on me."

While Jack described the little tragedy, the other allowed an understanding smile to bend his lips. He seemed engrossed, however, and when Jack had finished, he said:

"That was probably an ammophila wasp. *Sphex urnaria* Klug. Lovely but vicious little she-demon. Injects the poison from her sting into the caterpillar's central nerve cord. That not only paralyzes but preserves it. The victim is always stowed away with another one in an underground burrow. The wasp attaches one of her eggs to the body of a worm. When the egg hatches, the grub eats both of the worms. They're alive, but they're completely helpless to resist while their guts are gnawed away. Beautiful idea, isn't it?

"It's a habit common to many of those little devils: *Sceliphron cementarium, Eumenes, coarcta, Eumenes fraterna, Bembix spinolae, Pelopoeus . . .*"

Jack's interest wandered. His informant was evidently one of those transies who spent long hours in the libraries. They were ready at the slightest chance to offer their encyclopaedic but often useless knowledge. Jack himself had abandoned his childhood bookwormishness. For the last three years his days and evenings had worn themselves out on the streets, passed in a parade of faces, flickered by in plateglass windows of restaurants and department stores and business offices, while he hoped, hoped. . . .

"Did you say you spied on the camp?" Jack interrupted the sonorous, almost chanting flow of Greek and Latin.

"Huh? Oh, yeah. For two weeks. I saw plenty of transies rucked in, but I never saw any taken out. Maybe they left in the rocket."

"Rocket?"

The youth was looking straight before him. His face was hard as bone, but his voice trembled.

"Yes. A big one. It landed and discharged about a dozen men."

"You nuts?"

"I saw it, I tell you. And I'm not so nutty I'm seeing things that aren't there. Not yet, anyway!"

"Maybe the government's got rockets it's not telling anybody about."

"Then what connection could there be between rehabilitation camps and rockets?"

Jack shrugged and said, "Your rocket story is fantastic."

"If somebody had told you four years ago that you'd be a bum hauled off to a concentration camp, you'd have said that was fantastic too."

Jack did not have time to reply. The truck stopped outside a high, barbed wire fence. The gate swung open; the truck bounced down the bumpy dirt road. Jack saw some black-uniformed Bohas seated by heavy machine guns. They halted at another entrance; more barbed wire was passed. Huge Dobermann-Pinschers looked at the transies with cold, steady eyes. The dust of another section of road swirled up before they squeaked to a standstill and the engine turned off.

This time, agents began to let down the back of the truck. They had to pry the pitiful schizo's fingers loose from the wood with a crow-bar and carry him off, still in his half-crouch.

A sergeant boomed orders. Stiff and stumbling, the transies jumped off the truck. They were swiftly lined up into squads and marched into the enclosure and from there into a huge black barracks. Within an hour each man was stripped; had his head shaven, was showered, given a grey uniform, and handed a tin plate and spoon and cup filled with beans and bread and hot coffee.

Afterwards, Jack wandered around, free to look at the sandy soil underfoot and barbed wire and the black uniforms of the sentries, and free to ask himself where, where, where-wherewhere? Twelve years ago it had been, but where, where, where, was . . . ?

III

How easy it would have been to miss all this,
if only he had obeyed his father. But Mr.
Crane was so ineffectual. . . .

"Jack," he had said, "would you please go
outside and play, or stay in some other room.
It's very difficult to discuss business while
you're whooping and screaming around, and I
have a lot to discuss with Mr.—"

"Yes, Daddy," Jack said before his father
mentioned his visitor's name. But he was not
Jack Crane in his game; he was Uncas. The big
chairs and the divan were trees in his
imaginative eyes. The huge easy chair in
which Daddy's caller (Jack thought of him
only as "Mister") sat with a fallen log. He,
Uncas, meant to hide behind it in ambush.

Mister did not bother him. He had smiled
and said in a shrill voice that he thought Jack
was a very nice boy. He wore a light grey-
green Palm Beach suit and carried a big
brown leather briefcase that looked too heavy
for his soda straw-thin legs and arms. He was
queer looking because his waist was so
narrow and his back so humped. And when he
took off his tan Panama hat, a white fuzz
exploded from his scalp. His face was pale as
the moon in daylight. His broad smile showed
teeth that Jack knew were false.

But the queerest thing about him was his
thick spectacles, so heavily tinted with rose
that Jack could not see the eyes behind them.

The afternoon light seemed to bounce off the lenses in such a manner that no matter what angle you looked at them, you could not pierce them. And they curved to hide the sides of his eyes completely.

Mister had explained that he was an albino, and he needed the glasses to dim the glare on his eyes. Jack stopped being Uncas for a minute to listen. He had never seen an albino before, and, indeed, he did not know what one was.

"I don't mind the youngster," said Mister. "Let him play here if he wants to. He's developing his imagination, and he may be finding more stimuli in this front room than he could in all of outdoors. We should never cripple the fine gift of imagination in the young. Imagination, fancy, fantasy—or whatever you call it—is the essence of mainspring of those scientists, musicians, painters, and poets who amount to something in later life. They are adults who have remained youths."

Mister addressed Jack, "You're the Last of the Mohicans, and you're about to sneak up on the French captain and tomahawk him, aren't you?"

Jack blinked. He nodded his head. The opaque rose lenses set in Mister's face seemed to open a door into his naked grey skull.

The man said, "I want you to listen to me, Jack. You'll forget my name, which isn't important. But you will always remember me and my visit, won't you?"

Jack stared at the impenetrable lenses and nodded dumbly.

Mister turned to Jack's father. "Let his fancy grow. It is a necessary wish-fulfillment play. Like all human young who are good for anything at all, he is trying to find the lost door to the Garden of Eden. The history of the great poets and men-of-action is the history of the attempt to return to the realm that Adam lost, the forgotten Hesperides of the mind, the Avalon buried in our soul."

Mr. Crane put his fingertips together. "Yes?"

"Personally, I think that some day man will realize just what he is searching for and will invent a machine that will enable the child to project, just as a film throws an image on a screen, the visions in his psyche.

"I see you're interested," he continued. "You would be, naturally, since you're a professor of philosophy. Now, let's call the toy a specterscope, because through it the subject sees the spectres that haunt his unconscious. Ha! Ha! But how does it work? I'll tell you. My native country's scientists have developed a rather simple device, though they haven't published anything about it in the scientific journals. let me give you a brief explanation: Light strikes the retina of the eye; the rods and cones pass on impulses to the bipolar cells, which send them on to the optic nerve, which goes to the brain . . ."

"Elementary and full of gaps," said Jack's father.

"Pardon me," said Mister. "A bare outline should be enough. You'll be able to fill in the details. Very well. This specterscope breaks up the light going into the eye in such a manner that the rods and cones receive only a certain wavelength. I can't tell you what it is, except that it's in the visual red. The scope also concentrates like a burning-glass and magnifies the power of the light.

"Result? A hitherto-undiscovered chemical in the visual purple of the rods is activated and stimulates the optic nerve in a way he had not guessed possible. An electrochemical stimulus then irritates the subconscious until it fully wakes up.

"Let me put it this way. The subconscious is not a matter of *location* but of *organization*. There are billions of possible connections between the neurons of the cortex. Look at those potentialities as so many cards in the same pack. Shuffle the cards one way and you have the common workaday *cogito, ergo sum* mind. Reshuffle them, and, bingo! you have the combination of neurons, or cards, of the unconscious. The specterscope does the redealing. When the subject gazes through it, he sees for the first time the full impact and result of his underground mind's workings in other perceptics than dreams or symbolical behavior. The subjective Garden of Eden is resurrected. It is my contention that this specterscope will some day be available to all children.

"When that happens, Mr. Crane, you will understand that the world will profit from man's secret wishes. Earth will be a far better place. Paradise, sunken deep in every man, can be dredged out."

"I don't know," said Jack's father, stroking his chin thoughtfully with a finger. "Children

like my son are too introverted as it is. Give
them this psychological toy, and you would
watch them grow, not into the outside world,
but into themselves. They would fester. Man
has been expelled from the Garden. His
history is a long, painful climb toward
something different. It is something that is
probably better than the soft and flabby
Golden Age. If man were to return, he would
regress, become worse than static, become
infantile or even embryonic. He would be
smothered in the folds of his own dreams."

"Perhaps," said the salesman. "But I think
you have a very unusual child here. He will go
much farther than you may think. Why?
Because he is sensitive and has an
imagination that only needs the proper
guidance. Too many children become mere
ciphers and paunches and round "O" minds
full of tripe. They'll stay on earth. That is, I
mean they'll be stuck in the mud."

"You talk like no insurance salesman I've
ever met."

"Like all those who really want to sell, I'm a
born   psychologist,"   Mister   shrilled.
"Actually, I have an advantage. I have a Ph.D.
in psychology. I would prefer staying at home
for laboratory work, but since I can help my
starving children—I am not joking—so much
more by coming to a foreign land and working
at something that will put food in their
mouths, I do it. I can't stand to see my little
ones go hungry. Moreover," he said with a
wave of his long-fingered hand, "this whole
planet is really a lab that beats anything
within four walls."

"You spoke of famine. Your accent—your name. You're a Greek, aren't you?"

"In a way," said Mister. "My name, translated, means gracious or kindly or well-meaning." His voice became brisker. "The translation is apropos. I'm here to do you a service. Now, about these monthly premiums . . ."

Jack shook himself and stepped out of the mold of fascination that Mister's glasses seemed to have poured around him. Uncas again, he crawled on all fours from chair to divan to stool to the fallen log which the adults thought was an easy chair. He stuck his head from behind it and sighted along the broomstick-musket at his father. He'd shoot that white man dead and then take his scalp. He giggled at that, because his father really didn't have any hairlock to take.

At that moment, Mister decided to take off his specs and polish them with his breastpocket handkerchief. While he answered one of Mr. Crane's questions, he let them dangle from his fingers. The lenses were level with Jack's gaze. One careless glance was enough to jerk his eyes back to them. One glance stunned him so that he could not at once understand that what he was seeing was not reality.

There was his father across the room. But it wasn't a room. It was a space outdoors under the low branch of a tree whose trunk was so big it was as wide as the wall had been. Nor was the Persian rug there. It was replaced by a close-cropped bright green grass. Here and there foot-high flowers with bright yellow petals tipped in scarlet swayed beneath an internal wind. Close to Mr. Crane's feet a white horse no larger than a fox terrier bit off the flaming end of a plant.

All those things were wonderful enough—but was that naked giant who sprawled upon a moss-covered boulder his father? No! Yes! Though the features were no longer pinched and scored and pale, though they were glowing and tanned and smooth like a young athlete's they were his father's! Even the thick, curly hair that fell down over a wide forehead and the panther-muscled body could not hide his identity.

Though it tore at his nerves, and though he was afraid that once he looked away he would never again seize the vision, Jack ripped his gaze away from the rosy view.

The descent to the grey and rasping reality was so painful that tears ran down his cheeks, and he gasped as if struck in the pit of the stomach. How could beauty like that be all around him without his knowing it?

He felt that he had been blind all his life until this moment and would be forever eyeless again, an unbearable forever, if he did not look through the glass again.

He stole another hurried glance, and the pain in his heart and stomach went away, his insides became wrapped in a soft wind. He was lifted. He was floating, a pale red, velvety air caressed him and buoyed him.

He saw his mother run from around the tree. That should have seemed peculiar, because he had thought she was dead. But there she was, no longer flat-walking and coughing and thin and wax-skinned but golden-brown and curvy and bouncy. She jumped at Daddy and gave him a long kiss. Daddy didn't seem to mind that she had no clothes on. Oh, it was so wonderful. Jack was drifting on a yielding and wine-tinted air and warmed with a wind that seemed to swell him out like a happy balloon. . . .

Suddenly he was falling, hurtling helplessly and sickeningly through a void while a cold and drab blast gouged his skin and spun him around and around. The world he had always known shoved hard against him. Again, he felt the blow in the solar plexus and saw the grey tentacles of the living reality reach for his heart.

Jack looked up at the stranger, who was just about to put his spectacles on the bridge of his long nose. His eyelids were closed. Jack never did see his eyes.

That didn't bother him. He had other things to think about. He crouched beside the chair while his brain tried to move again, tried to engulf a thought and failed because it could not become fluid enough to find the idea that would move his tongue to shriek, *No! No! No!*

And when the salesman rose and placed his papers in his case and patted Jack on the head and bent his opaque rose spectacles at him and said good-by and that he wouldn't be coming back because he was going out of town to stay, Jack was not able to move or say a thing. Nor for a long time after the door had closed could he break through the mass that gripped him like hardened lava. By then, no amount of screams and weeping would bring

Mister back. All his father could do was to call
a doctor who took the boy's temperature and
gave him pills.

IV

Jack stood inside the wire and bent his neck
back to watch a huge black and silver oyster
feel the dusk for a landing-field with its single
white foot and its orange toes. Blindingly,
lights sprang to attention over the camp.

When Jack had blinked his eyes back to
normal, he could see over the flat half-mile
between the fence and the ship. It lay quiet
and glittering and smoking in the flood-
beams. He could see the round door in its side
swing open. Men began filing out. A truck
rumbled across the plain and pulled up beside
the metal bulk. A very tall man stepped out of
the cab and halted upon the running board,
from which he seemed to be greeting the new-
comers or giving them instructions. Whatever
he was saying took so long that Jack lost
interest.

Lately, he had not been able to focus his
mind for any length of time upon anything
except that one event in the past. He
wandered around and whipped glances at his
comrades' faces, noting listlessly that their
uniforms and shaved heads had improved
their appearance. But nothing would be able
to chill the feverishness of their eyes.

Whistles shrilled. Jack jumped. His heart
beat faster. He felt as if the end of the quest
were suddenly close. Somebody would be

around the corner. In a minute that person would be facing him, and then . . .

Then, he reflected, and sagged with a wave of disappointment at the thought, then there was nobody around the corner. It always happened that way. Besides, there weren't any corners in this camp. He had reached the wall at the end of the alley. Why didn't he stop looking?

Sergeants lined the prisoners up four abreast preparatory to marching them into the barracks. Jack supposed it was time to turn in for the night. He submitted to their barked orders and hard hands without resentment. They seemed a long way off. For the ten thousandth time, he was thinking that this need not have happened.

If he had been man enough to grapple with himself, to wrestle as Jacob did with the angel and not let loose until he had felled the problem, he could be teaching philosophy in a quiet little college, as his father did. He had graduated from high school, and then, instead of going to college, as his father had so much wanted him to, he had decided he would work a year. With his earnings, he would see the world.

He had seen it, but, when his money ran out, he had not returned home. He had drifted, taking jobs here and there, sleeping in flophouses, jungles, park benches, and freight cars.

When the newly created Bureau of Health and Sanity had frozen jobs in an effort to solve the transiency problem, Jack had refused to work. He knew that he would not be able to quit a job without being arrested at once. Like hundreds of thousands of other youths, he had begged and stolen and hidden from the local police and the Bohas.

Even though all those years of misery and wandering, he had not once admitted to himself the true nature of this fog-cottoned grail. He knew it, and he did not know it. It was patroling the edge of his mind, circling a faroff periphery, recognizable by a crude silhouette but nameless. Any time he wanted to, he could have summoned it closer and said, *You are it, and I know you, and I know what I am looking for. It is . . . ? Is what? Worthless? Foolish? Insane? A dream?*

Jack had never had the courage to take that action. When it seemed the thing was galloping closer, charging down upon him, he ran away. It must stay on the horizon, moving on, always moving, staying out of his grasp.

"All you guys, for'ard 'arch!"

Jack did not move. The truck from the rocket had come through a gate and stopped by the transies, and about fifty men were getting off the back.

The man behind Jack bumped into him. Jack paid him no attention. He did not move. He squinted at the group who had come from the rocket. They were very tall, hump-shouldered, and dressed in light grey-green Palm Beach suits and tan Panama hats. Each held a brown leather briefcase at the end of a long, thin arm. Each wore on the bridge of his long nose a pair of rose-colored glasses.

A cry broke hoarsely from the transies. Some of those in front of Jack fell to their knees as if a sudden poison had paralyzed their legs. They called out and stretched out open hands. A boy by Jack's side sprawled face-down on the sand while he uttered over and over again, "Mr. Pelopoeus! Mr. Pelopoeus!"

The name meant nothing to Jack. He did feel repulsed at seeing the fellow turn on his side, bend his neck forward, bring his clenched fists up against his chest, and jack-knife his legs against his arms. He had seen it many times before in the transies jungles, but he had never gotten over the sickness it had first caused him.

He turned away and came almost nose to nose with one of the men from the rocket. He had put down his briefcase so it rested against his leg and taken a white handkerchief out of his breast pocket to wipe the dust from his lenses. His lids were squeezed shut as if he found the lights unbearable.

Jack stared and could not move while a name that the boy behind him had been crying out slowly worked its way through his consciousness. Suddenly, like the roar of a flashflood that is just rounding the bend of a dry gulch, the syllables struck him. He lunged forward and clutched at the spectacles in the man's hand. At the same time he yelled over and over the words that had filled out the blank in his memory.

"Mr. Eumenes! Mr. Eumenes!"

A sergeant cursed and slammed his fist into Jack's face. Jack fell down, flat on his back. Though his jaw felt as if it were torn loose from its hinge, he rolled over on his side, raised himself on his hands and knees, and began to get up to his feet.

"Stand still!" bellowed the sergeant. "Stay in formation or you'll get more of the same!"

Jack shook his head until it cleared. He crouched and held out his hands toward the man, but he did not move his feet. Over and over, half-chanting, half-crooning, he said, "Mr. Eumenes! The glasses! Please, Mr. Eumenes, the glasses!"

The forty-nine Mr. Eumenae-and-otherwise looked incuriously with impenetrable rosy eyes. The fiftieth put the white handkerchief back in his pocket. His mouth opened. False teeth gleamed. With his free hand he took off his hat and waved it at the crowd and bowed.

His titled head showed a white fuzzlike hair that shot up over his pale scalp. His gestures were both comic and terrifying. The hat and the inclination of his body said far more than words could. They said, *Good-by forever and bon voyage!*

Then, Mr. Eumenes straightened up and opened his lids.

At first, the sockets looked as if they held no eyeballs, as if they were empty of all but shadows.

Jack saw them from a distance. Mr. Eumenes-or-his-twin was shooting away faster and faster and becoming smaller and smaller. No! He himself was. He was rocketing away within his own body. He was falling down a deep well.

He, Jack Crane, was a hollow shaft down which he slipped and screamed, away, away, from the world outside. It was like seeing from the wrong end of a pair of binoculars that lengthened and lengthened while the man with the long-sought-for treasure in his hand flew in the opposite direction as if he had been connected to the horizon by a rubber band and somebody had released it and he was flying towards it, away from Jack.

Even as this happened, as he knew vaguely that his muscles were locking into the posture of a beggar, hands out, pleading, face twisted into an agony of asking, lips repeating his croon-chant, he saw what had occurred.

The realization was like the sudden, blinding, and at the same time clarifying light that sometimes comes to epileptics just as they are going into a seizure. It was the thought that he had kept away on the horizon of his mind, the thought that now charged in on him with long leaps and bounds and then stopped and sat on its haunches and grinned at him while its long tongue lolled.

Of course, he should have known all these years what it was. He should have known that Mr. Eumenes was the worst thing in the world for him. He had known it, but, like a drug addict, he had refused to admit it. He had searched for the man. Yet he had known it would be fatal to find him. The rose-colored spectacles would swing gates that should never be fully open. And he should have guessed *what* and *who* Mr. Eumenes was when that encyclopedic fellow in the truck had singsonged those names.

How could he have been so stupid? Stupid? It was easy! He had *wanted* to be stupid! And how could the Mr. Eumenes-or-otherwise have used such obvious giveaway names? It

was a measure of their contempt for the
humans around them and of their own grim
wit. Look at all the double entrendres the
salesman had given his father, and his father
had never suspected. Even the head of the
Bureau of Health and Sanity had been
terrifyingly blase about it.

Dr. Vespa. He had thrown his name like a
gauntlet to humanity, and humanity had
stared idiotically at it and never guessed its
meaning. Vespa was an Italian name. Jack
didn't know what it meant, but he supposed
that it had the same meaning as the Latin. He
remembered it from his high school class.

As for his not encountering the salesman
until now, he had been lucky. If he had run
across him during his search, he would have
been denied the glasses, as now. And the
shock would have made him unable to cry out
and betray the man. He would have done what
he was so helplessly doing at this moment,
and he would have been carted off to an
institution.

How many other transies had seen that un-
forgettable face on the streets, the end of their
search, and gone at once into that state that
made them legal prey of the Bohas?

That was almost his last rational thought.
He could no longer feel his flesh. A thin red
curtain was falling between him and his
senses. Everywhere it billowed out beneath
him and eased his fall. Everywhere it swirled
and softened the outlines of things that were
streaking by—a large tree that he
remembered seeing in his living room, a
naked giant, his father, leaning against it and

eating an apple, and a delicate little white creature cropping flowers.

They were not yet gone. He could feel the hands of the black-clad officers lifting him up and laying him upon some hard substance that rocked and dumped. Every lurch and thud was only dimly felt. Then he was placed upon something softer and carried into what he vaguely sensed was the interior of one of the barracks.

Some time later—he didn't know or care when, for he had lost all conception or even definition of time—he looked up the deep everlengthening shaft of himself into the eyes of another Mr. Eumenes or Mr. Sphex or Dr. Vespa or whatever he called himself. He was in white and wore a stethoscope around his neck.

Beside him stood another of his own kind. This one wore lipstick and a nurse's cap. She carried a tray on which were several containers. One container held a large and sharp scalpel. The other held an egg. It was about the size of a hen's egg.

Jack saw all this just before the veil took on another shade of red and blurred completely his vision of the outside. But the final thickening did not keep him from seeing that Doctor Eumenes was staring down at him as if he were peering into a dusky burrow. And Jack could make out the eyes. They were large, much larger than they should have been at the speed with which Jack was receding. They were not the pale pink of an albino's. They were black from corner to corner and built of a dozen or so hexagons whose edges

caught the light.
    They twinkled.
    Like jewels.
    Or the eyes of an enormous and evolved
wasp.